Christie Ridgway is a *USA TODAY* bestselling author of more than thirty-five contemporary romances. Known for her stories that make readers laugh and cry, Christie began writing romances in fifth grade, inspired by the Harlequin books she loved to read. Later, after marrying her college sweetheart and having two boys, she left the geeky field of computer programming and returned to what she loved best—telling stories of strong men and determined women finding their happy-ever-afters. Christie lives in California. Visit her on the web at christieridgway.com.

New York Times and *USA TODAY* bestselling author **Leslie Kelly** is known for her delightful characters, sparkling dialogue and outrageous humor. Since the publication of her first book in 1999, Leslie has gone on to pen dozens of sassy, sexy romances for Harlequin Temptation, Blaze and HQN Books. This award-winning writer lives in New Mexico with her hubby Bruce—her real-life romance hero—along with their children. Visit her website at lesliekelly.com and look for her on Facebook and Twitter.

New York Times and *USA TODAY* bestselling author **Tanya Michaels** writes about what she knows—family, community and lasting love! Her books, praised for their poignancy and humor, have won numerous awards and honors. Tanya is an active member of Romance Writers of America and a frequent public speaker, presenting workshops to encourage aspiring writers. She lives near Atlanta with her husband and two children plus a household of quirky pets. Check out her website at tanyamichaels.net.

New Year's Resolution:

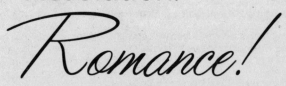

Romance!

USA TODAY BESTSELLING AUTHOR
CHRISTIE RIDGWAY

NEW YORK TIMES & USA TODAY BESTSELLING AUTHORS
LESLIE KELLY & TANYA MICHAELS

HARLEQUIN® ANTHOLOGY

ISBN-13: 978-0-373-83808-0

New Year's Resolution: Romance!

Copyright © 2015 by Harlequin Books S.A.

The publisher acknowledges the copyright holders of the individual works as follows:

Say Yes
Copyright © 2015 by Christie Ridgway

No More Bad Girls
Copyright © 2015 by Leslie A. Kelly

Just a Fling
Copyright © 2015 by Tanya Michna

Recycling programs for this product may not exist in your area.

Printed in U.S.A.

www.Harlequin.com

CONTENTS

Dear Reader,

The new year seems a natural time for new beginnings. The heroine of "Say Yes," Ashley Walker, is ready to start anew after four lonely years as a young widow. But she's thinking of putting on dresses again and going to parties, not taking the scary risk of falling in love. When she meets wealthy money manager Chase Bradley, she figures he's as cautious as she is, until he seeks a midnight kiss... and then more.

If you've not visited the setting for this story, Blue Arrow Lake, through my Cabin Fever series for HQN Books, I hope you'll enjoy this glimpse of peaks and pines just a couple of hours from Southern California's stunning beaches and sunny glamour. It's where the celebrated rich go to relax and where the more humble mountain men and women exult in their incredible natural surroundings. It's a clash of types that causes sparks that result in passion that just might possibly end in love!

Wherever you are, whenever you're reading this, I wish for you health, happiness and great reading.

All the best,

Christie Ridgway

SAY YES

Christie Ridgway

CHAPTER ONE

ASHLEY WALKER STEPPED out of the florist's van and shivered in the New Year's Eve air. Though this was Southern California, the five-thousand-foot mountain elevation meant real winter weather. An unusual white Thanksgiving had made for happy times at the nearby ski resorts, and the numbers of skiers and snowboarders lining up for the lifts continued to surge. The wealthy patrons who owned second homes surrounding private, posh Blue Arrow Lake had been flocking up the hill from their usual Los Angeles environs to celebrate the holidays before roaring fires and on powdery slopes.

With a quick glance at the Tudor-inspired mansion she'd visited on this same day for the past three years, Ashley snatched a knee-length smock from the passenger seat and slid her arms through the cotton sleeves. As a coat, it didn't provide much warmth, but it would protect the little black dress she'd put on in advance of her evening plans.

Before she could get to those, however, she had to deliver the arrangements for the Bradleys' traditional house party, which was why she'd pulled up beside the side service entrance. They hosted the weeklong event every year, inviting couples who were also favored clients of their financial firm to enjoy a vacation in the luxurious lakeside home. It was a massive place, with

twenty bedrooms and more bathrooms than that, set
in the middle of expansive grounds that butted up to
a sandy beach and double docks on the water. Ashley
always enjoyed her little peek into how the other half
lived—something she never grew accustomed to even
though her job in a florist shop in the nearby village
meant she often visited the premier showplaces in the
area. As a mountain woman born and bred, she accepted
that their peaks-and-pines economy needed the überrich
Angelenos so the full-timers here could make a living
in this area of stupendous natural beauty.

Her phone rang as she walked to the rear of the van.
She fished it from the smock's patch pocket, checked
the screen and then held the device to her ear. "What's
up, Suze?"

"What are you wearing to my party tonight?"

Ashley glanced down at the strip of fabric revealed
by the flapping sides of the garment she wore over it.
"Borrowed a dress from my cousin. Black, knee-length,
sleeveless. Has a full skirt with a black lace overskirt."

"Really?"

Her friend's surprise rankled a little. "I know how
to dress up. I have on black lace stockings, too, and my
black heels."

"I don't think I've seen you in anything but jeans
and T-shirts in more than four years."

"I work in a florist shop. A business suit would be
impractical."

"You know what I mean," Suze said.

Yes, Ashley knew what the other woman meant. She
hadn't had an occasion to wear anything besides jeans
and T-shirts in more than four years because she hadn't
gone anywhere but to work and the grocery store since

her husband, Stuart, had died. Now, as a twenty-seven-year-old widow, she'd decided it was time to get out more. "I told you, Suze. I've turned over a new leaf. I'm making a resolution. This is going to be my year of yes."

"If I get you drunk enough tonight, I may have it tattooed on your forehead. That way you'll see it every morning as you brush your teeth."

"I'm not going to get any kind of drunk tonight." Ashley pulled open one of the van's back doors. The combined scent of various flowers wafted out, the fragrance dominated by the deep sweet smell of the roses with just a hint of cinnamon from the carnations.

"Oh, you might want to reconsider that," Suze said, in an airy, casual manner that put Ashley on high alert. Suzanne was her best friend since fourth grade, and she knew all her moods and sneaky subterfuges.

"What have you done?" The ensuing pause was long enough for Ashley to take inventory of the flowers stowed in the back of the van. There were arrangements for every bedroom and bathroom and others for the living areas. Mrs. Bradley had called in her order and left it up to Ashley to make decisions when it came to the particular flowers and greenery.

"I trust your judgment," the older woman had said. "And you'll set them around for me, won't you? My older daughter is expecting her second child soon into the new year so I'm staying with her until the very last minute."

Ashley reached in to tweak a bit of Queen Anne's lace that was out of place and put a stern note in her voice. "Suzanne Janice Reynolds, don't think I can't detect the guilty vibrations coming over the line."

"Isortofarrangedadateforyou."

She said it so fast Ashley couldn't separate the syllables. "What?"

"Isortofarrangedadateforyou."

This time her brain managed to decipher the sentence. She dropped to take a seat on the back bumper as heat bloomed on her nape and over her face, dissipating the late-afternoon chill. "Suze!" she said in an irate tone. "You promised—"

"And you promised me that you were ready to climb out of your shell."

"I can't do a date. You know that. It's too soon—"

"Four years," Suze pointed out.

Four years and seventeen days. "Still—"

"Climbing out of your shell," Suze said again.

"A date on New Year's Eve is more like…like… bursting out of a birthday cake!"

"Calm down," her friend advised.

Ashley pressed her hand to her stomach. "I feel sick. I don't think I can make it to the party after all."

"Coward."

"Cautious," Ashley countered. "Who is this guy anyway?"

"A gym friend of Jackson's."

She groaned. "It's going to be one of those men who stares at himself in the mirror, grunting with every biceps curl."

"That's not so bad."

"Haven't you ever noticed how they dead drop the free weights so that everyone in the room looks over? I hate that type."

"When was the last time you were in a gym?"

Guilt nibbled at Ashley. She supposed she had no choice but to come clean. "Um…look. I've been taking classes every morning. Alternating between spin and Pilates."

There was another long silence on the other end of the phone. "We have a pact," Suze finally said with a lacing of hurt. "You broke the pact."

It was true. When they were fourteen, they'd taken a solemn vow to tackle any new exercise or diet regimen together. There'd been those four days when they'd eaten broiled bologna at every meal. The training for the 10K that had gone well until Suze sprained her ankle. The weeklong cabbage soup cleanse that upon mutual disgust they'd ended after seven hours. If one was going to commit to concerted calorie restriction or sweat production, they were supposed to do it together.

Ashley hung her head. "Suze, I'm sorry."

"My fat behind is sorrier." Her friend blew out a sigh over the phone. "Well, as payback, you'll make an effort with Moose."

"Moose?" Ashley nearly shouted the word. "He's called *Moose*?"

"It's just a nickname."

"I don't only feel sick to my stomach," Ashley said. "Now I have a migraine."

"That's no excuse to avoid the first stop on your year of yes."

Ashley thought hard, hoping to come up with something better than feigned illness. Because…*Moose*!

"When are you going to get here?" Suze demanded. "I have all the ingredients for your special dip—you know, the one Jackson loves—and I need you to make it."

Ashley rolled her eyes. "You rip open the packet, pour it into the sour cream container. Stir."

"With a spoon or a fork?"

"Suze—"

"It's past time for a change, honey, and that change starts with tonight's party. Come concoct the dip."

"I'm at the Bradley estate now. I have to deliver the flowers. After that—"

"It's yes time."

With a sigh, Ashley slowly nodded her head, though it felt as if she was agreeing to disaster. *Moose*. "All right. It's yes time."

ASHLEY DREW OUT a rolling cart from the van and filled it with the first round of arrangements. She cast a glance at the mansion's side door, certain it was unlocked. The caterer's truck was parked nearby, the one that read Fare by Fanny on the side. She knew Fanny. Ashley's stomach growled a little because even as she thought of the other woman, the smell of her famous beef bourguignonne tickled her nose. Maybe she could beg a bite or two after she finished up with her own duties.

The cart rattled across the flagstone drive toward the immense house made of rock, stone and wood. She ducked under an arch and found the door she wanted indeed unlocked. More delicious smells were drawn into her lungs as she entered an expansive, rectangular mudroom. As Ashley continued into the kitchen, pushing her flower arrangements in front of her, Fanny glanced over.

"Happy New Year," the older woman called out. She wielded a wooden spoon, and a butcher apron was wrapped about her apple-round middle. Her gaze inspected the profusion of floral beauty. "Those look wonderful."

"Just my first load," Ashley said. "Everything going all right with you?"

"Well…" Fanny grimaced. "I'm afraid this isn't going to be like other Bradley parties," she began, only to be interrupted by the musical ring of her cell phone. One finger went up as she half turned to take the call.

Not like other Bradley parties? The warning made Ashley's brows rise a little, but she shrugged off her concern and kept moving her cart forward. There was dip in her future. Moose. Suze, whom she couldn't in good conscience disappoint. And after today, two weeks off from work. The florist shop always closed in January to accommodate the owner and her family's ski vacation.

So Ashley needed to take care of the task at hand and then move…

…on with her life.

Ignoring the uneasiness that idea brought on, she began looking for signs of the Bradleys' arrival. Nancy had said she and her husband, Arthur, would be arriving only shortly before their guests, but she was an attentive hostess, and Ashley wouldn't be surprised to find her fussing with the position of the furniture or reviewing the calendar she had planned for the week ahead. A whimsical and charming woman, she was known for the unique parties she organized every year.

The place seemed deserted, however. Ashley strolled about, her heels clicking on the wooden floors as she tucked small arrangements on bathroom windowsills and larger ones on the occasional tables in the cavernous room with the forty-foot ceilings that was referred to as the great hall. Then she moved to the dining room, where she placed centerpieces along the massive dining table that could seat thirty. For all its size, the home still felt…well, homey, with its velvet-upholstered furniture in muted shades and the lovely, mantel-topped fireplaces. There was one in the dining room and another in the library. The third in the great hall took up an entire wall and was big enough to roast an ox. Flames leaped and jumped in them now, splashing golden light to counter the growing dusk.

Cart empty, she pushed it back toward the kitchen. She'd load up and finish the first floor. After that, she'd take the service elevator to the second and third. Another twenty minutes or so and she'd be back on the road.

Fanny was still on the phone when Ashley exited, but was finished with her call when she returned with another round of flower arrangements. She paused, still curious about the caterer's earlier comment. "So… what's going to be different about the party this year?"

Okay, so the question was kind of *Downton Abbey* of her, but face it, wondering and gossiping about the owners of the estate was nearly impossible to resist.

It didn't help that Fanny cast a look around as if they might be overheard by the lord of the manor. "The Mr. and Mrs. won't be here this year."

Ashley blinked. "Arthur and Nancy?"

Fanny nodded. "Grandbaby came early."

"Well, that's nice," Ashley said. "But…they didn't cancel the party?"

"Nope. It's an especially important one this year. They just announced Arthur Bradley's retirement. They want to show their best clients that things aren't going to change under the tutelage of the new head of the firm."

"Oh," Ashley said. "And the new head of the firm is...?"

"Chase, of course."

Of course. Chase Bradley, Arthur and Nancy's son. Dark-haired, lean-bodied Chase Bradley, who strolled about with a bone-deep confidence that no woman could fail to admire. She'd never met the man, but on the occasions she'd delivered flowers to the house, she'd caught glimpses of him. While she wasn't normally a timid titmouse of a person, she'd always found herself scurrying away from his oh-so-masculine presence.

This time she'd do no different, she thought, putting her weight behind the cart. It was time to finish her duties and skedaddle. Then a horrible noise had her drawing up short. Her gaze flew to Fanny. "What the—"

The blood-curdling sound of female frustration and rage came again. Ashley jumped. "Should we call the police?" she wondered aloud.

Thumps sounded, as though a body had been pushed and was now tumbling down the grand flight of stairs. Her hand rose to her throat. "Oh, my God," she said, and ran toward the sound with Fanny at her heels.

They stopped in the hallway, peering around a corner to the staircase. It wasn't a body broken at the bottom, but a suitcase, its contents spilled in a profusion of bright colors. A beautiful, sleek woman was on the landing, hands on her hips, the red talons of her nails standing out against her navy peg-leg pants. She was staring at the mess of clothes as if her gaze could ignite them on fire. Then she glanced up to the top of the stairs and hissed.

"This is all your fault." Her malevolence was now aimed at the calm man standing above her, one shoulder propped against a wall and his ankles crossed, as if he had all the time in the world for the murderous little drama the blonde was clearly preparing as her starring vehicle.

"Who's that?" Ashley whispered to Fanny.

"Apparently the woman on her way out of Chase's life."

CHASE BRADLEY COULD only blame himself for the current situation. Not that he hadn't always made his non-intentions very clear to Brianna, but he'd realized quite early in their short relationship that she suffered from selective listening. She simply didn't hear anything that would counter her world view—the world that revolved around her.

He frowned. What did it say about him that he'd continued to see her for three months after coming to that conclusion?

It said he'd been too consumed with the changeover in the family business to take care of personal business. Hell, he should be smarter than that.

He tuned back into Brianna's rant. She was stabbing her arm in the direction of the exploded suitcase. "Who?" she demanded. "Who is going to take care of this?"

Since he wasn't the one who had kicked the piece of luggage down the stairs, it wasn't going to be him. "Brianna, calm down," he said mildly.

Her face turned a mottled shade of red. "You do realize I'm leaving?"

"It's what you shouted right after I said I wasn't planning on proposing."

Brianna slammed her arms over her chest. "But I

told you New Year's Eve would be the perfect time for an announcement," she fumed.

Chase shook his head. Where had she gotten the idea that they were marriage bound? That he hadn't seen this coming only made him curse himself more. "Brianna, I'm sorry. Truly. I'm sorry if you had the impression we were aiming toward the altar. That's not going to happen."

"Then I'm *really* leaving you!"

To be fair to himself, until today, she'd been mostly undemanding and understanding. Self-centered, maybe, but he'd actually appreciated the email she'd sent with links to the Christmas presents she'd expected him to give her last week. Chase abhorred pretense, and he'd counted her honesty about that list as a feature, not a defect. "I'll have Gregory bring the car around. He'll be happy to take you back to LA."

Though Chase usually avoided all the car-and-driver nonsense, this time he'd taken one of the company limos, thinking it might come in handy for his guests during the week at the lake house. Now it was coming in handy for him.

The expression on Brianna's face indicated she wasn't mollified by the offer. Chase watched her haul in a large breath and he braced for the next onslaught. "I'm not going without my clothes," she declared in a strident voice.

"I wouldn't dream of suggesting you should," Chase replied, and he could see his reasonable tone was only further infuriating her. "I'll let Gregory know to be ready if you'll tell me how long it will take you to repack."

"*Me?*"

Wow. Now she was acting as if she regularly had a handmaiden to attend her. Chase held on to his own kindling temper. "Brianna—"

"Mr. Bradley?"

He turned his head slightly in the direction of the hesitant voice. Peeking around a corner downstairs was the caterer. "Yes, Mrs. Erwin?"

"Is there something I could do to help?" There was a look of concern on her motherly face.

"Thank you, but no," he said firmly. "I'm sure you're quite busy as it is in the kitchen."

A brief pause, and then she turned, presumably heading back to her domain. But another movement caught his attention, and he narrowed his eyes, tilting his head to get a better look. Someone was in Mrs. Erwin's wake. She had a glossy head of espresso-dark hair and wore a sort of robe thing that didn't detract from a pair of excellent legs dressed in decadent lace.

"Who was that?" Brianna asked, her voice suspicious. She craned her neck to see where he'd been looking.

Perhaps that niggle of interest he felt was showing on his face. He wiped it clean. "The caterer." And someone else. An employee of Mrs. Erwin? No matter, he thought, dismissing the minor mystery. He was trying to smoothly detach from one woman, not get entangled with another.

It took several more minutes to usher Brianna from the house. She finally ended up throwing her clothes back in her suitcase with ill grace. Chase hunted up a couple of bungee cords to keep the thing together since the latches had broken on its tumble. As he carried the luggage out to the car, he endured her parting shots.

It wasn't pleasant, but then it was over.

As the car disappeared down the drive, he tried to scare up a holiday mood. His guests would arrive soon and they'd expect him to be a genial and entertaining host. But the scene with Brianna lingered in his mind as he climbed the steps to the front door. His gut had let him down, he decided, and that wasn't good. It should have been talking to him from the beginning with her, sending out warnings on a regular basis.

Stifling a sigh, he turned the knob and pushed on the paneled wood to let himself into the house. His gaze instantly caught on a pair of lace-wrapped legs climbing the staircase. Their owner's thick, wavy hair bounced against her shoulder blades with each step. The clean, enticing scent of flowers lingered in the air.

His gut began clamoring. *Follow that one. Find out who she is. See where she's been all our life.*

Oh, sure. *Now* it started talking. Which just went to prove the current out-of-whack state of his instincts. With a busy week ahead, this was not the time to be distracted by a pretty pair of legs. Even a stupendous pair of legs, which hers actually were.

Deliberately turning his mind from that fact, he wheeled left and headed toward the office on the first floor. It was time to go over the guest list and the plans his mother had laid out for the week. His phone vibrated and he pulled it free from his pocket, grinning when he saw the photo his brother-in-law had texted. His new niece, Larissa Larue. Leave it to his sister to come up with such a fanciful name—she took after their mother that way.

He texted back, A beauty! And she was, even with

that scrunched little face and the pink stocking cap pulled down nearly to her nonexistent eyebrows.

Feeling more upbeat, he settled behind the big desk and pulled up the files he wanted on his laptop. The house party would total twenty-four—no, twenty-three now that Brianna had decamped. Eleven couples and himself. Mrs. Erwin would be in the kitchen every day, ensuring they all were well fed. A handful of servers in her employ would help at the meals. A local cleaning service would send a daily crew to take care of the housekeeping.

He wondered if Lacey Legs was attached to either the caterer or the cleaners. Would he have the opportunity to see her every day? Would her front be as attractive as her back?

On a silent groan at his own lack of control, he spun his chair to look out the mullioned windows at the view overlooking the lake. It was nearing dark, but he could still make out the winter blue of the water. At this time of day, it was almost slate-colored, with the fir trees a dark contrast against the white slopes of the surrounding mountains. It never ceased to amaze him that a couple of hours away were LA's famous beaches and graceful palm trees, while here it was craggy peaks and towering conifers. His mind wandered again. Had Lacey Legs grown up in the mountains?

All right. Time for a better distraction. Good smells had made their way from the kitchen, and he decided he had very good reasons to check in with Mrs. Erwin. The bar should be set up in the great hall shortly and he could ask her about that, too, though a bartender would do all the heavy lifting once the guests arrived.

In the kitchen, he found the caterer bustling about,

instructing servers in black pants and white shirts about where to find the serving trays. Two of them were young men. The young women had their hair in neat ponytails. None of them wore lace or had that shiny hair that he couldn't free from his thoughts.

Mrs. Erwin turned to him. "Is there something you need?"

"The bar—"

"George is just getting on it," she said, pointing to one of the men. George gave him a two-fingered salute.

"Okay. Great." He glanced around at the other three young people. "You have enough helpers?"

"Oh, yes," the older woman was quick to assure him. "Ruth, Carl and Ellen will handle it just fine."

Chase nodded. So Lacey definitely wasn't part of the waitstaff. So why *was* she here?

As if to answer his question, she came through the mudroom and into the kitchen. Well, he assumed it was her, because he could see the legs. The rest of her was obscured by an immense flower arrangement in cool blues and white. Long, thin curling stick things gave it even more drama. Chase leaped forward. "Here, let me get that," he said, taking it from her grasp.

The action gave him a view of her face.

He felt as if he'd been hit in the solar plexus. He stared at her, breathless, until he coughed to get oxygen moving into his lungs again. With a little more effort, he managed a smile. "I'm Chase Bradley."

Her face was heart-shaped, and as he watched, pink color infused her cheeks. She had a snub of a nose, thick lashes, a full mouth and eyes the same slate blue as the lake water. "I, um…" Her hands dipped into the pockets of the apron/coat thing she wore over a black dress.

He smiled at her again. "You're, um…?" he prompted.

The color on her face deepened. "Sorry. Ashley Walker. From the florist."

"Ah," he replied, and hefted the flowers. "That's a surprise."

A brief smile flashed over her face, but her gaze danced away from his. "Oh, I guess not."

Who knew he could be charmed by shy? "Where should I put this?" he asked.

"I can take it. Really," she said.

"You'll trip over your toes. It's bigger than you are." She was a petite thing, and the hell of it was it only served to make him feel more…protective. Or was that predatory? Bad Chase.

In an attempt to dial down the attraction, he made his tone brisk. "Why don't you lead the way? I'll follow."

She did just that. But losing the front view didn't diminish his interest in her one bit. The *tap-tap-tap* of her heels on the floor only drew his attention to those incredible gams of hers. The fragrance of the flowers in his nose only made him wonder what *she* smelled like. He wanted to press his mouth to her throat and breathe her in. He wanted to bury his face in that glossy hair and determine if it was as silky as it looked.

His gut was nagging at him again, and Chase didn't think it was going to shut up anytime soon. *Follow Ashley Walker*, it ordered. *Find out where she's been all our life.*

CHAPTER TWO

ASHLEY WISHED SHE'D done her job and gotten out of the house before drawing Chase Bradley's attention. As she proceeded down the hall, the man carrying the massive arrangement behind her, she could feel his presence like a warm tickle on the back of her neck. When facing him, she'd felt his magnetism elsewhere.

He had the kind of looks that heated a woman.

His face was all planes and angles: sharp cheekbones, blade of a nose, square jawline. His broad brow was revealed by the business cut of his nearly black hair. His eyes were gray, surrounded by inky lashes. His very white smile flipped her stomach and filled her with an odd, wild yearning.

That was the kind of effect he likely encountered—and expected—from all females.

It vexed Ashley to acknowledge that. She'd never liked being one of a crowd. Not that she enjoyed standing out, either. That had been her husband, Stu. Cocky, reckless, flashy Stu. Thinking of him no longer tore at her heart. It just informed her head, reminding her to go slow, be cautious, take her time. Even if Moose turned out to be The One—fat chance, because *Moose*—she figured she'd casually date the next man in her life for a few years before even contemplating something the slightest bit serious.

It was possible that she'd never fall in love again, and the idea of that didn't make her feel as lonely as it might. It felt...smart. Safe.

They'd reached the foyer.

A round table, gleaming from a good waxing, sat precisely in its center. She pointed to it. "There," she said.

He placed the ceramic pot with its profusion of flowers in the middle and stepped back.

"Thank you," she said, moving forward without looking at him. She began fussing with the stems and leaves, hoping he'd read her actions as a polite dismissal.

He didn't move.

Without wanting to, she glanced over her shoulder. He wore gray jeans, a light blue dress shirt and a darker blue slim-cut, suit-styled jacket over it. What every successful young executive wore to greet guests at his vacation estate. She tore her gaze off him and went back to working on the arrangement of white roses, miniature irises and muscari.

"Lovely," Chase murmured.

"Thank you. I'll pass along your compliment to my boss, the owner of the shop." Another few seconds passed and he was still there and she was still pretending to be conscious of only the flora in the room when the male fauna nearby was completely derailing her thought processes.

What should she do? How could she get him to go away? For some odd reason, she didn't want to face him again.

"Is there anything else you need?" she asked, still with her back turned. "Otherwise, I'm on my way."

"You must have big plans for tonight."

Since he couldn't see her face, she grimaced. Moose. "Sure. It's New Year's Eve."

"And you're already dressed for a party. I like the lace stockings."

She fought the urge to cross one leg over the other. But a flame shot up the back of both, like a fiery seam. "Um, thank you." How could she begin to conclude this conversation? "I hope you have a nice time tonight yourself."

"It'll be all right, I suppose, even though I lost my hostess."

There was no way she couldn't respond to the comment. She turned around, because it would seem inhuman and impolite not to. "I'm sorry. Your goodbye seemed…"

"Awkward? Uncomfortable?" he supplied, grimacing. "Inconvenient?"

She offered her own suggestion. "Hurtful?"

He shook his head. "Not to me. And if Brianna's pain goes beyond her pride, I'd be surprised. Yet I'm still sorry I didn't see that she was taking us much too seriously. I guess I've been too caught up in my work."

"Your kind of job must require a lot of focus." She didn't know exactly what it entailed, but she figured investing other people's money would make a man sober and prudent. Unlike Stu, Chase Bradley would look before he leaped.

"I'm getting used to my new role in the company," he said. "I hope this week goes off without a hitch."

"So do I," she said. She'd always liked his mother and his father, the few times she'd interacted with them, and Chase…well, she was a trifle more accustomed to

him now, even though she could almost taste his masculinity on her tongue. It was coming off him in waves.
"I wish your family well."

"Do you?" One of Chase's brows arched.

Ashley got a funny feeling in her stomach—not quite
queasy, but close. "Sure." Deciding there was nothing
more to say, she gave a last glance at the flowers, then
strode toward the hallway that would take her to the
side entrance and from there to her van. Chase got in
her way.

Halting, she pressed her palms against the thin cotton smock, and dared to look at his face. A black ring
surrounded the gray of his irises. It gave the impression
of being looked at through binoculars, or maybe dual
microscopes, she decided, and felt her stomach take
another woozy turn. With a hand, she made a vague
gesture. "I need to get to my party." When he just continued to look at her as if he could see through her skin
to her racing blood and her jumping nerves, she cleared
her throat. "I'm making dip."

"What kind?"

Surely, he didn't care what kind of dip she made.
It wasn't anything fancy, like he was undoubtedly accustomed to. But she humored him, because otherwise
she'd have to push past him and run down the hall like
a spooked rabbit. "You mix a packet of stuff into sour
cream. Stir. With a fork, a spoon, a knife. I've even used
my finger," she said, demonstrating.

"That sounds…messy."

"Not so." Before she even knew she was going to
do it, she had the digit in her open mouth and she was
pretending to lick it clean.

Pretending to lick it clean!

The heat of a thousand suns burst over her face and she quickly pulled her finger from between her lips and tucked both hands into the pockets of her smock. Where had that move come from? It was pure…flirtation, and she'd never been coquettish. Stu had been her boyfriend before she'd been old enough to learn any flagrant moves. Since his death, the only way she could have picked up any would have been through osmosis, those few times she'd met Suze at bars before the woman married Jackson.

Ducking her head, she made to scoot around Chase. "I've got to go," she mumbled.

"Wait." He caught her arm. His touch hummed along her nerve endings, vibrating from wrist to shoulder as the tiny hairs on her skin stood at attention. "I have a proposition."

Her head jerked up.

"Not that kind of proposition," he said, humor putting new light in his eyes. "Unless—"

"No, thank you." She drew back her elbow, freeing herself from his hold. This time, she managed to skirt his big body, and then she *clack-clack-clacked* out of the foyer, her high heels moving even quicker than her pulse.

She breezed through the hall, sped along the kitchen floor, and was then out in the brisk air, where she breathed in great gulps of calming oxygen. Her hand was on the cold chrome of the door handle when he spoke from behind her.

"I'm serious," Chase said. "I need a hostess. Could you help me out?"

"You're joking," she said without turning around.

"No." He came close enough that she could smell

the expensive cologne he wore—or maybe it was just expensive soap because it was a clean scent and not a clingy one. "I'll pay you well."

Now she chanced a glance over her shoulder. "For what, exactly?"

His eyebrows shot toward his forehead. "Why, Ashley, we've only just met. Nothing indecent, okay? I'm a businessman, and this offer is entirely on the up-and-up."

It wasn't disappointment that sluiced through her. "You'd better spell it out."

"Come live here for a week. Even out the numbers of men and women at the house party. Smile. You might even have a little fun."

"Why would you want me?" she asked, finally turning to face him.

"It's not such a crazy impulse, I promise you. The thing is, you're dressed for the occasion."

"Well, true," she acknowledged with a slight nod of her head. "Though it's for an entirely different party." With chips, dip and Moose.

"Are you married?" Chase asked.

Stu. With his streaky blond hair and his snow tan. He'd burned through life too soon. "Not anymore."

"Boyfriend?"

She shook her head.

"Well, there you go. I need a single female pretty much immediately, and you're already here. Plus, I'm a generous employer." He named a sum.

She nearly gasped. "I couldn't accept that."

Chase frowned. "Now I see you *need* to take me up on this. Your negotiating skills are severely lacking. I can teach you a thing or two, I'll bet."

A shiver tiptoed down her spine. Ashley ignored it. "For all that I'd be grateful for it," she said, her voice sugar-sweet, "we both know that a big, bad businessman like yourself can handle a week on his own just fine."

"Also true."

A laugh bubbled up from her belly. He was confident, all right.

"But…" He drew a fingertip along her cheek, and when she shivered, unable to hide it this time, he frowned and stripped off his jacket. Dropping it over her shoulders, he tugged the lapels close beneath her chin.

Though his warmth instantly enveloped her, she still had to fight another betraying shiver. "But?" she prompted.

His serious gaze caught hers. "Here's the thing, Ashley. I guarantee if I don't have a woman by my side, one of the clients will feel as if *she* has to step up. And this week isn't about requiring any of those who work with us to take on responsibilities. It's about shedding them. They're supposed to have a good time and relax in the capable Bradley hands. It makes them feel more comfortable with our firm."

That actually made sense, Ashley thought. It was a logical, very legitimate, business-backed argument. Hadn't she already supposed a man with his kind of success in his line of work would make rational and shrewd decisions?

Maybe she *should* let that rub off on her. And if she did… Well, she had two free weeks. Grabbing up this opportunity to make a fistful of cash during one of them would give her some cushion in her bank account. At the very least she could buy outfits other than T-shirts

and jeans for that shell-stepping-out-of she'd said she'd
be doing in the new year.

In her year of yes.

She hauled in a breath that smelled of lake and snow
and just a little bit of Chase Bradley. It was an intelligent choice, she thought. Not a crazy impulse, as he'd
assured her. She would be taking no kind of risk at all,
really.

"You've got yourself a deal."

CHASE CONGRATULATED HIMSELF a few hours later for his
powers of persuasion. Ashley Walker had been a fine
snap decision. And even though she'd started a fire inside him by that little mime with her finger—something
he'd noted she'd instantly regretted—he'd managed to
come up with a sensible argument that got her to agree
to be his hostess.

It had paid off.

She'd greeted his guests smoothly, helped to make
sure everyone had drinks during the cocktail hour,
kept talk flowing during dinner with those closest to
her at the table. While not a loud, lampshade-on-her-
head, life-of-the-party type—thank God—her shyness
seemed strictly reserved for him. With everyone else she
was easy with her smiles and her conversation.

As the only local in the group, she was called upon
to dispense nuggets of the area's history and to suggest
nearby attractions. The party was made up of people
who possessed a high degree of wealth, but she didn't
appear intimidated nor did she pretend to be anything
but a woman who worked with her hands and enjoyed
doing so.

She fascinated him.

And it wasn't lost on Chase that he'd have an opportunity to kiss that fascinating mouth of hers at midnight. It was tradition, right? And he wanted to taste her in a way he found most distracting. So he figured getting that taste out of the way as soon as possible would be beneficial for his plans for the rest of the week. He'd satisfy his curiosity and then get on with the more important task of cementing integral business relationships for another year.

But it also wasn't lost on him that the locking of lips wouldn't happen unless he got her more comfortable around him.

His mother had arranged for a pianist to play on the grand piano in the great hall after dinner. Muted TVs in other rooms were tuned to the big countdown shows, but most people opted for getting another drink from the bar and enjoying the live music. The musician played a classy selection of tunes: Gershwin to Billy Joel, Sinatra standards to Broadway songs.

When a handful of couples took to the dance floor while the man played "New York State of Mind," Chase looked for Ashley. She stood alone by the windows, sipping sparkling water as she stared out at the view toward the lake. Fairy lights had been strung through the trees and wrapped the rail surrounding the deck. The light snow on the ground glittered. A winter wonderland.

"Pretty, huh?" he asked, coming up behind her.

She started, glancing around. "Sorry, I was woolgathering."

"The beginning of a new year is conducive to deep thought," he said, aware that she edged away to put more inches between them. "Were you working on world peace or a solution to global hunger?"

"You're giving me much more credit than I deserve."

"So, what *were* you thinking about?"

Her pretty mouth pursed. "What I'm going to have to do to make up my absence to my best friend, Suze. It was her party I was going to tonight."

"Think she'll understand?"

Ashley shrugged. She'd taken off that robe thing before the guests arrived. Underneath it was a ladylike party dress that still made him sweat because it was so damn proper. It revealed slender, bare arms, and combined the creamy flesh of them with her lace-covered legs... "You should dance with me," he said.

She appeared not to hear him. "It's worse because of Moose."

"She has a moose?"

"Moose is a man. She asked him to be my date tonight."

"You'd date a man named Moose?"

"I'd do just about anything for Suze. She...she's gotten me through tough times."

At her now-worried expression, Chase could tell she didn't want to elaborate on the "tough times." So he found her hand and pulled her toward the music. "Dance with me."

She made some sounds of protest, but he ignored them. The pianist had segued into "You'll Never Walk Alone" and when he drew her against him to lightly sway to the music, her body was stiff in his arms. "I wanted to talk to you about the coming week. Your duties," he lied.

"Oh." Ashley relaxed a fraction.

Chase wished she'd look at him like a man, not an employer, but clearly that wasn't to be just yet. "So far, you've done a great job."

"Thank you."

"If you'd continue in this same vein for the rest of the week I'll give you a bonus."

"Chase…"

Now it was his turn to ignore her. "Just continue being yourself and seeing to the comfort of the guests."

"I can do that."

"Each day has a theme that my mother settled upon and an activity or two to support that theme."

The corners of Ashley's lips quirked upward. "Your mom."

"Yeah." He smiled back, moving his feet so it was more like dancing and not just shifting. "Her imagination is a little offbeat, but everyone ends up enjoying her ideas."

Ashley was following along, letting him lead. "So what do I need to do?"

"Like I said. Be yourself. Be relaxed." With his palm at the small of her back, he nudged her closer to him. Once he'd been at a wedding where the guests were given fresh rose petals to throw at the bride and groom. His handful had been slightly bruised, and that was what she smelled of—crushed, clean sweetness.

"I can do that." But wariness had overtaken her expression again, and she pulled back to put more room between their bodies.

So, not ready for a kiss, Chase thought, and decided to change tactics. "Hey, I want you to meet a couple of people. They slipped in during the second course, and I don't think you've had the opportunity to speak with them."

Stepping away from the other dancers, he took her hand and tucked it into the crook of his elbow. He scanned the room and found the Sargeants just turning from the bar, each of them with a glass of ruby wine. With a smile, he drew her in their direction.

"Arch." He moved from Ashley to give his old friend a back-thumping half hug. "June, beautiful as ever." She got a kiss on the cheek.

"We're so sorry we were late," June said, her curious glance sliding to Ashley and then back to his face.

"She had to go back to her parents' house twice in order to say more goodbyes to the twins," Arch said.

His wife bumped her elbow against his ribs. "If I recall correctly, it was you who needed to make sure that my dad knew how to install the car seats in his SUV."

Grinning, Arch rubbed his side. "We're disgustingly besotted with our offspring," he confessed, his eyes bright with good humor and fixed on Ashley's face. "I'm Arch Sargeant," he said, holding out his hand.

"Ashley Walker. And anything I can do to make your stay more pleasant, please let me know."

His friend's wife looked ready to burst with curiosity. "I'm June." Her glance shifted to Chase. "So…I thought Brianna was going to be here. Glad to see she isn't."

Arch groaned. "So much for subtle, sweetheart."

"Brianna had to leave unexpectedly," Ashley put in smoothly. "Chase hired me to take over as hostess."

"Hired you?" Her eyebrows climbed high on her forehead, and her gaze darted between Chase and Ashley.

"I work for a local florist," Ashley explained. "And I happened to be at the right place at the right time—

meaning here at the house—when Chase found a need for someone to help out."

"Found a need," Arch echoed.

At the smirk in his voice, Chase sent him a quelling look. "Ashley, Arch is my former college roommate. And June—"

"Has this sudden need for some girl talk."

Ashley looked alarmed. "Oh, I—"

"Actually, I need help pinning a strap," June said, plucking at the silk of her slinky red dress. Her smile beamed wide and guileless. "You'll help, won't you?"

And with that, Chase saw his hostess head off into the metaphorical sunset with his best friend's wife. Frowning, he glanced over at Arch. "I don't want her scaring Ashley away."

"She'll just pump her for all her personal information," Arch said in a cheery tone.

Chase groaned. "That's what I mean."

"What *else* do you mean?" his friend asked. "Brianna takes off and an hour later you've got Ashley moved in?"

In less than an hour, Chase thought. "Just for the week," he assured himself and his best buddy. He shrugged one shoulder. "I saw her and it…it seemed like a simple solution."

Arch was gazing at him.

"What's with the pitying expression?" Chase demanded.

"Nothing's simple when it comes to women, you should know that."

"Hell," Chase said. "Don't go there, please? Sure, she's pretty and all." Beautiful. "But I asked her because I needed the assistance."

Not true. What he needed was that midnight kiss he was planning, just to satisfy his curiosity and so he could neutralize this odd fascination she held for him. Once that was out of the way, he could devote his attention to the important business of the rest of the week.

He managed to get Arch onto other topics and then included some others in their light conversation as the musician continued to play. It was when the servers began circulating with trays of crystal flutes filled with liquid bubbles that Chase realized midnight was nearly upon them. June was standing near her husband, her arm around his waist as they swayed to the music.

Ashley was nowhere in sight.

As the countdown began, he was torn. Leave his guests or seek out his hostess? It would be better to stick with the crowd, he decided, ignoring a spurt of disappointment. Foolish to feel it, especially when the last time he'd been so eager for a New Year's kiss he'd been thirteen years old. At Tammy Martin's house, he remembered. Her parents were out for the evening and she'd been babysitting her little brother and sister.

"Ten," the people on the dance floor chanted, arranging themselves in a circle.

Ridiculous to want to look into Ashley's upturned face as the clock struck twelve.

"Nine."

No, it wasn't imperative that he dive his fingers into her flowing hair.

"Eight."

Would her breath hitch as his mouth neared?

"Seven."

He'd trace his nose across her warm cheek, drawing in her crushed-petal scent.

The voices of the people surrounding him rose. "Six."

Shoving his hands into his pockets, he rooted his feet to the ground, even though his gaze wandered, looking for any sign of her.

"Five."

He recalled Tammy's kiss—his first—and hadn't that changed his life? A boy taking his first step to becoming a man.

"Four."

Move, his gut piped up. *Find out where Ashley's been all our life.*

On the crowd's roar of "three," he bolted from the great hall.

At "two" he saw movement in the library at the end of the passage.

"One" sounded in the distance when he breached the doorway. Ashley, who had been standing contemplating the small fire burning in the grate, whirled. The notes of "Auld Lang Syne" drifted into the room, wrapping around them like ribbons, he thought, then instantly shoved away the fancy.

Still, her big eyes and her tense posture drew him forward. Her fingers clutched the lace overlaying her skirt. Chase hauled in a slow breath as he came to a halt before her. "You're missing midnight," he said softly as if his voice might spook her.

She smiled a little. "The clock ticks on without me."

It seemed to come to a standstill to Chase as he stared down at her upturned face, her sooty lashes a perfect frame for her expressive eyes. There was wariness in them.

"Don't be afraid of me," he whispered.

Her gaze slid to the side. "Of course not," she scoffed. "Or shy."

Her gaze flicked back to his for a moment. "I'm not."

Only with him, he thought, and for some reason he liked the idea of that.

The last notes of the song died out. The guests' voices stopped singing and they went back to chatting. In the background, the pianist continued playing the traditional song, embellishing the original melody. Chase stepped closer to Ashley and cupped her bare shoulders in his hands. "Happy New Year," he said, and, bending his head, placed his lips on hers.

She tasted like champagne and roses. But it wasn't that which got him. It was the tremble that racked her frame. Something moved in his belly, lust and another emotion that reached up to clutch his heart like a fist. His tongue touched her bottom lip, and even as she trembled again, she opened her mouth. He took a tender foray inside, not pressing but trying to please instead.

When her hand came up to wrap around his wrist as if she had to hang on for dear life, it was Chase who shuddered. *Sweet*, he thought. *So damn heady and sweet*.

Because he was desperate, suddenly, to move closer, he drew back. She stared at him with those big eyes, her mouth still damp from his. That fist around his heart tightened.

His curiosity was not sated, Chase knew. His fascination with her not put to rest. It would take more than a kiss to do that. Much more.

Chase Bradley wanted Ashley Walker in his bed.

CHAPTER THREE

WALKERS WERE NOT COWARDS, Ashley reminded herself, sitting in the back of a limo that was taking her from the florist to her own small house. She'd dropped the van in the parking lot behind the business. Now, once again in her New Year's Eve dress but sans the stockings, she was headed home to pack a bag for her week at the Bradley estate.

She could do this, she assured herself again, despite that midnight kiss.

Her gaze slid toward the man sprawled on the seat beside hers. "You didn't need to escort me, you know," she said.

He'd been looking out the window and now turned his head. "Maybe I was afraid you'd change your mind."

"We made a deal."

"Right." He crossed his legs at the ankle. Today he wore a pair of black boots, black jeans and a cashmere sweater the same gray as his eyes. At least she thought it was cashmere. She'd have to touch it to be positive about that, and she sure as heck wasn't going to be reaching out and fondling him anytime soon.

Last night she'd squeezed his hard arm as he'd taken her mouth in the softest, yet most carnal kiss she could imagine. Her toes curled just thinking about it, and she quivered.

Chase's hand went to the climate controls. "Cold? I'll edge up the heat."

Exactly what he'd done the night before. Edged up the heat.

But she said nothing as warmer air blew through the vents. "Over there." She leaned forward to speak to the driver. *A driver!* "The bungalow with the wreath on the door."

The man pulled into the rutted driveway alongside her little house. She didn't have a garage, but the one-bedroom was spacious, and she didn't cringe too much when Chase followed her inside. Sure, it wasn't a fancy home like he was used to, but it was hers.

He looked around as he stood in the tiny foyer, taking in the living room that opened to the updated kitchen. "I like this," he said, and walked toward her fireplace, his gaze trained on the photos sitting on the mantel. None of Stu or of Stu and her. She'd put those away years ago in a fit of self-preservation. These were black-and-whites of the Walker ancestors, posing with shotguns, wearing low-slung hats and the wooden expressions typical of the times.

"They seem nice," Chase commented, glancing over his shoulder with a small smile.

Even that quick flash of white teeth made her knees soft. She slipped out of her shoes to pad toward her bedroom at the back of the house. "The Walkers came to the mountains a hundred and fifty years ago, traveling up the hill with oxen and wills of iron."

Behind her bedroom door, she quickly slipped out of her dress and hung it in her closet. In seconds she was in jeans, a sweater and a pair of suede boots. Chase's mother had taken her themes for the house party from

the designated "holidays" of the month. Besides being
New Year's Day, Ashley had been told, January 1 was
"Daydreamer's Day." Before they'd left the Bradley
estate that morning, Chase had led her to a room on
the third floor, an immense space she hadn't been instructed to fill with flowers. Instead, table after table
held buckets of plastic bricks, wooden blocks and hun-
dreds of pieces of railroad systems, including houses,
trees, people and locomotives. The plan was to encourage the guests to "play" to their heart's content by creating worlds from their imaginations.

As Ashley gathered clothes and toiletries in stacks on
her bed, she smiled at the idea of it. Where one would
find all those toys for a temporary period she didn't
know, but she knew she'd enjoy experimenting with
them. Wasn't that what she did with flowers every day?
Creating things from the pictures in her head was a delightful way, she'd found, to make a living.

And to escape.

She ventured back to the kitchen and the utility closet
there. "I won't be much longer," she called to Chase.
"Just have to get my suitcase and fill it."

He strolled into the room, distracting her. How could
he look so good? A quarter-inch of the ribbed neckline
of a blinding white T-shirt showed at his throat. The
sleeves of his sweater were pushed up to expose powerful forearms she didn't think he'd achieved by merely
working a calculator on a daily basis. His attention was
on the framed photo in his hand.

She stared at him, noting the bristle of whiskers on
his jaw. He hadn't shaved that morning. If he kissed her
now, the small, scratchy hairs would leave a telltale trail
of reddened skin in their wake. Then she'd be able to

see proof of the meeting of their lips. When she'd been in her assigned bedroom the night before, she'd studied herself in the mirror.

There'd been no overt sign of the first kiss she'd experienced in more than four years. But she'd touched her mouth with her fingertips, aware her lips felt puffy and oversensitized. Thinking of that, it had taken her a long time to fall asleep in the nightshirt that Chase had unearthed from somewhere. His sister's, he'd said of the utilitarian flannel. Thank goodness it hadn't been something silky or sheer she'd have to assume was left behind by an old girlfriend.

He looked up now and almost caught her staring. She let her gaze drop to the frame he held and she drifted closer to glance at it. "Uncle Handlebar," she said. "Aunt Clunky Shoes."

"Not their real names, I take it," he said, grinning.

"Mustache," she said. "Clunky Shoes is obvious."

"They're really part of your family?"

"Oh, yeah. We go way back at Blue Arrow Lake. Came early, have scrambled for years to keep our toeholds in the mountains."

"Something we have in common," Chase said. "You have a family history in a place. I have a family history in a business."

"Oh?"

"Bradley Financial was established by my great-grandfather." He narrowed his eyes as if thinking. "Based on photos I've seen, I think we can call him Grandpa Potbelly."

"A fan of beer?" she guessed.

"No idea. More likely he enjoyed whiskey and cigars. But he definitely had the expansive midsection."

Ashley couldn't help but take a quick glance at Chase's lean hips and flat abs. "You're not carrying on the family tradition."

His slow smile appeared gratified. "Not in that particular way, I hope."

With a quick turn, Ashley directed herself away from him and his ever-so-attractive features. "Did you feel pressure to take that on?" she asked, pulling open the pantry door. "Your position in the company, I mean."

"No." She could feel him coming up behind her. "I have a head for numbers. I like the game of finance."

Frowning, she glanced at him. "Surely it's not a game. In your business I'd think you have to take it all quite seriously. Be levelheaded at every moment. Ponder all the possibilities before making your decisions."

"Whatever you say," he murmured. "Here, let me get that."

On tiptoe, she was reaching for the suitcase hanging from a heavy utility hook overhead. "No, I can…"

But he was already crowding her farther into the corner closet, his chest brushing her back. As she turned to protest again, he shoved the picture frame into her hand and stretched to lift the piece of luggage down. "Where should I take this?" he asked.

He was so close she could smell his skin, his toothpaste, a hint of laundry detergent. The T-shirt, she figured, because the cashmere sweater was too refined to have any kind of odor at all. With the photograph against her breasts like a shield, she just gaped up at him. The quarters were too close…but deliciously so.

Chase's eyes heated. "Ashley…"

The note of desire in his voice snapped her out of

her trance. "I'll take it to my room," she said. "The suitcase."

"I'll carry it." He strode across the kitchen with her following behind. "This way, right?"

"Mmm," she said, distracted again by the wide pair of shoulders that made the narrow hall that much more constricted. Come to think of it, no man had ever been in the passage leading to her bedroom. She'd had Jackson and Suze and a few others over for dinner sometimes, but no male had gotten so close to her inner sanctum. She'd moved to this house after Stu's accident. The room Chase just stepped into had always been her private place.

Her retreat.

It would never be the same, she thought with a sudden clutch to her stomach, now that he'd brought his tall and broad presence into her feminine space. Feigning calm, she gestured toward the bed. "You can set it there. Then maybe you can go, um, wait in the living room. I'll bring it out when I'm done packing."

His brows came together. "I'll wait here. Take it for you once you're finished."

No one had ever carried her luggage for her, she realized. Well, maybe her dad when she was a little girl. But Stu hadn't. He'd considered her perfectly capable of carting things around, whether it was when she was hauling in groceries or lugging her snowboarding gear about. "I'm not a weakling," she told Chase now, thinking of how he'd grabbed the flower arrangement from her yesterday afternoon.

"It's not a question of muscles, Xena."

She shook her head at the reference to the warrior princess.

"I don't mind doing things for you," he continued. "I *like* doing things for you."

What to say to that? Ashley didn't try to come up with anything. Instead, she wished she hadn't spent the past four years home alone nearly every night. If she'd gone on a date or two, maybe she'd be able to handle Chase's smoothness, his charm, his sophistication with a bit more aplomb. As it was, he just bowled her over in every way.

Or maybe no experience could provide her with the skills to manage the way this man made her feel.

"Ashley," he said now, his voice quiet. "Will you look at me?"

See? Even now he overcame her reluctance. Though she didn't want to, she found herself turning to face him. "What?"

"You don't have to come back to the estate," he said. "If you don't want to go through with our deal, I won't hold it against you."

But it would go against her resolution! She couldn't say no to the first thing that came along during her year of yes, right? Walkers weren't cowards. "It's fine," she said. "I'm fine. I'm not afraid or anything. A deal's a deal. Walkers don't renege."

Her face heated. She was babbling, right? He had to realize she was babbling.

His eyes were doing that binocular/dual microscope thing again, giving her the feeling he was watching every doubt flash through her brain, every desire cross her heart. "Ashley?" he said, his voice so soft it was almost tender. "Should we talk about last night's kiss?"

She jolted, the backs of her knees hitting the end of the bed. "Oh, no. Not necessary. Not at all. New

Year's. Just a midnight kiss." Then she whirled to toss her clothes into the case.

Her palms were sweating and her heart was hammering, as they used to do when she was poised at the top of a black diamond run. It was then Ashley realized that though the Walkers might be brave, it didn't mitigate the bad feeling she had that all the courage in the world wouldn't keep her free from danger.

CHASE DESCENDED ON the breakfast buffet the next morning in a cheerful mood. His guests had enjoyed themselves the day before, settling in and then venturing to the third floor to check out the goings-on in the playroom. Even the most reserved of them had ended up devising elaborate communities from the bricks, blocks and railroad parts. A contemporary of his father's, Declan Hart, had talked another man into a joint development, and Chase couldn't help but laugh when they decided to charge a fee to anyone wanting access to the amusement park they'd built.

The fourteen dollars that had been collected was promised to charity, but Chase wouldn't be surprised if Declan didn't consider his pocket a legitimate 501(c)(3).

Ashley had seemed to have a good time, too. She'd constructed a fantastical skyscraper upon which butterflies built of plastic blocks had decided to roost. It reminded him of her flower arrangements: colorful, eye-pleasing and worth a second look.

As was she, of course. He hadn't dropped his intention of getting her into bed.

But yesterday he'd left her mostly alone, allowing her a chance to catch her breath. He'd known she was nervous after their New Year's kiss, so his strategy was to back off. Just a little.

His conscience wasn't bothered in the least by making this play. At her house, he'd given her ample opportunity to back out of the hostess deal. She could even have lied and expressed distaste of his kiss. He wouldn't have pushed any further then.

But he remembered her taste and her trembling body at midnight. And he'd watched her pack her bag and come with him anyway. This attraction wasn't one-sided.

As if to underscore that fact, when he entered the dining room, his gaze went directly to her, standing by the sideboard. Her eyes hit his, too, and he saw her twitch at the same time that becoming color flushed her face. She was dressed in tight dark jeans and brown boots. A long, oatmeal-colored thin-knit sweater covered her torso, but when she turned back to continue filling her plate, he saw that the loose garment buttoned up the back. It was half sliding off one shoulder, revealing more creamy skin and parts of a skinny-strapped tank top.

"Good morning," he said, strolling up to her side. As yet, they were the only two in the room.

"Morning." She kept her head down as she scooped up Mrs. Erwin's famous egg-and-potato scramble.

"Again, great job last night. Thanks for getting the washer and dryer going when Lynn wanted to take care of that spill on her corduroys."

"No problem." As she sidestepped to get to the next chafing tray, the ends of her hair swept across her shoulder blades and he wondered what they would feel like tickling his naked chest.

Then he wished he hadn't wondered, because the idea of nakedness and him and her was leading to other thoughts. Before breakfast. When they were in the dining room and both fully clothed.

Damn, but she got to him.

He cleared his throat. "Still, I didn't expect you to take on laundress duties."

She peeked at him through her thick lashes. Her eyes were still that winter-water blue. "No problem."

"So accommodating," he murmured, and smiled at her with a wiggle of his brows.

A dimple poked a little dent in her cheek. Triumph! he thought. His small foray into flirtation didn't immediately turn her shy.

"What's the agenda for today?" she asked.

He followed her to the table, where he placed his plate beside hers. Then he reached for the nearby carafe and poured her a cup of coffee. "Did you know it's National Science Fiction Day?"

There was that dimple again. "I had no idea."

Seated, she unfolded her napkin and spread it across her lap. He liked how she moved, precise and controlled. The man in him wanted to destroy that precision, wreak havoc on that control. If he brushed aside her hair and nuzzled her neck, would she drop her fork? Would he taste the heat on her skin?

"…Chase?"

Taking the chair beside hers, he forced his mind away from fantasy. *Take it easy, Bradley. You've got hours before you can get her alone to do what you've been dreaming of.* "Sorry. Say again?"

"What are we doing on National Science Fiction Day?"

Lifting his coffee, he blew across the top, hoping it

would cool him down some, too. "Not that much, really. The library has been raided for all the Ray Bradburys and Ursula K. Le Guins, etcetera. They're upstairs, along with an easel and an oversize pad of paper. For those to whom inspiration strikes, we're to try our own fiction story, one sentence at a time."

"How?" She frowned, putting a crease between her brows.

He rubbed at the little line with his forefinger, and a jolt transferred from her flesh to his and back again. When she gasped, he just said, "Yeah," and dropped his hand.

"Chase…"

His steady gaze met her anxious one. "Yeah," he repeated with a little more force. "I felt it, too."

When she shifted her glance to her plate, he continued on as if the moment hadn't happened. "To answer your question," he said, "one person writes a sentence, then a second person picks up the pen. I think there's a rule that there must be three additional sentences before the first author can write another, but I'm not going to count."

Because I'll be too busy counting the minutes until bedtime, when I intend to escort you to my room where we'll take care of all this wanting and wondering.

"I'm not sure how good I'll be at that," Ashley said.

He shrugged. "Critiquing is outlawed." Leaning close, he put his mouth an inch from her ear and breathed in the cool, sweet fragrance of crushed roses. "And for the record, I think you'll be very good. As a matter of fact, I'd bet on it."

She froze, and then her chin lifted. "You're very

practiced at that," she said, her little smile communi-
cating she wasn't taking him seriously.

"I—" But he was forced to break off before his de-
nial could be fully uttered as a handful of couples wandered into the room, calling out greetings.

Ashley moved into hostess mode, and the moment
was lost. People began peppering her with questions
about the nearby ski areas.

"I'm guessing most everyone will hit the snow
today," he said.

"Arch and I are going snowboarding for sure," June
put in. "What about you, Chase?"

Drawing his friends' cups closer, he poured them
coffee. "Not this time. I'll stick around and entertain
anyone who stays at the house."

June turned her attention to Ashley. "How about
you?"

She shook her head. "I don't."

"Don't?"

"Hit the snow."

June's brows rose over her pretty brown eyes. "I
would think everyone who lives in the mountains skis
or boards."

"Nope." Ashley's lips curved, but it wasn't a smile.

What it was, Chase thought, was weird. But before
he could give it further thought, more guests arrived,
and he was drawn into other conversations. A few hours
later, he'd sent the bulk of the visitors off with gear or
with directions of where to rent gear, and the house had
quieted. He found Declan and his wife, Miriam, playing
cards in the library. Another older couple was perus-
ing the books arranged on the tables upstairs in honor
of National Science Fiction Day.

It didn't appear he was needed.

Maybe now he could get to work on his own agenda: Ashley in his bed.

No daytime nookie—he still had enough hold on himself to wait until the cover of darkness—but he could seek her out. Soften her up a little.

Tease her in preparation for the night to come.

But she'd disappeared. It wasn't until afternoon, when the first of the guests returned to the house, that she made her way down the stairs and went about offering up the hot tea, coffee and cookies that Mrs. Erwin had prepared for a snack.

Delicious smells of dinner cooking were drifting from the kitchen, and Chase and the bartender were setting out glassware in the great hall when the house's landline rang. He strolled toward the phone in the library. Ashley was closer, and he nodded to her when she glanced his way.

"Bradley residence," she said into the receiver. Then she grabbed the back of her desk chair as her face drained of color.

Alarmed, Chase rushed forward. "What—"

She held the phone his way. "The ski patrol. Asking for you."

He continued to watch her with concern as he took the call. The information imparted relieved him somewhat, but he remained puzzled by Ashley's wan face as he set the receiver back in its cradle. "Are you all right?" he asked, placing his hand on her stiff shoulder.

"What's happened?" she asked, her voice low.

"David Albright," he answered, naming one of the guests. "He fell, and in doing so sprained an ankle and busted his cell phone."

"He's okay other than that?" She searched his face with anxious eyes. "You're sure?"

"He'll be fine. I'm going to the ski resort in the limo and I'll settle him into the rear seat. Then I'll take the wheel of his car and drive it here. Can you handle drinks and hors d'oeuvres until I get back?"

"Sure." She released her death grip on the chair and managed a weak smile. "I've got this. Don't worry."

But he did, both going to and returning from the Mountain Magic Resort. At the Bradley house, David managed to get himself into the great hall just fine on a pair of crutches. As a matter of fact, he looked better than Ashley, who still appeared shaken. She soldiered on through dinner, though, only to disappear on Chase again.

Carrying a snifter of brandy in each hand, he searched the house for her as most of the guests tromped up the stairs toward the playroom in order to try their hand at science fiction. Chase was interested in storytelling, too—but Ashley's story...the one that had caused her distress.

Maybe he should question this protective side she brought out in him. But instead, he wanted to question *her*.

It took him several minutes to discover her hideout. As a matter of fact, he'd walked past the half-lit kitchen three times, presuming it was empty because Mrs. Erwin and her staff had left an hour before. But finally he found Ashley, seated at a banquette in one corner of the large kitchen, tucked behind the table and sitting in near-dark.

"There you are," he said, keeping his voice soft so as not to startle her.

She started anyway, and then glanced over. "Did you need something—"

"Only to find you," he said, and realized it was true. Skirting the table, he seated himself on the cushioned bench beside her. Not touching, but close enough to settle his unease a little. "I was concerned."

"About me?"

He took a sip of one brandy and placed the other snifter in front of her. "Why do you sound so surprised? You've seemed...off since this afternoon."

"I didn't think anyone would notice."

"I don't think 'anyone' did. Just me." Another truth. From the moment he'd seen Ashley, he'd been attracted. But upon talking to her, he'd somehow...found her wavelength. Or she operated on the same as his. Chase didn't know. He'd never experienced this with any other woman, this heady rush of recognition.

He recalled a night out with Arch, very soon after he'd met June. The other man had been drinking heavily, and Chase had come to understand it was because he'd been so knocked on his butt by the brown-eyed woman whom he'd been introduced to at the wedding of mutual friends.

We just...worked from the first moment, Arch had said, as if he could hardly believe it. *Our edges line up. She fits with me like a baseball in that old glove of mine.*

At the time, his friend and his baseball analogy had amused Chase. He wasn't laughing anymore.

Slightly unnerved, he focused on Ashley once again, nudging the brandy toward her. "Have a drink of this."

Maybe she was getting sick, he thought, and lifted his hand to press the back of his fingers against her cheek.

She drew away. "What are you doing?"

"Checking if you have a fever." Good God, he wasn't going to admit it was the same move his mother had made when he was a kid. What was it about Ashley that made him want to care for her so? He looked about the room. "Are you cold? Should I get you a blanket?"

"I'm fine."

"You hardly ate any dinner." Now he really *did* sound like his mother. But the thought didn't stifle his concern. "Ever since that call..." His voice petered out as he realized there was his answer. Since the ski patrol had phoned, she hadn't been the same. "What's going on, Ashley?"

She shook her head.

He struggled against his impatience. "Okay. Let's start over." Whatever was wrong, he'd fix. "Are you sick?" Whatever it took, he'd make her well.

She shook her head again.

"No? You're not sick?" He might have growled. "Ashley, talk to me. Your silence is making me nuts."

"I'm not sick," she said, looking down at the snifter she was cradling in her hands. Lifting it, she took a sip, then set it down as she shifted her gaze to his. "What I am...is a widow."

"A widow," he repeated. A *widow*? How could someone so young have been married and then...not?

"It happened four years ago last month."

"I'm—" no, he was never speechless "—so sorry for your loss."

"Thanks," she whispered. "I've had time to get used to it."

"But something about today..."

He saw her fingers tighten on the snifter. "We only

had a season together." She glanced up at him again. "We have those here, you know, not like in other parts of Southern California. We have four true seasons. Stu and I had an autumn of married life."

"His name was Stu." Maybe Chase should tell her he didn't want to hear any more, but of course he did.

"Stuart Phillips. Mountain kid, like me."

"You loved him."

"Of course," she said, lifting her hand. "My first and only love."

Those words felt like five separate stabs. And he asked for more pain when he questioned her again. "What happened?"

"He was an avid snowboarder. That year...it wasn't like this one, when snow came early. The white stuff didn't come down for the first time until mid-December. We were both excited to get on the slopes. Stu couldn't wait."

Ah. "You used to go with him? Snowboard?"

"Yes, though not that last time. The conditions weren't good and I was willing to postpone gratification until another day."

"But not Stu."

She smiled a little. A sad smile. "Stu was not about postponing gratification."

"What was he about?"

"Flash. Fun. Speed." She sipped from the brandy again. "Everyone loved him."

Chase decided not to tell her that he didn't because it was ridiculous to feel like this—jealous, he could admit only to himself—about a dead man. "You like the reckless type."

"Not anymore. I've learned my lesson." She sighed.

Tossing back the rest of his brandy, Chase decided he had to know everything. "So what happened?"

"He was racing with a friend. Those two were always egging each other on." Her finger traced the rim of the snifter, going around and around and around. "It was nearing dark and they should have headed back much earlier. They took a short cut… He hit a rock and ended up slamming into a tree. The impact caused a massive head injury."

"He wasn't wearing a helmet?"

"As you said, reckless." She addressed the brandy instead of Chase. "Today, when I took that call…I was reminded of when the ski patrol phoned me."

Chase couldn't stand the inches of distance between them. Reaching out, he drew her close. She went stiff for a moment before relaxing against him, her cheek to his chest. Her warmth and her willingness did little to assuage the ache in his heart. He pressed his cheek to the top of her head. "I'm sorry," he murmured. "And I'm sorry you took that call today."

Her arms came around him, their light weight propped on his shoulders. She lifted her chin. "Thank you," she whispered. "I—"

His mouth came down on hers, stifling anything else she might have said. Chase told himself it was a kiss of comfort, like the hug, but that was only so much baloney. Not when he traced his tongue over the seam of her lips. Not when his heart exulted when she opened for him. The taste of brandy combined with the light scent of roses evaporated his good sense. He hauled her closer, into his lap, as his mouth ate at hers.

Greedy. He was greedy for her.

She made a noise deep in her throat. A moan? He

cupped her cheek in one palm to change the angle of her head. His thumb brushed over her soft, heated skin and he felt wetness. *No. God, no.*

Breaking the kiss, he stared at her. There were tears on her face. As he watched, another rolled over the rim of her eye, caught for a moment in her bottom lashes, then trailed toward her chin.

Oh, God, he thought again, as knowledge hit him like a snowplow knocking over a mailbox. As much as he might want her well, it wasn't in his power, was it?

Although she wasn't "sick," she was definitely hurt. And how could he possibly fix that? Chase was helpless when it came to healing Ashley's heart.

CHAPTER FOUR

THE NEXT MORNING, Ashley woke to learn it was J. R. R. Tolkien Day. Most of the Bradley guests who'd been skiing or snowboarding the day before were in various states of pain. David was milking his sprained ankle, begging more of Mrs. Erwin's cinnamon rolls to be served to him by his wife. "Everyone knows they're the best medicine." Others hobbled about, too, complaining of sore muscles or bruises in uncomfortable places.

She knew *The Hobbit* movie and *The Lord of the Rings* trilogy were playing in a nonstop loop in the media room, so she suggested over breakfast that relaxing while watching them for a few hours might be just the thing. But at the other end of the long dining table, Chase had a different idea. His suggestion: a short drive that would take them to an even shorter trek through the snow to natural hot springs. There, they could soak their aches away. It seemed the guests had been aware of the possibility because they all had bathing suits with them…except Ashley.

"I'll stay here, then," she told Chase as breakfast wound down.

"Good," he said, his voice curt and his expression remote.

She tried not to take offense. He had things on his

mind. A houseful of people to please. That she'd shared something so personal last night didn't mean he had to be her BFF today. Still, it stung a little, and she felt the back of her neck go hot as he walked away from her. It seemed the man regretted knowing so much about her.

The rest of the day, she puttered about. First she changed the water in all the flower arrangements in the public portions of the house, pinching off any tired blossoms or leaves. Then she joined Fanny Erwin in the kitchen, watching as the caterer wound twine around pieces of beef that she'd stuffed with a concoction that smelled garlicky and delicious.

"How are you getting along?" the older woman asked, glancing at Ashley over her shoulder.

"Do you think I'm stupid to take on the job?" The question burst out.

Fanny shot her another quick look. "Now, why would I think that?"

"You know." She waved a hand. "This whole group is out of my league."

The older woman's eyes narrowed. "Has anyone made you feel less...or less than welcome?"

"No," Ashley muttered. Except Chase didn't seem as...warm to her as he'd been in the days before. Last night, after she'd shared that second kiss with him, he'd practically bolted from the kitchen. He'd said something about checking on the guests upstairs, and she'd thought she'd understood—hosting was his first priority, after all—but now she just didn't know.

"Well, they'd better not," Fanny said hotly, returning to her food preparation. "Money doesn't make one person better than another."

Ashley didn't try to hide her smile. Here was the

thing about being born and bred in the mountains—
especially for people like Fanny and the Walkers, who'd
been in the area for generations—they considered themselves the richest in the world for the privilege of having
a legacy tied to this amazing landscape. The part-timers,
to their mind, held the shorter end of the stick.

The innate arrogance of the mountain people meant
they were never intimidated by the wealth and fame of
those they came in contact with—whether as florists,
caterers, restaurant workers, cleaning people, whatever.
Ashley's own cousin, Poppy Walker, was engaged to a
famous Hollywood movie star and the only thing that
awed their family—the women in the family anyway—
was his matinee idol good looks.

Ashley wasn't sure she'd stay among the peaks and
pines forever, but they would forever be part of her.

By late afternoon, everyone was back in the house.
It was buzzing with new energy, because they'd been
informed the evening meal would be Middle-earth-
inspired. To make it more fun, they were instructed to
come in costume. Dozens of pieces hung in the playroom for the guests to choose from.

Once again, Ashley was impressed with Chase's
mother's novel ideas for entertainment. The grown
men and women seemed as eager as eight-year-olds
to dress up.

Before they retired to their rooms for their transfor-
mations, most hung around the bar with drinks in hand.
The majority of the time Chase was surrounded by a
bevy of people, but when she saw him wander toward
the windows, she approached. "How was your day?"
she asked him, trying to sound friendly.

He glanced over. "Fine."

She waited, thinking he'd take up the conversational ball. When he didn't, a wave of humiliated heat washed over her skin. Why had she told him about Stu? When he hadn't known, Chase had been warm and attentive. He'd made her feel like a desirable woman. They'd shared a couple of amazing kisses, and she'd been sure he felt that same sizzle from them that she did.

A sizzle that had made her feel alive.

Now she was only embarrassed.

"Well, I'll talk to you later," she mumbled. Turning to go, she felt his hand on her shoulder.

"Ashley."

She looked back. "Yes?"

"Are you all right?" His gaze studied her face. "Better?"

"I am," she said.

"Good." His hand fell away. His expression revealed nothing more.

On her way up to her room to change, Ashley brought with her a glass of wine. She nursed it along with a spurt of temper. What was with the hot-cold-hot-cold? She might not have a lot of experience with different men, but she knew something was off. Or was this just Chase's way?

Jerk, she decided, if that was true. Look what her year of yes had gotten her into so far!

Gazing at herself in the mirror, in the filmy gown she'd chosen with a braided girdle and matching circlet for her head, it was hard to hold on to her regret, though. The pale blue of the low-cut long chiffon dress complemented her eyes. The skirt was made up of light layers that moved when she walked.

It was an otherworldly outfit, and she added glittery shadow and dark liner around her eyes to go with it. Several coats of mascara added to the drama. Her mood lifted by the primping and the pleasing reflection of herself, she nearly danced down the stairs to the great hall. There, she found that June was the only other person waiting for the evening to begin.

The other woman wore a black dress with a calf-length handkerchief hem topped by a quilted vest resembling armor. Her boots were something that a Doc Martens elf might have designed. "Wow," Ashley said, in admiring tones. "A warrior."

June's grin was cheeky. "Is this fun, or what?"

"I know I'll count on you to defend my honor," Ashley said with a nod to the short sword tucked in the sheath hanging from the belt buckled around June's waist. Then she looked around. "Where is everyone?"

"I'm hoping Legolas will show," June said, leaning near. "But it won't be Arch. He refused to snag the platinum wig that's upstairs."

"Legolas!" Ashley had to frown. "I'm an Aragorn girl."

"Takes all kinds," June said, smiling. Then she sobered. "Hey, is everything okay? You didn't join us last night after dinner. Our science fiction story could have used more authors."

"I…" She looked down. Her feet were bare except for sparkly nail polish on her toes. Then, instead of making some excuse, she heard herself speak the truth. "When the ski patrol called, I had a bad moment. You see…I'm a widow." She peeked at June, saw the sympathetic expression overtake the other woman's face. "My husband died in a ski accident four years ago."

"Oh, that's awful," June said, and stepped forward to hug Ashley. "It's a terrible thing. I'm so sorry."

"Thank you." She pushed back from the other woman as the oddest feeling of lightness infused her being. "You're…you're only the second person I've ever told."

June frowned. "What? It's a secret?"

"There are no secrets when you live in a small place like this," Ashley answered. "Everyone that matters has already known from the beginning. The information came to them almost as quickly as it came to me."

"Well…" June's brows drew together. "Should I be sorry that you had to tell me?"

"No. The opposite, actually." Ashley looked up. "I don't know if I can explain this, exactly, but…it feels good to say it. Like its weight is no longer pressing so heavily on my chest. Don't get me wrong—I loved my husband, and I wish you had known him. He was a great guy." She sucked in a breath.

June held out her hand.

Ashley grasped it. "Stu was a great guy," she said again, and gladness filled her being as she shared it. A smile broke over her face. "I feel good," she added with a note of wonderment. *Really good.*

"I'm glad," June said.

"Me, too." The sound of footsteps on the stairs had them both looking over.

Chase and Arch descended, the two big handsome men laughing. Arch had on a long tunic, leggings and boots. A crown sat on his head. "Very regal," Ashley murmured. "Aragornish," she said to tease the other woman.

But her smile died when she noted what their host had on for the evening. A very modern, very un–

Middle-earth pair of dark gray slacks and a collared sweater. With or without a costume, he was so good-looking Ashley's stomach tightened.

And resentment grew. How stupid she'd been to think they had some special…connection. It was his fault, she decided. His masculinity was just too alluring. His confidence like a nectar that Ashley couldn't help but want to taste.

She glanced at June. "Why didn't he dress up?"

"Well…he doesn't like to, um, put on a costume."

"What? Why?" Ashley didn't try to hide the bitter note in her voice. "Was there one bad Halloween when the poor little rich boy didn't get all the candy he wanted?"

"That's not it," the other woman said quietly.

The men were heading toward the bar and had yet to notice the women who stood in the corner of the big room. Ashley crossed her arms over her chest, wishing she didn't find the dark-haired, gray-eyed man so appealing. What was *wrong* with her?

June cleared her throat. "He has an aversion to… camouflage, I'd guess you'd say. He doesn't like deception of any kind."

Frowning, Ashley turned her attention to the other woman. "It's just costumes."

"Not to Chase. I don't know if I should tell you this…"

Please do, Ashley silently urged.

"He had a girlfriend in college," June whispered in a rush. "A fiancée, actually."

"He's been married?"

"No. It didn't get that far. Because…it was at a costume party. Figures in history or famous movie characters was the theme. There were, like, a gazillion

Cleopatras." June made a face. "I went as Margaret Thatcher. What was I thinking?"

"That it was more comfortable to attend in a stodgy suit than something slinky?"

"I still had this itchy wig, though," June said, pointing to her head. "*Any*way, Chase was looking for his Cleo as the party was getting rowdier and he wanted to leave. Glancing in a half-open bedroom door, he saw the Queen of the Nile doing the nasty with a guy dressed as Chewbacca. Try to get *that* out of your head."

"He saw it was his Cleo," Ashley guessed.

"Not right then. Fifteen minutes or so later. That's when she came to Chase, acting all sweet and lovey-dovey."

"So how'd he know what she'd done?"

"Clumps of fur in her wig. And when he asked, she told him it was true. Just a one-time thing, she assured him. It didn't matter, she said."

"It mattered to Chase."

"Oh, yeah, big-time," June agreed. "He's not been eager to tie himself down since."

Issues, Ashley thought. He had issues, just as she did. Sympathy and understanding cleared away all the dark clouds inside her. Hearing of her loss had probably reminded him of his own. No wonder he'd had a change of mood.

"Thanks for letting me know, June." He'd been her shoulder the night before. It was her turn to make him feel better. Maybe the magic of Middle-earth would provide her with an idea of how to do just that.

INSPIRATION DIDN'T STRIKE Ashley until after everyone had retired for the night, and it was necessity that ac-

tually took her to Chase's bedroom door. Pasting on
a friendly smile, she gave a light rap on it with the
knuckles of her free hand. The other was pressed to
her bodice.

It took a moment, but then he stood in the open doorway.

Her breath caught. Chase's chest was naked. Dressed
only in slacks, his feet bare like hers, he looked at her,
one brow rising over an eye.

"Um…" She hoped she wasn't gawking. But, goodness! He was chiseled. Every muscle was carved to
masculine perfection. Broad shoulders, defined biceps.
Pectorals that were slabs of tough muscle dusted with
dark hair. A toy boat could ride the ripples of his ab-
dominal muscles.

Yanking her gaze from the trail of hair disappearing downward, it caught on the dusky circles of his
nipples. Heat prickles rose on her back. Had she ever
noticed those on a man before? Ashley curled her free
fingers into a fist to prevent herself from reaching out
and touching one.

"Can I help you?" he asked.

"I don't know the location of anyone else's room but
yours," she said, finally glancing at his face. "I didn't
want to go around knocking indiscriminately."

Amusement etched lines in the corners of his amazing eyes. "By all means, let's not be indiscriminate."

At that sign of humor, her clutching stomach eased
a little. "I need help."

"What kind?"

Turning, she presented him with her back. "My hair
is caught in the dress's zipper."

In a breath, he'd pulled her into his room and shut

the door. She glanced around, and the low illumination from the bedside lamp revealed a massive four-poster, the lake view beyond French doors, the attached bath. The space smelled like him, that expensive, clean scent that reminded her of clear water and night air.

"I need to see better," he said, and towed her toward the bathroom.

In there, he flipped on the overhead light. The mirror over the double sinks reflected her image—flushed cheeks and big eyes. Chase lined himself up behind her and studied the dress situation with a serious expression.

"How bad is it?" she asked, craning her neck to look over her shoulder.

"Pretty bad," he replied. She felt his fingers at the midway of her back, the farthest point she'd managed to draw down the zipper before realizing her hair was caught in its teeth. As he worked on the situation, his knuckles bumped her spine and goose bumps broke out all over.

Chase stilled. "Really bad."

"Oh, no." She bit her bottom lip. "Tell me you don't have to cut my hair."

He cleared his throat and went back to fiddling with the zipper. "I don't want to make any promises."

She sighed, and tried not to squirm under the onslaught of his inadvertent touches. *He doesn't mean to do this*, she told herself. *He's not intending to stir you up.*

But she was stirred up anyway, heat and heaviness pooling in her body. Her breasts felt swollen and the tips were hard. Ashley's free hand gripped the edge of the granite countertop, and she hoped he didn't notice her state.

"You looked very beautiful tonight," he said.

Oh, how glad she was that he'd noticed that! Trying to play it cool, though, she lifted one shoulder. "Um, thanks. I'm usually in jeans and T-shirts, so this was outside my realm of experience. As a matter of fact, everything that's happened since I met you has been outside my realm of experience."

"I made you cry last night."

"What?" She glanced at him in the mirror. His focus was still on her uncooperative dress.

"I'm sorry."

"But…" She tried to rein in her thoughts. "Before the zipper predicament, I was going to come to you and thank you for last night."

He looked up now, and their gazes caught in the glass. "You were sad."

"Yes, at first. But telling you…it made me feel better. I haven't had to say the words before, did you know that? News travels fast in Blue Arrow. So it made me feel better to know I could tell you. It was liberating."

"Okay. That's good. But I shouldn't have kissed you."

"Why not?" Ashley demanded. Then an unsettling thought occurred to her. "Was it a pity kiss?"

"Definitely not pity." He grimaced. "I tried telling myself it was for comfort, but then…"

"Then it became very hot," she whispered.

He nodded. "And it made you cry. I wanted to kick myself."

"Oh, Chase." She pressed her lips together because she felt like crying again. "I wasn't sad anymore. Those tears…they were tears of joy."

His eyes narrowed. "What?"

"Of relief, too. I was gratified to know I could respond to another man. It proves to me that I've made it to the other side of grief."

A strange expression crossed his face and his gaze zeroed in on her face. Because she still had one hand holding up the bodice of her dress, she could feel how that look made her heart pound. It thrummed against the center of her palm, and she pressed harder, hoping she could keep it inside her chest.

Chase cupped her shoulders and drew her back against him. She could feel his bare skin against her spine. His mouth touched her temple. "You know I want you."

She wanted him, too. So much. And it was her year, right? Her year of… "Yes," she told him.

His hands tightened on her. Then he turned her to face him. His eyes studied her face. "You said your husband was your one and only love."

"He's gone now." She traced Chase's lips with her fingertips. "And I don't want him to be my one and only love."

"Then he won't be."

Her mouth turned down. "I'm still stuck in this dress."

"I managed to free your hair. The zipper's all the way down," Chase said. He touched the back of the hand still plastered to her chest. "Let go, Ashley."

LET GO. CHASE watched Ashley mouth the words, then her hand drifted away, and the dress dropped.

Hot blood shot like fire through his veins.

"Ashley," he groaned, his gaze roaming all over her

bare, creamy skin. Under the dress, she'd worn nothing but a pair of tiny lace panties. It made him crazy, thinking all night that she'd been just a few feet away, nearly naked.

His hand lifted and he drew the backs of two fingers along the gentle slope of her shoulder. Her lashes drifted down, casting shadows on her pink-tinged cheeks. So lovely.

His knuckles traced the outer curve of one breast and she trembled, but stayed in place as the circle spiraled, spiraled. When he touched the hard knot of her upright nipple, she gasped.

"Shh," he soothed, leaning down to press his mouth to her temple, her cheek, the shell of her ear. "You smell so good." He'd wake in the morning with her scent on his skin, he thought. It would be a pleasure.

But before that, other pleasures.

His palm brushed her nipple, back and forth, as the other curved under her bottom to fit her closer to him. Lips trailing across her cheek, he went for another kiss. She opened for him immediately, and he tasted her deeply, his tongue moving forward in dominant surges.

Just like sex.

But then he slowed himself. *Think of her, Bradley.* If he'd understood her right, she'd had only one other man in her bed. Not that he cared about numbers. But he cared about Ashley, and if this was her first time being with someone in four years, he had to make it good. Great.

One of her arms wound around his neck and her other hand slid between them. *Hell!* He jerked into the touch, his body disconnecting from his mind.

"No," he said against her mouth, and grabbed for her wrist.

"No?" She arched against him, and he felt her hard nipples against his chest like tiny brands.

"Okay, yes." *Yes, yes, yes.* "But later."

"What now?" She drew her bare heel up the back of his calf and thigh to twine his hip with her leg. On tiptoe, she pressed against the placket of his pants. The heat was scalding-good. "What can I do now?"

Chase closed his eyes, groaning again, and slid his hand downward to hold one silken cheek. Lust raced through him and he took her mouth again, plundering. She melted against him, compliant, a rose-scented treasure.

He had to do this right. Take it slow. Make it good.

Swinging her up in his arms, he reminded himself this was for her. All her.

She deserved a lover. A considerate lover. Not an animal that was driven by savage want. Chase was too controlled for that anyway. He used his brains, even in bed.

That was where he took Ashley.

Placing her on the downturned sheets, he studied the picture she made there, forcing his lungs to suck in oxygen and expel it again in a calming sequence. Her hair was spread on the pillow, and he didn't let himself remember the fantasies he'd had of it. On the pillow, just like that, or the ends tickling his ribs, or of his face buried in it.

Okay, he *was* thinking of them.

But then she was moving, shimmying that little scrap of lace down her legs, and Chase couldn't get the rest of his own clothes off quick enough. Then he pounced, and she giggled like a girl as he covered her. He grinned at the sound, struck by the carefree aspect of it. "You make me happy," he said.

Then he froze. Where had that come from? She made him happy? He was supposed to be making *her* happy. Sex-happy. There was nothing here about happy-happy. Not the heart kind of happy.

Her fingers speared his hair and moved over his head, as if discovering its shape. "You make this easy."

That sounded better.

Chase applied himself to making it even easier, with his lips, his tongue, his hands. She was warm as candle wax and as pliable. He turned her this way and that, finding the secret cove behind her knee, the dimples at the small of her back, the notch at her throat. When he flicked it with his tongue, she cried out, and he could tell she was close to the edge.

So he took her closer. Now he went for the obvious places—her breasts, her belly, the hot and tender skin of her inner thighs.

A wildness thrashed inside him. It wasn't his way. But Ashley...she did something to him.

Oh, he didn't turn rough or savage or anything like that. It was his pulse that turned riotous, his heart that pounded with unruly abandon in his chest. He took her mouth again, a messy kiss that had her clutching his shoulders and moaning. His hands roamed her body, intrepid travelers of a foreign land that wanted to map every hill and every valley. She opened for him, her arms flung wide, and he felt all his sophistication fracture, then fall.

He kissed her, listened to her unsteady breaths and sensed her tightening muscles. She was climbing closer, and when he covered himself then drove into her wet heat, the sound she made caused him to drive faster into her, harder.

They felt so good together. A seamless alignment of bodies and desires.

His tongue invaded her mouth, and as she lifted into his every thrust, he put his hand between them, explored their joining and then sent her flying.

He continued his rhythm as she rode out the release, his face in her rose-scented hair, his body reaching for his own release. When the crisis came upon him, his mind shattered.

It took a long time to come back to that bed, the tangled sheets, the woman breathing in his ear. It hadn't gone as he'd planned, he realized. He hadn't been thinking of her, as he'd promised. And not himself, either.

No, it was more serious than that. As he'd been sheathed in her body and was driving them both over the edge, he'd thought…he'd thought about a "them."

CHAPTER FIVE

WHEN ASHLEY AWOKE the next morning on the pillow beside Chase, he was staring at her, and it was as if he could read the first question that came to her mind. *How will we handle it?*

"This is going to be easy," he said with a promise in his voice. "We'll get up, have breakfast, begin another day of charming the guests."

She had the covers in her fists and pulled up to her chin, and though she wanted away from this awkward moment in the worst way, she asked him a question. "Is that how you look at it...that you're here this week to win them over?" It seemed a little calculating, but he was a numbers guy, after all, and was heading up an important company.

"Not really," he said. "Most of these people I've known for years and they're considered family friends. I like them. I hope they like me. My grandfather and father taught me managing people's investments is a responsibility...I'm a guardian of their present and their future. So they need to trust me to handle their money wisely, and because of that I try to be—God I hate this word—*authentic*."

Ashley thought of June telling her how he despised camouflage. He wasn't the kind of man to pull the wool over people's eyes. She believed that—and she could see him, definitely, as a guardian. He was a steady guy whose job meant playing it safe. It was one of the reasons she felt comfortable with him.

And it turned out he was right about the easy part.

No one seemed the least bit suspicious about what they'd been up to the night before. Breakfast proceeded like every other day. Good food, laughter, the sharing of plans. Chase was going onto the slopes with a party of guests whose muscles no longer shrieked at them. He met Ashley's eyes over the carafes of coffee and the small pitchers of cream. "Want to go along?" he asked.

She shook her head, glad that he didn't push it.

Instead, she spent the morning with a deep conditioner on her hair, an avocado mask on her face and her nose buried in a book. If every once in a while her mind returned to the night before, she didn't blame herself. A woman could cherish some memories.

At first, she'd wondered if maybe she'd feel guilty for going to bed with Chase, as if she'd betrayed Stu's memory. But he'd been about living life, as hard and fast as a person wanted. He'd likely be more annoyed that she hadn't ventured before now. Anyway, it was just sex. Not like she was thinking of a relationship with Chase Bradley or anything. After this week was over, she'd never see him again. Well, possibly next year... though she could ask her boss to deliver the flowers on New Year's Eve, she decided. By then she might be regularly dating.

Moose could turn out to be just what the doctor ordered.

Yeah, right.

After dinner, everyone made their way to the playroom upstairs. It was National Trivia Day, and Chase's mom had arranged a tournament. Several of the guests groaned. June said she only excelled at science questions, while Arch rarely fumbled a literature one, but as they weren't partnered, their chances appeared doomed.

Ashley held her own for a while because she and her partner, a gentleman in his sixties, did well enough when the categories were History—he was a buff—and Latin—Ashley had a familiarity due to her knowledge of flower names. In the end, though, it came down to two contenders: Chase and Declan Hart.

The rest of the guests ringed the two at their table. Along the way, Declan had put money on the game, and there was a small wad of cash in the middle. At the outskirts of the circle, Ashley and June exchanged amused glances. "Do the words *just a game* never penetrate?" she murmured.

"Miriam," Declan called out at one point. "Get over here. I need a little luck from my lady." He patted his knee.

Ashley's gaze sliced to Chase. What if he did the same? What if he called her over and…claimed her in that way? Her face went hot thinking about it. Then he glanced at her and, embarrassed about her thoughts, she pointedly looked in the other direction.

Miriam, elegant and silver-haired, glided toward her husband, even while shaking her head. "This isn't high-stakes poker like Las Vegas," she said.

"You're right," her husband replied, eyeing the pot. "We need to make this more interesting." His fingers went to the expensive-looking watch strapped around his wrist. He deposited it on the cash with a flourish. "What are you willing to gamble, young Bradley?"

Ashley's thrifty soul spun like a corpse in a grave.

She shot out her hand and gripped June's wrist. "This isn't good," she murmured.

The other woman frowned. "You wouldn't catch me wagering like that, but what's got you so concerned?"

Arch looked over, tuning in to the women's conversation. Ashley switched her gaze to him. "Can't you put a stop to this?"

Her anxiety only jumped higher when she watched Chase begin to unlatch his own timepiece. What did she know about luxury accessories? Only enough to figure Chase wore the best.

"Arch? Please."

Chase's friend sidled closer. "I don't get it."

Didn't Arch understand Chase as she did? He wouldn't be comfortable pushed into this kind of activity, even if Declan was an old family friend. The "authentic" Chase Bradley, the guardian of presents and futures, didn't take chances. "He's not a gambler," she told the other man. Maybe she was overreacting, but she couldn't help herself. "He doesn't take risks."

Arch glanced over at his wife, then back at Ashley. "Of course he does."

"The nature of his work—"

"Includes making bets on the market. Educated bets, of course, but in the end…"

Her palms going clammy, Ashley stared at him. "No."

"He's raced cars. He pilots his own plane. I can't tell you how many times he's skydived."

Ashley's stomach stalled then rolled, like an out-of-control aircraft. Chase…Chase wasn't the sober, steady, play-it-safe guy she'd imagined? She glanced over at him to see him scooping the winnings toward himself, the game apparently over. In his favor. He was looking at her with puzzlement on his face.

Miriam Hart announced to the crowd that the Patek Phillipe watch her husband had just lost was one he'd never liked anyway. "My mother gave it to him," she said, and everyone laughed.

Except Ashley. She was preoccupied by the silent sound of the gates to her heart slamming down. Okay. All right. *Whew.* That was good. For a moment there, she'd been a bit too close to liking Chase a bit too much. Now that she knew he wasn't her type she was safe again.

Not that he wanted to get any closer to her, she reminded herself, feeling more relief. It had been a one-night thing, so there was no way that a single evening between the sheets was going to mess her up. Their... connection was done now. Over. Forgetting about him would be no problem. All she had to do was keep out of his way.

This is going to be easy.

After Trivia Day it was National Bird Day, and Chase kept his distance from Ashley during most of both. Sure, he couldn't help wanting her again in his bed, but if his own reaction to their intimacy had spooked him a little, the way she avoided him made it clear she was downright agitated after being with him.

Still, he didn't like leaving things this way between them. Their week together was almost up.

The highlight of National Bird Day was a contest that coincided with happy hour to see which of the house-guests could identify the most bird calls. The quiz was available on the internet, and as with every other activity his mother had arranged, the guests responded—and participated—with enthusiasm. It was no surprise that mountain girl Ashley won the first and second cycles of the competition. As hostess, though, she bowed out of the prize-winning round and stood on the outskirts of the crowd chatting with June as a couple of old coots listened to…well, coot calls.

Without shame, Chase hovered nearby, eavesdropping on the women's conversation. They spoke of returning to their regular lives in a couple of days, and that sent June off with her phone to find privacy. "I need my twin fix," she said. "They should be getting ready for dinner just about now."

Chase stepped into the empty spot beside Ashley. She cast him a look and then focused her attention back on the contest.

He should leave her alone, Chase thought. But he didn't, not when he wanted to normalize the situation between them. "So," he said, leaning close. "I couldn't help but overhear you and June talking about next week. Are you looking forward to getting back to work?"

She shifted a shoulder. "I actually have another week off. My mother-in-law—she's the owner of the shop where I work—her husband, and the rest of the family are skiing in Colorado."

"You work for your mother-in-law?" He shouldn't care, he thought. He shouldn't care, he shouldn't care, he shouldn't care.

"Mmm."

"Is that…" He reminded himself it was none of his business.

She glanced over. "Is that what?"

Fine, he'd say it. "I don't know. Healthy?"

Her mouth curved, rueful. "I get that a lot."

"From who?"

"Oh, mostly my passel of Walker cousins. The girls anyway." She ticked off names on her fingers. "There's Poppy, Shay and Mackenzie. My boy cousin, Brett, he's more of the strong-and-silent type. But the consensus is that I'll stay mired in the past if I stay at my mother-in-law's shop."

"What about Suze? What does she think?"

She shot him another look. "You remember Suze?"

"Fixed you up with Moose for New Year's, right?"

"Right."

"You going out with him next week?" Chase asked with a close eye on her face. It would be good for her, he decided, ignoring the protests of his gut: *She doesn't belong with some other guy!* Chase had only been after physical pleasure with her, and one night of that would have to suffice. "Maybe Moose is just the man you need in your life."

Her shoulder went up in another shrug and her expression gave nothing away. "Probably not. If I'm going to move on with my life, I've been toying with actually moving on. Moving someplace else, I mean. Dating a person from the Blue Arrow area might delay that."

"You'd leave here?" From what he knew of the natives, they were nearly impossible to pry from their pines and lakes and purple mountain majesties.

"It's my year of yes."

"Ah." Things clicked into place, and then something ugly clawed at his heart. "So that night with me…it was, what, a test of your dedication to the notion? Was sex an item on your year-of-yes agenda?" Why did the thought of it anger him so much? Hadn't *he* put *her* on his to-do list?

She turned to him, and her winter-blue eyes flamed like fire. "Is that what you think of me? I used you because sex was on my...my schedule? Oh, and I get paid for it, too. Let's see..." Tapping her chin, she pretended to think. "What does that make me?"

"Damn it, Ashley—"

"Damn *you*, Chase," she said, and swept off.

Frustrated, he stared after her until Arch arrived with two cold beers. "Want to go break some rocks? Your fists look ready to take on the challenge."

Chase forced his fingers to relax and grabbed one of the bottles from his friend. "Women," he muttered. "What the hell are they good for?"

Arch's brows rose. "If I have to explain that to you, then I must have been more out of it during those long weekends in college than I thought."

"We have nothing in common," Chase said.

"*We* who?"

He slashed out with his free hand. "Men. Women." His gaze shifted to the last place he'd seen his hostess. "Ashley and me."

"We're talking about Ashley now?"

"I haven't done any better with her than I did with Brianna."

"Well, she was a peach."

Chase glanced at his friend. "Why do I have such lousy luck with women?"

"What are you talking about? With the exception of your college fiancée—who I remember you had many doubts over—you've had perfect luck with women. They've been in your life until they weren't. The breakups were mutual, or at least undramatic. You don't have a stalker I don't know about, do you?"

"Brianna threw her suitcase down the stairs."

Arch's expression didn't change. "Like I said, a peach." At Chase's grimace, he punched him lightly in the arm. "Don't be so hard on yourself. You're thirty-two and you've been with some pretty nice women over the years."

"Ashley's nice." And he'd just insulted her. Lifting his bottle, he clunked it against his skull. Why had he done that?

"Very nice," Arch said mildly.

"She's been hurt."

"June explained that to me. That shouldn't deter you. You'd make a great protector."

Chase looked over at Arch, realized he was serious. "I never saw that as my role… I guess I never got to a place with a woman before where I wanted to…take care of her like that. Shield her."

"It's not bad, you know," Arch said, and lifted an arm to show off bunched biceps. "Makes a guy feel all manly."

"You're an idiot."

His friend's arm dropped to his side. "Even better, when you care like that…and she cares back…you feel half of something that's bigger than one times two."

Chase stared. "You always were lousy at math."

"Why you take care of my money." Arch took a swig from his beer. "It's great, you know?"

"What is?"

"To have someone who listens, who laughs, who will clasp your hand in the dark. When you find the person you want at your side when bad news strikes or whom you'd want to shower with gifts if you ever won the lottery—you'd better hold on tight."

Rubbing his chest, Chase turned to face his friend. "What the heck are we talking about, Arch?"

"We're talking about love, buddy." And with a grin, he tapped glass bottle against glass bottle. "We're talking about love."

CHAPTER SIX

THE NEXT MORNING, Ashley stumbled toward her bedroom door, ready to get on with the next-to-final day of the house party. Sleep hadn't come easy until about dawn, and then she'd woken late to find it was snowing hard outside her windows. That meant being housebound, she supposed, and she wondered about the day's theme.

As she pushed open her door, she saw something was tied around the outer knob. A posy, wrapped in a man's handkerchief, then knotted to stay in place. Embroidered initials in navy could be seen on one fluttering edge of pristine cotton. CDB.

A voice spoke from her left. "It's Sherlock Holmes Day."

Ashley glanced over. Chase was more casual than she'd ever seen him, in worn jeans, running shoes and a UCLA sweatshirt. Her fingertips brushed the small bunch of flowers. "Is that why I've been given an early morning mystery? Who could be CDB?"

Chase leaned one shoulder against the hallway wall and smiled at her. She pretended it didn't heat her blood and bump against the fortress surrounding her heart. "Guilty."

That was her, still finding him so annoyingly attractive when he wasn't the type of man she wanted at all.

When she'd had her one night and that should be plenty with someone who had raced cars and piloted a plane and—God—*skydived*.

"Am I supposed to guess, then," she said, "*why* you left these for me?"

His expression sobered. "You know why. I screwed up last night. I didn't mean to insult you, but…" He ran his hand through his hair. "My mouth got away from me."

She thought of it, his mouth, skating across her cheek and running along her neck and closing over her breast, his tongue teasing her. She threw a casual arm over her chest and told herself she wasn't blushing. "All right."

"I'm sorry."

"Me, too," Ashley said, half turning to unknot the handkerchief. "I'm not usually so prickly."

"We probably shouldn't have had sex."

She froze. "You regret it?"

"No." His hand scraped through his hair again. "I'm not making any sense. I didn't sleep well last night."

"Must be going around," she murmured.

"I just, uh, feel lousy about what happened. You did me a favor, agreeing to play hostess, and then I…"

She glanced over as the flowers came free. "You what?"

He shrugged. "I can be a bad man."

Not in the least. But she smiled a little and shook the posy under his nose. "You're a flower thief. Is one of my arrangements looking underdressed?"

His mouth turned up in a grin. "Not that you'd notice. I moved stealthily about the house and only took one or two blossoms from here and there."

"Clever."

"So...you forgive me?"

"I don't even know if I was really mad," Ashley confessed. "I was just...confused. I mean, I'm glad I took that step, but it left me a little rocky."

"I understand that." He hesitated. "When I started thinking about it, I worried that you'd feel as if you'd been disloyal. If it seems to you that you betrayed your husband's memory by being with me... I'd hate to think our night together caused you that kind of distress."

Did he have to be so nice? "It didn't. I'm okay."

He let out a breath. "Good." He glanced down at his feet and then back at her. "I think the problem is we didn't make time for a morning-after talk."

Panic bubbled. He wanted to talk about it? "I know it didn't mean anything. It was a one-night deal." How did people *do* this kind of thing? In the light of day, it was so difficult to discuss.

"Still..." Reaching out, he cupped one of her shoulders and urged her a step closer. "I should have told you how absolutely lovely you were that night." His voice was a low whisper. "You smelled so good. You *smell* so good."

"Um, thank you." Her pulse thrummed and she felt heat crawl all over her skin. "You smell good, too."

He smiled and traced the arch of one of her eyebrows with his forefinger. "I know it had been a long time for you—since you'd been with a man."

She glanced away.

His knuckle tucked under her chin to force their eyes to meet. "I should have told you how much you pleased me. How amazing you felt."

His focus was intense, and she thought he was looking through her once more, seeing secrets that she didn't want to admit to herself. Heat raced again over her skin. "Thank you. I was, uh, pleased, too."

"I think I got that," he said, cocky grin reappearing. "All that moaning and sighing."

"You." She pushed away from him, though the teasing tone put her, strangely, more at ease. "You're trying to embarrass me."

He shook his head. "I'm trying to get us past the insult and the awkwardness."

"All right," she said, "consider it done." Then she smiled at him.

His right hand brushed her cheek. "That dimple. It does something to me."

Under his touch, Ashley stilled. Their gazes met again and it was there, that connection, that attraction, the invisible tie that had no place in her life.

Chase's hand dropped. "Arch thinks he knows everything."

At the non sequitur, she blinked. "Um…okay."

"But he doesn't. Take my word for it." His tone was brisk now.

"Whatever you say."

"I say we're friends. Right?"

"Right." She nodded. "Friends. Sounds great."

Except it didn't. Because there was no sense in being friends with a man she'd never see again.

As MOST OF the guests tromped up the stairs at the end of Sherlock Holmes Day—notable for several rounds of the board game Clue and a fancy English high tea—Chase decided he could already call the week a success. Tomorrow afternoon the visitors would head down the hill. He'd follow the next day, another New Year's house party behind him.

In the media room, Arch turned on the television. The opening credits to the 1959 version of *The Hound of the Baskervilles* began to play. It continued to snow outside, but the fire was glowing in the grate, and June and Ashley came in with a plate of brownies and a pot of tea.

Without a word, Arch got up to pour a couple of snifters of brandy and passed one to Chase. They toasted each other silently, and Chase took a healthy swallow. Yeah, a successful week.

His friend set his glass aside and rubbed his hands together. "I love this movie." He plopped down on the sofa and patted the cushion while mock-leering at his wife. "Come here, my pretty."

That left the love seat for Chase and Ashley. He drew up a pair of ottomans so they could stretch out their legs. Without a word, she took her place beside him. They kept several inches of distance between their shoulders and thighs. Her attention on the screen, she clasped her fingers in her lap.

A few minutes later, both she and June let out light screams, bouncing on the cushions. Arch glanced at Chase, winked. "Just like junior high," he said, and slung an arm around his wife to draw her close. "Scare the girls so you can cop a feel."

Chase didn't respond. But he did mimic his friend's action and pulled Ashley against his side. She stiffened, but then settled in. "I hate spiders," she said, shivering. "That tarantula…" Her voice drifted away as she returned her attention to the movie.

Hitching her closer, Chase watched her instead of

what was playing on the big screen. Colors washed over her face and he thought of all the moods he'd seen reflected there in the past days: shyness, sadness, determination, desire.

When he managed to make her smile or laugh…

He remembered what he'd said to her in his bed. *You make me happy.*

And he remembered what Arch had said. *We're talking about love, buddy.*

We're talking about love.

Stilling, Chase waited for a cold wash of trepidation to roll over him. He expected to feel panicked or, at the very least, uncertain.

Instead, everything inside him shifted for an instant, shifted again, and then the world around him seemed exactly right. Balanced. *Our edges line up.*

He was in love, Chase realized. *I'm in love with Ashley.*

His gut had been telling him that all along, from the first moment. While he'd never before believed in love at first sight, he believed in listening to his instincts.

She was it for him.

As the movie continued playing, and she burrowed closer with each new suspenseful twist and turn, Chase considered his next step. Doing nothing was not an option. He wanted love in his life, this certainty, this *happiness.* This woman.

But Ashley…

He tried to engage his brain to figure out a solution, a strategy. She was an investment, more important than any other he'd ever nurtured. She was an asset he wanted to hold on to long-term. She was his future; he hers. *Go slow, think this through.*

But his heart was impatient, and its needs took over.

Without a word, he pulled her from the media room, dragging her to the library, where he shut the door behind them and then turned to face her. His breath caught as she stared at him, her blue eyes wide, her mouth parted. God, so beautiful. So, so the right one.

"This is special," he said, wrapping his fingers around her upper arms. "This thing between us."

She swallowed. "It's been nice—"

"It's not 'nice,' and it's not over. It's not going to *be* over."

Her body quivered in his clasp. "You live in LA."

"And you said you were thinking of moving. But we can come here as often as you want. In any case, I'm sure we'll figure that part out."

"W-we?" she whispered.

"We." How odd, but also how delightful, to be so certain. "I'm in love with you, Ashley."

She jerked, breaking free of his hold. When he stepped forward, she held up one hand. Her eyes were huge, and she looked at him as if he was a huge hairy spider. He tried a reassuring smile. "Sweetheart…"

Her feet stumbled back again. "I'm not your sweetheart."

"Yes. Yes, you are."

She crossed her arms over her chest, the gesture defensive. "You can't want me."

"Do you mean *you* don't want *me*?"

Her head bobbed up and down. "Yes, that's it. I can't want you."

"That's not the same as not wanting me," he pointed out. When she looked ever more disturbed, he softened his voice. "It's okay, sweetheart. I won't hurt you. There's nothing to be afraid of."

She stared at him. "You should be afraid of love."

"Ash—"

"You should really be afraid of love." Whirling, she rushed toward the windows. "You think…you think it's like that," she said, pointing outside. "You think it's snow coming down like marshmallows that will make the fall soft and easy."

Oh, baby, he thought, shredded by the fear in her voice. "But?"

"But it's really ice and brittle hearts and broken bodies and broken promises."

He shook his head. "I won't break a promise to you if I make one."

"You don't know that," she said. "You *can't* know that."

Of course it was clear where this was coming from, and he could only hope he had the words to reassure her. "I can't promise to live forever, Ashley. But I'll promise to love you as long as I live."

CHAPTER SEVEN

MEN WERE IMPULSIVE, terrifying, risk-taking creatures, Ashley thought, kindling her anger to keep the tears at bay as the limo and driver took her home. Last night, she'd run from the library, and Chase had let her go. At first light, she'd been grateful to see that the snow had stopped falling, and she'd grabbed the opportunity to escape him altogether.

To return to her real life.

Everything that's happened since I met you has been outside my realm of experience.

That explained it all in a nutshell. Once she'd been plucked from her world and landed in Chase Bradley's, her emotions and her sense of self had been rattled. Her year of yes should never have started with him.

Confident, beautiful Chase Bradley.

Once at her house, she hefted her suitcase over the threshold and watched through the window as the limo receded in the distance. *There*, she thought when she could see it no longer, *I'm out of trouble now.* Chase was out of her life.

In love with her, indeed!

Hot tears pricked the corners of her eyes, but she stomped to her room with her luggage, ignoring the watery view. After unpacking, she schlepped her suitcase toward the closet in the kitchen while trying to kick aside the memory of Chase taking these same steps. She should never have let him in, she thought. She had been right to worry the place would never be the same again.

That she'd never be the same.

Perturbed by the idea, she flung the small case into the back corner of the closet. Like a bowling ball, it knocked over a bicycle rack, which toppled a stepladder that took out a stack of plastic bins and revealed a navy blue nylon ski bag and the matching tote that held her boots. After Stu's death, she'd given away her snowboarding gear but held on to this stuff.

She couldn't say why.

The skis seemed to be whispering to her now. *Take me. Take me flying.*

"No," she said aloud. "Not doing it. I made a vow." Never to return to the snow. Never to give her heart to the wrong kind of man.

Impulsive, terrifying, risk-taking.

She backed out of the closet and firmly shut the door.

But as she moved into the kitchen and made coffee, the voice continued to nag at her. *Take me. Take me flying.*

"Not a good idea," she told the refrigerator as she pulled out a questionable carton of milk, then dumped its spoiled contents into the sink. "I haven't been on the slopes in over four years. I'll probably fall on my butt and break a leg."

Which would prevent her from running back to Chase.

"Or hit my head and end up with amnesia."

Which would make her forget all about Chase.

Maybe it was a good idea after all, she thought, and found herself drifting back toward the closet.

During the long, lonely nights, she'd often dreamed of it—of being back on the snow. So it didn't seem altogether real as a half hour later she climbed out of her car and, gear in hand, trudged across the parking lot's asphalt to pay for her lift ticket. She was one of the first to arrive so was one of the first on the mountain, deposited on her feet by a chairlift that she'd been able to take up alone. No singles needed to partner yet this morning.

At the top of the run, she hesitated. When a boarder brushed by, she sidestepped out of the main thoroughfare and looked out at a view she'd been familiar with her entire life. White peaks glistened as if they'd been carved out of sugar. Fir trees gathered close in valleys as though they were huddling together for warmth.

The cool wind stung her cheeks, but she barely noticed. Instead, as she gazed out onto the immenseness of the mountains surrounding her, she was aware of the gaping loneliness inside her chest, that big empty space that had yawned inside her for the past four years. It was colder there than snow.

More frightening than death.

With a small whoop, a pair of young children set out down the mountain, taking it on as she had when she'd first learned, skis set in the snowplow position, without poles and without inhibitions. She eyed them as they traversed the slope and saw it happen. One came too close to the other and they both tumbled, sliding until they slowed to a stop, their gear strewn around them.

Without thinking, Ashley skied to the pair, her alarm dying as she saw they were giggling while lying flat on their backs in the snow. "Are you all right?" she asked anyway.

More giggles.

"We used to call this a yard sale," Ashley said, bending to snatch one's mitten and another's hat. Two pairs of ski goggles rested another few feet away.

In moments, they were accessorized and off again. She tagged them with her eyes, watching them all the way down. Maybe they felt her gaze, because at the bottom, they turned, waved.

She waved back.

"Hey, thanks," a voice said behind her.

She twisted around. A man shushed to a stop at her side. His face was ruddy with the cold and he had green eyes that matched the dark olive of his watch cap. "Uh, you're welcome?"

He smiled. "Those are my niece and nephew. I had a little trouble with my ski at the top and they got away from me."

"They seem to have survived their fall just fine."

"Hurts less when you're young."

"Yes." Like she'd tried to explain to Chase, she was too brittle now to chance a tumble...especially into love.

The man brought his glove to his mouth and jerked it off with his teeth. "Nice to meet you," he said, holding out his bare hand. "Moose Carlisle."

She blinked. Could there be more than one Moose in the Blue Arrow area? "I'm Ashley Walker."

"Ah." He squeezed her fingers and smiled. "Ashley."

The first thing that came into her head popped out of her mouth. "You don't look like a Moose." She winced. "Sorry."

He laughed. "I hear that a lot."

It wasn't that he wasn't big, but he was athletic-looking, not hulking. Fit, not fat. "Sorry."

"My real name's Marcus. My younger brother, the

dad of those scamps, couldn't say my name when he was little. It came out sounding like Moose, which stuck."

More people were gliding over the snow now and were forced to swoop around them. "Shall we go?" he asked, nodding down the hill.

What could she say? She couldn't stand in one place forever.

Like you've been doing for the past four years. Her damn skis were speaking again.

Maybe they'd be too breathless to talk if she made them do a little work, she decided, then pushed off.

It wasn't like riding a bike. But it came back to her all the same, and she felt as if the rush of the air was lifting her and lifting away the last of the grief she'd been carrying around with her. In the blue sky she saw Stu's blue eyes, his blinding grin in the bright snow, his devilish love of speed and fun in the exhilaration she felt even at her much tamer pace. Behind her sunglasses, tears pricked at her eyes, but they didn't stab at her soul. When she stopped at the bottom, the rooster tail of snow from her skis looked like a burst of fresh, clean hope.

She'd been right. It was time for her to step back into life.

Looking over, she exchanged a smile with Moose, who came to rest just a few feet away. "I'm sorry about New Year's," she said.

"Me, too." He glanced at his niece and nephew, signaling them to stay. "I better catch up with the monsters. But…how about we reattempt a night out together soon?"

What reason did she have to refuse? Staring at the handsome guy who was friends with her friends and who seemed kind to small children, she couldn't think of one. Or she could think of *only* one.

Chase. He wasn't Chase.

It seemed he'd ruined her for every other man.

Tears stung her eyes again and she pressed her mitten beneath her nose. "I, uh, I'll let you know," she said, trying to work up another smile.

Maybe she did okay with it, because he nodded, sketched a small wave and skied away.

Instead of regret, she only felt relief. While she might be ready to venture into life again, no way was she ready for love. She couldn't take that gamble again.

I can't promise to live forever, Ashley.

That cold hole in her chest would be the companion with whom she shared her days.

Her skis seemed to be out of words, so she decided to return home. She'd not even had her morning coffee. A quick stop at the market for fresh milk and then she'd be in her kitchen with her mug of java, snug and safe.

Between the ski resort and her small house, she noted the line of cars heading up the hill for a day on the slopes. Flatlanders, of course, two lanes of them, bumper-to-bumper even though the roads were slick and icy in some spots. Ashley was careful with her own speed, steering carefully and then slowing for the left turn into the grocery store's parking lot. Turning up the radio, she waited for a break in the double line of cars. When she saw it, she goosed the accelerator. At the same time, a car pulled out of the lot into one of the lanes she was attempting to cross. She braked to slow herself just as her eye caught on an immense SUV speeding along the right shoulder to circumvent the stilled traffic.

It was aimed directly at her smaller vehicle.

Time didn't seem to slow, but her ability to absorb detail heightened. The radio played an ad for a local restaurant. "Steak and seafood Saturday nights!" The driver of the oncoming car was turned in his seat, talking with a passenger in the back. Her right thigh cramped as she put all her weight onto the brake pedal.

At the first crunch of metal on metal her car began to spin.

CHASE SAT AT the library desk, his head in his hands. His father came into the room and Chase looked up. "Hey, Dad." He tried to smile. "You and Mom made it."

Arthur Bradley pulled up a chair and sat down, propping one ankle on his knee. "We wanted a chance to say goodbye to your guests."

"I'm sure they're happy to see you."

"I ran into several already. Your praises are being sung."

"Ah." His head felt like a percussion section was playing inside. "Mom did an outstanding job organizing, as usual." He rubbed at the spot between his eyes. "How's Larissa Larue? And her mom and dad and big brother?"

"Doing very well. So well that your mother only shed a few tears on the way up here."

"That's good."

"She wants more grandchildren."

"I think Annie and Doug need a few weeks before starting the whole process again."

His father laced his hands behind his head, his gaze studying Chase's face.

He told himself he was far too old to squirm.

"What's the matter?" the older man asked.

She left me. My gut steered me wrong and I laid it all out for her and scared her right out of my arms. "I'm thinking perhaps now's not the right time to make a changeover at the helm of the business, Dad."

Arthur quirked a brow but didn't look the least bit perturbed. "Because...?"

"Maybe I've lost my mojo."

His father snorted. "Tell me what's really going on."

Chase was in love with her. He'd been certain she felt the same way. That she'd run had shaken him—shaken his confidence. "I lost the most precious commodity to come into my life."

His dad started to say something, and then his attention shifted to the library door. A slight figure stood there, swaying a little.

Chase's throat closed down and he stared, wondering if she was a figment of his deep desire for her. "Ashley?" he croaked. The figure was backlit by light streaming through the windows in the room across the hall. He shoved to his feet. "Ashley?"

His father rose, too, and pulled a small box from his pocket that he slid onto the desk. "Arch called. Suggested to your mother she might want to bring this with us."

Chase glanced at the velvet box and then watched his father hesitate on his way out the door. "Son," he said, looking back. "She's injured."

"What?" He sped around the desk.

Ashley stood with one hand braced on the doorjamb. Her hair was disheveled, there were butterfly bandages over an inch-long cut on her cheek, a reddish-purple bruise colored her jaw. He reached out, and then dropped his hands, afraid to touch her. "Are you all right?"

"Mostly," she answered.

"What happened?" His mind was racing. "Do you need to sit down?"

"It was a car accident," she said. "I don't have room for any passengers now. Whole side crumpled."

"Oh, God," he said as his belly pitched. "*I* need to sit down."

She stared at him with a bemused expression. "You do look pale."

He took her hand and guided them both to the leather couch. Her fingers were icy in his hold. "Honey, do I need to take you to the hospital?"

She continued to study his face. "I didn't know I could make such a strong man weak."

He laughed, and it sounded shaky. "From the first moment we met."

"It happened then for me, too. Weird, huh?"

"No," he said. "Right." He was steadier now, and hope was beginning to fill him.

"I was stopping for milk," she told him.

He chafed her still-cool hand with both of his. "All right," he said, not sure where she was going with this.

"Just a little errand."

"Okay."

"It shouldn't have been dangerous at all."

"Ah." He brought her fingers to his mouth and kissed them.

"I could have missed out on my future thanks to a quart of skim."

"Yuck, Ash. You should at least buy two percent."

She smiled, just as he'd intended her to. "I could

have missed out on the chance to tell you that I love you back."

With those words, his heart, which had felt just as bedraggled as she looked, underwent a miraculous healing. He pulled her close, breathing in her crushed-petal scent, convincing himself this moment was real by pressing his face to her throat and the pulse beating there. "You make me happy," he said. "You make me so happy."

One of her hands stroked over his hair. "I'm sorry I ran away."

"But you came back. That's what matters."

"I had to. I love you," she said. Then her adorable dimple peeked out. "And of course I needed to know today's theme."

"It's—" He lifted his head, grinning as a great idea came to him. Straight from his gut, which seemed to be back in working order. *Strike while the iron's hot.*

"It's?" She tilted her head, a smile playing at the edges of her pretty mouth.

Chase left her a moment to scoop up the box his father had deposited on the desk. "It's Old Rock Day."

Ashley blinked. "There's an Old Rock Day?"

"Look it up. It's real. Just like us." He opened the box, plucking out the diamond engagement ring that had been his grandmother's. "Just like this. Our old rock."

She glanced at the diamond, then up to his face. In her wide eyes, winter-water blue had never looked so beautiful. "Are you…?"

"Marry me, Ashley. Take a chance on us."

"Chase…"

He could see she was trembling, but there was a light

in her eyes that didn't signify fear. Cupping her cheek in his hand, he pressed his mouth to hers. "Say yes."

Her tears didn't alarm him this time. The taste of them and of her, the salty-sweetness of the two, reminded him of life. Of risk, of reward, of loss, of love.

Of a future they had to believe in to make true.

"Yes," his beloved whispered then. "A thousand times, yes."

* * * * *

Dear Reader,

When I was asked to contribute a novella to a fun-and-flirty New Year's collection, I immediately thought of writing about Amelia, who'd appeared in my recent Blaze story, *Oh, Naughty Night!* She was such a good girl, sweet and kind, and I really wanted her to meet a guy who deserved her. But what kind of guy would that be? He couldn't be as super-sweet and nice as she is...in fact, who better to seduce a good girl than a very bad boy?

Then the wheels really started churning. What if this bad boy had sworn off bad girls? And what if Amelia had gotten tired of being the good girl and for once wanted to be super bad?

Well, everything gelled in my mind right then and there. Lex was born—the perfect complement to lovely Amelia—and their whole story played out in my thoughts long before I put my fingers on the keyboard to write it.

I do hope you enjoy Amelia and Lex's story and that it gets your New Year off to a fun and sexy start.

Best wishes,

Leslie Kelly

NO MORE BAD GIRLS

Leslie Kelly

To my readers.
Happy New Year to you all—
and good luck keeping those resolutions!

CHAPTER ONE

"You know what your problem is, Lex?"

Hearing one of the most dangerous-to-answer questions ever voiced—right up there with *Does this make me look fat?*—Lex Rollins frowned. Little would stop his buddy Ryan from sharing his opinion when sober. Now, after several New Year's Eve/Stag Party drinks, there'd be no shutting him up. Meaning Lex had no choice but to be educated on what, exactly, his problem was.

"You have lousy taste in women."

The three other guys at the table, one of them tomorrow's groom, the others his groomsmen, nodded their agreement. *Traitors.*

"That's ridiculous. I've dated some beautiful women."

"Beautiful maybe," said Ryan. "But also seriously whacked."

"God, remember the chick who slashed his tires? The blonde, what was her name?" asked Tony, sounding far too amused.

"No, the blonde was the one who keyed his car," said Matt. "It was the redhead with the pierced eyebrows that slashed his tires. Or was it the crazy-as-a-bedbug brunette with the monster truck?"

"Hey, watch it, that one was my sister," said Dean.

Lex didn't comment. Dean's sister, whom he had dated in grad school, was indeed as crazy as a bedbug.

"But it's true," said Ryan. "You do have a habit of hooking up with women who are…um…not exactly nice."

Nice girls? Since when had that been a requirement for this crew? Well, except for Matt, who was getting married tomorrow to an angel. Oh, and Ryan, whose wedding would be on Valentine's Day. Come to think of it, Tony's girlfriend was great, as was Dean's new guy.

Crap. He *was* the odd man out. His best friends had all found their Ms.—or Mr.—Rights. Lex, meanwhile, had been stuck in the land of wrong for most of his life. Why, he couldn't say. Bad luck? Bad timing? Bad job, since he often interacted with sports groupies? Or, crap, were his buddies right, did he really just have bad taste? The idea stung.

"Nice girls are overrated," he muttered.

"They don't slash your tires, key your car or alienate your friends so you never see them anymore," said Matt.

Tony jumped in with the coup de grâce. "They also don't wait for you to go to work, then back a U-Haul into your driveway and steal everything that's not nailed down."

Lex took a deeper pull of his beer. The subject definitely required it. The scabs from his last relationship, which had ended four months ago, hadn't disappeared… unlike his big-screen TV, Xbox, iPad and most of his kitchen appliances.

Damn, he really missed his Keurig.

"We're not talking about that."

Ryan was courteous enough to change the subject.

"I've told you, my future sister-in-law is supercute and sweet."

Ryan—the Valentine's Day groom—had been trying to set Lex up with his fiancée's sister for weeks. Lex couldn't work up much interest in a girl named Amelia—was that even a name anymore?—who owned a craft shop. Yarn and teddy bears didn't exactly turn him on. Then again, neither did getting robbed.

Ryan wasn't finished, though. "It's New Year's Eve. Why not make a resolution to steer clear of wild women and bar babes, and try to find someone who's not gonna cheat on you, maim you or rob you?"

"Wow, I don't know if I'm worthy of such perfection."

Fortunately, the guys moved on to another topic, but Lex fell silent.

Looking back, he guessed he'd always been attracted to the bad girl, ever since first grade when Mindy Myers had dragged him in the coatroom to show off her *My Little Pony* panties. Considering the example his father had set, with five marriages and a revolving door of stepmothers for Lex, he wondered if a shrink might have a good idea where the urge came from.

Or maybe it wasn't the stepmothers. Hell, the only woman who'd ever truly broken his father's heart had been Lex's mother—wife number one. She'd been a doctor, who everybody had believed was the kindest, noblest woman ever born. She'd been so kind and noble, she'd decided working with the poor and sick in the third world was more important than staying with her husband and son. *So long, boys, I'm off to devote myself to the entire human race. Except you, I'm sure you'll do fine.*

She'd left when Lex was five, keeping in touch only with the occasional birthday card, but not every year. Hence the stepmothers.

His father's next four wives had been very different—certainly less noble. His old man had married them, but usually hadn't gotten too attached. Neither had Lex. So their hearts were never completely shattered again. Well, not until wife number five. But that was another story.

Damn. There might be something to this…perhaps his bad girl thing had its roots in his childhood. Maybe it was time to make a change, and this might be the night to start. New year, new attitude. New everything.

The group broke up before midnight. It was early for a Stag Party/New Year's Eve outing, but the wedding was in the morning, and the others didn't want to get caught in the holiday crowd pouring into DC. Since Lex had recently moved nearby, into Dupont Circle, he didn't care and offered to wait for the overworked server, who had yet to bring the check.

As Ryan stood, Lex said, "About your fiancée's sister…"

Ryan grinned. "You'll do it?"

"I hate blind dates," he insisted. "But I guess I'm in. A week from Friday, if she's available."

"Excellent! I'll fix it up and give you the details."

Lex nodded, eyeing his friends, forcing himself to go a step farther. "And I guess I'll try this resolution thing."

Tony chortled. "No more wild women? Nice girls only?"

Lex sighed, wondering if he was crazy. "No wild women. Nice girls only. From here on out, it's bowling dates and picnics."

His friends eyed each other with amused and skeptical expressions. "You swear, man? No spying some hot chick on the way out the door tonight and changing your mind?" asked Ryan.

"I swear. After midnight, I'm a Boy Scout."

"Okay, we're holding you to it."

His friends said their goodbyes, and he followed them ten minutes later, after settling the bill. Weaving through the crowd, Lex swam upstream as the holiday partyers poured in through the door. He wasn't halfway to the exit when he was elbowed by a red-nosed dude who looked as if he'd been celebrating since Christmas Day. Lex found himself lurching onto the crowded dance floor, and instinctively put his hands out to steady himself.

They landed on something warm, soft and silky.

"You could just ask me if I want to dance," a woman's voice said, the tone almost as smooth as the green dress brushing against his fingers.

Lex froze, his senses battered. The voices, music and clinking glasses deafened him, but he barely noticed. He was instead focused only on the delightful feel of soft, curvy female beneath his hands, and the sight of the biggest, bluest eyes he'd ever seen. His quick, surprised inhalation brought with it an evocative, sultry scent—part perfume, part woman—and he swallowed hard, stunned by his own immediate reaction to her.

His hands were on her waist. He should let her go, he knew, but something made him tighten his grip and tug her closer. Close enough to study the thick, wavy curls—gold, with red highlights—that fell over her shoulders in a lush tangle, and to note the beauty of her face.

He realized it wasn't midnight yet, meaning his resolution hadn't started, and said, "Wanna dance?"

She nodded slowly, staring at him with a steady intensity that made his heart beat faster. As if she was trying to figure him out, or figure out what to do about him. Hearing her soft exhalation, seeing the close attention she paid to his mouth—as if she were already thinking about what it would be like to kiss him—he doubted she would meet the good-girl requirements he'd just promised to seek out. Still, something wouldn't let him turn away, not while he had a few minutes left.

The cacophony continued around them, but his attention remained on those blue eyes, that delicate, heart-shaped face, the full red lips. She was stunning—delicate, but sexy as hell. Even without the dramatic makeup, her eyes would have been unforgettable, and that mouth was incredibly kissable.

Without a word, she lifted her arms to encircle his neck. Lex cupped her hips, holding her tight to him. He pulled her even closer, and they began to move to the music—a hot, steady thrum that vibrated the floors and pounded through his body. He lost himself to the hard beat, to the heat and the colors and the noise. Mostly to the feel of her, this glorious stranger, pressed against him, her fingers twining in his hair and her soft curves melting against every inch of him. There was no subtlety, no holding back. She was aggressive, certain of her sexual power and using it to push every thought out of his head except for one: *God, why didn't I meet her before tonight?*

"I'm Lex," he finally said, remembering he had a voice.

"Are you carrying Kryptonite?"

It wasn't the first time someone had made a Superman quip about his nickname. "Why? Is it your weakness?"

"It might explain why I couldn't resist dancing with you."

"I assumed that was my charm."

"You haven't charmed me yet."

"Give me a minute," he said, laughing softly, liking that she had an answer for everything. "What's your name?"

"I'm...Lia."

"Are you alone?" he asked.

"No. My friends and I just arrived." She nodded toward a table crowded with laughing young adults. "This is our typical weekend spot. I don't remember seeing you here before."

"First-timer," he admitted, wishing he'd been here before tonight, if only so he could have met her sooner. Because, damn, how badly did it suck to stumble across a sexy goddess on the very night he'd sworn off bar-pickups and bad girls?

"It's not a bad place—not usually this crowded."

"So, your friends over there, are you with one of them?"

Her smile coy, she replied, "I'm with all of them."

"I meant one of the guys."

"Do you think I'd be dancing with you if I were?"

"Only if he's stupid."

She hesitated. His heart skipped a beat.

Finally, she broke the tension. "I'm not with anyone."

Not tonight anyway. But he doubted this woman was without male company too often. How lucky for him that he'd met her at exactly the right moment.

Then he remembered his resolution…and had a hard time thinking of himself as lucky.

"So, if you're here all alone, who do you plan on kissing at midnight?" he asked, brushing his cheek against her soft hair.

She looked up at him, her expression direct, almost challenging, not coy or flirtatious. "I guess you'll have to stick around and find out."

And although he'd been on his way out the door, though he had to get up early, though he had no interest in being in a crowd of strangers and though he'd just made a resolution that he was done with this kind of seductive woman, Lex knew he wouldn't be going anywhere at least until after the clock struck twelve.

WHO ARE YOU and what have you done with the real Amelia?

Wrapped in the arms of one of the handsomest men she'd ever met, Amelia Jones found the questions hard to answer.

Had she let her best friend, Viv, talk her into layering on a pound of makeup and styling her normally ponytailed hair into what Viv called the "primal cavewoman" style? Had she then borrowed a slinky dress so low cut the V-neck might as well be called an *X*, and thrown herself at a sexy man who'd accidentally bumped into her? And was she really flirting with him, as though she had enough confidence to believe he would stick around to kiss her when the ball dropped and the New Year was oh-so-enjoyably rung in?

Yes, to all of the above. She, nice girl, craft-store owner, knitter extraordinaire, had done all of those things.

After being designated the best-friend type, the one who never drove a guy wild, she'd decided to start the New Year with a change: she'd stop being the girl guys could take home to mama and become the aggressive woman guys wanted to take home to bed.

Of course, she didn't actually intend to go that far into some stranger's bed. Although, right now, pressed close against a guy so hot he should grace the cover of a Sexiest Man Alive magazine spread, she had to think his bed wouldn't be such a bad place to end up. But no matter how much makeup she put on, or how low-cut her dress, she wasn't the one-night-stand type. Still, her at-least-six-dates-before-sex rule would be tested quickly by this stranger.

Oh, who was she kidding? She hadn't had six dates with a guy in more than two years. Meaning it had been more than two years since she'd had sex. No wonder Viv called her a born-again virgin. Her hymen might well have grown back. That's if she'd ever lost it to begin with. Her college boyfriend hadn't been the most, er, equipped lover.

"So, are you in the habit of grabbing strange women on the dance floor?" she finally asked, raising her voice to be heard above the music.

"Sorry. I got shoved and put my hands out. Your perfect body happened to be where they landed."

She half lowered her eyes to disguise her reaction to his words. Nobody had ever called her perfect before. Pretty, maybe. Nice, patient, friendly, loyal…but not perfect. And while the line should have sounded practiced or smarmy, the genuine warmth in his voice made her believe he'd meant it.

"I suppose I should say I'm sorry about that."

"Are you?"

"Nope."

The normal Amelia might have blushed or looked away. But tonight was about pushing outside her boundaries, being less inhibited and more daring. So she replied, "Neither am I."

"I'm glad."

"You should be," she pointed out. "Your hands could have landed on a six-five former Marine and then you'd be doing a different kind of dance altogether."

"While I have great respect for members of the military, I'm sure he wouldn't have been as good a dancer as you."

The flirtation was coming easily to her, which made Amelia feel better about what she was doing. She'd come out looking for an adventure, something wild to kick off a new year and a new, less safe and practical, her. One of her friends had found the love of her life in this same bar on Halloween night; maybe the place, Shady Jo's, would work the same magic for Amelia. In any case, at least she could have an adventure. She was tired of always being the best friend, the one guys asked for advice about other, more glamorous women.

The last straw had landed on her back earlier in the week when her neighbor, a cute guy she'd thought might be interested in her, had asked her to help him pick out what to wear for a blind date. A blind one obviously being better than a fully sighted one with Amelia, whom he knew was single.

Yeah. Definitely time for big changes.

And considering she was in the arms of the most attractive man she'd ever seen, she'd say her resolution was off to a good start. The thick hair tangled in her fingers was a rich brown, but she caught streaks of gold when the lights above them hit it. His eyes were gorgeous, a pale green, gleaming in the semidarkness. They were emphasized by long lashes and dark brows. High cheeks with slashing hollows complemented a square jaw with a small sexy cleft. He had a great mouth, wide and smiling, meant for good humor and great kisses.

"This feels nice," she said, her voice throaty, though she hadn't done it intentionally. He brought out something in her—something reckless and elemental. Maybe she was channeling Viv.

"You feel nice."

He pulled her closer, until their legs tangled, one of his thighs sliding between hers. Her breath was stolen from her lungs and she could barely think, unable to focus on anything except the feel of him, all hard, powerful and warm. Lord, it had been a long time since she'd been this close to a man.

"So, what did Santa bring you?" he asked.

A soft gurgle of laughter burst from her lips. Here she was imagining all kinds of wicked things and he was talking about Christmas. She had to wonder if the segue was intentional—if he, too, was affected by the surge of instant attraction and was trying to normalize things.

"Not the lottery jackpot I asked for."

"I didn't get my trip to the space station, either."

"If I win next week, I'll buy you a ticket."

"Deal."

Their soft laughter mingled, and she wondered at how natural it seemed. Maybe it was because, despite the attraction, they were immediately at ease with each other. Sexual tension danced between them, but so did an instinctive liking.

"Did you get coal in your stocking?" she asked.

"How'd you guess?"

"Something tells me you might be a bit naughty."

He grinned. "Something tells me it takes one to know one."

Ha. The naughtiest Amelia had been lately was when she'd cheated on one of her favorite TV shows by checking out another in the same time slot. DVR had saved some of the most important relationships in her life. But she wasn't about to reveal that. Let him believe she was utterly wicked…that was, after all, what tonight was all about, wasn't it? Shedding her good-girl image? And oh, what a man with whom to shed it.

He went on. "Did you get coal in your stocking?"

No, she'd gotten three skeins of cashmere yarn, violet, lemon and pink, not that she was about to tell him that. "Maybe I don't want to discuss my stockings and their contents."

He licked his lips, picking up on the innuendo. "Are your stockings red and fuzzy? Or more soft and silky?"

She couldn't believe she was inviting him to speculate on what she wore beneath her slinky dress, but she took a deep breath and went with it. "Now what could they possibly hold if they were too soft and flimsy?"

"Special treats."

Nobody had ever called her thighs treats, though her legs were pretty nice. Usually nobody saw them, though, since she wore plain, simple dresses that had Peter Pan collars and fell to midcalf. But she suddenly found herself wanting a second opinion.

"Too bad Christmas is over. There's nothing left to unwrap."

His smile widened, growing more wicked, and Amelia shivered. Although she was enjoying dancing close, she couldn't help shifting back so she could stare up at him, drinking in the features of the face a few inches above her own.

"Are you really here alone?" she asked him, wondering why on earth this guy was flying solo on New Year's Eve.

"I was with a group of guys, but they left."

"Did they move on to the next bar without you?"

He shook his head. "No, everybody's heading home. One of my buddies is getting married tomorrow. This was his Stag Party."

"I didn't notice any girls leaping out of cakes as I came in."

"He's totally tamed. Has eyes for nobody but his bride. I'm surprised he came out with us at all, or that she let him."

"My sister's getting married in February. She's the same way—everything's sunshine and roses. Ugh."

She wasn't unhappy about her sister's happiness. She just wished she didn't have to see so much of it, at least on the romantic side. Romance hadn't been in Amelia's repertoire in a long time.

"Why is it when somebody gets engaged they suddenly want all their single friends to be tied down, too?" he asked.

"Misery loves company?"

They laughed together, easy, comfortable. Yet even as they chatted, Amelia found herself growing more fascinated by him. She was utterly in tune to every sensation, shocked and thrilled by the press of his hard, masculine body against her softer, feminine one. His powerful hands were possessive at her waist, and when he'd brushed his lips against her temple, she'd gone weak in the knees.

It was crazy, sudden and fierce. But she wouldn't step away from him if somebody screamed "Fire" in the crowded bar.

"Anyway, the party broke up and I was about to head home when I got bumped right into this dance." Cutting her off before she could ask, he added, "Not that I regret it."

"You were heading home before midnight?"

"I'm not much of a New Year's Eve partyer."

"My cop uncle always calls it Amateur Night."

He lifted a quizzical brow.

"People who know better but still drink and drive."

"Your uncle's a police officer?"

She nodded.

"Should I be nervous?"

"Are you planning to swindle me or steal my car?"

"Not on the agenda." A twinkle appeared in his springtime-green eyes. "At least, not so far anyway."

"I drive a beat-up old minivan."

"I have my own car," he murmured. "And I'm not a swindler."

"I bet you'd be talented at it, though."

He eyed her in confusion.

"I mean, you're good-looking enough to be a con man," she explained, though she regretted the words immediately.

"Thanks. I think."

Oh, damn, she was reverting to her usual crappy flirting style.

"So, Lia," he said in that throaty, husky voice that made her tingle right down to her toes, "what do you do when you're not being grabbed by strangers on crowded dance floors?"

She did not reply that she owned a craft store, was a yarn expert and taught knitting classes. She loved what she did, and supported herself rather well, if simply. But the crafty girl never got the man. The sexy, mysterious temptress did.

"Oh, this and that," she replied, hoping she sounded vague and enigmatic. She wasn't exactly lying, since her shop, located a few blocks from here, was called This 'n' That. "You?"

His eyes gleamed. "This and that."

So he was being mysterious, too. Tonight, that suited her fine. The old Amelia had played by the rules and learned everything there was to know about a man before going to first base with him. The new one—for tonight at least—was rewriting the entire rulebook.

The song ended, and Lex said, "Can I buy you a drink?"

She raised a coy brow. "I thought you were going home."

"I've suddenly decided I can't bear to ring in the New Year on my own." He glanced at his watch. "Ten minutes to go."

Ten minutes until she had a chance to share a New Year's Eve kiss with a perfect stranger…emphasis on perfect. That was definitely worth waiting for. "All right."

She deliberately chose not to lead him to the table

where her friends were gathered, a couple of them watching wide-eyed. Instead, they headed toward the bar. One empty bar stool stood on the far end, and he claimed it, picking her up and setting her on it before she had time to react.

Amelia's heart fluttered. She wasn't the type of girl who was swept up off her feet, figuratively or literally. She never had been. And she liked it more than she'd ever have expected.

She couldn't help remembering that her friend Lulu had ended up sitting on this stool on Halloween night, with a sexy charmer of her own. If history was repeating itself, she, too, might be having a daring, exciting encounter tonight. Though, unlike Lulu, it wouldn't be in a bank vestibule. Amelia wasn't that adventurous.

"What'll you have?" he asked.

"How about champagne to toast with?"

He nodded and ordered them each a glass, then stepped in close, bracing an arm against the bar. They were alone, nestled in the corner. Although the music surged and talk filled the room, she was aware only of the quick beat of her heart. Each breath was filled with his spicy, masculine scent, and though the bar stool was tall, she had to tilt her head back to look up at that handsome face.

She searched for something to say, something other than, *So will this New Year's kiss be of the French persuasion?*, and then found herself mumbling, "Vive la France."

"What?"

"Uh…what's your resolution?"

He looked down at her, his smile tightening. He let out a long, slow breath, and then swept a hand through his thick hair, tousling it even more than her fingers had. She wondered why her simple question had touched such a sore spot.

A frown tugged at his brow, and he clenched his jaw. "I don't want to think about my resolution until after midnight."

Meaning he'd resolved to do something unpleasant in the New Year? Or to stop doing something he enjoyed? Strange. "Well, you only have about a minute left to not think about it."

Before he could reply, the bartender pushed two glasses of champagne across the bar toward them. "Almost time!"

She reached for her glass, and Lex did the same, but as they did so, their hands touched on the sticky surface of the bar. Amelia sucked in a breath as a spark of electricity leaped between them, sharp evidence of the excitement that had been building from the moment he'd bumped into her.

Around them, she heard voices begin to count down to midnight. *Ten. Nine. Eight.* But she didn't speak, and neither did Lex. Their fingers were still touching ever-so-lightly, and his whole body was still close to hers, his hip brushing against her thigh, his warm exhalations reaching her temple.

Then, as if both of them were working under the same strange instinct, they moved together. She turned on the stool to face him, and he bent toward her. Amelia didn't close her eyes, losing herself in his deep green ones, as their mouths came closer and closer. Until, as the crowd shouted, "Happy New Year," their lips brushed, parted and then met again.

He cupped her cheek, and she lifted a hand to tangle

in his hair. The kiss deepened, tongues tangling delicately, deliberately. It was sweet and hot and sexy and tempting, the kind of kiss that wasn't going anywhere, wasn't leading to anything, but was delightful in and of itself. He tasted warm and spicy. Waves of pleasure rolled through her as she felt the kiss right down to the tips of her toes.

Around them, other couples were doing the same thing—kissing in the New Year—but Amelia barely noticed. When Lex drew her off the stool to pull her against his body, she went easily, loving being back in his arms, and the kiss went on and on.

Finally, they drew apart. She saw something warm and wondering in his green eyes as he murmured, "Happy New Year."

"Happy New Year to you," she replied, a bit stunned.

"Tell me, are you *really* the bad girl you seem to be?" he asked, his tone flirtatious, but also a little curious… as if he'd somehow sensed her innocence in that kiss.

She hid a groan. Lord, she did not want another man to back away from her because he thought she was too nice, too sweet, too untouchable.

She didn't want to be nice, or sweet. And she definitely didn't want to be untouched.

"I'm as bad as you want me to be," she said, which wasn't really an answer, but wasn't a lie, either. She was, after all, being intentionally naughty tonight. That she wasn't a bad girl the rest of the time was something he could find out later.

Oh, did she hope there would be a later.

But fate seemed to have something else in mind.

"I have to go," he told her, a deep frown pulling at

his brow. His jaw had tightened again, and his expression was genuinely regretful.

"You...huh?"

He brushed his thumb against her cheek one more time, and then shook his head and dropped his hand, as if forcing himself to do something he didn't want to do. "It was nice meeting you, Lia. But the New Year has started and I have to get out of here."

"Oh," she mumbled, trying not to reveal her disappointment.

"Believe me," he said, brushing his fingertips over her cheek in a caress as tender as it was fleeting, "if I hadn't made a promise, I'd never be walking out of here."

"Does this promise mean you won't be coming back, say, next weekend?" she asked, hoping she sounded sexy and inviting, not needy and pathetic. *Pathetic be damned. No guts, no glory.* "I sometimes hang out here on Friday or Saturday nights."

He clenched his jaw; she could see he was gritting his teeth, forcing himself to do something unpleasant.

Like turn her down.

"I'm sorry, Lia, I wish I could. Believe me, I do."

Although disappointment stabbed her, Amelia noticed he didn't sound happy. His reservations must be pretty important, and he must be a man of his word.

Knowing that didn't make her feel any better, though, when, with one more sigh and a sad smile, he spun and walked away, out of the bar, and out of her life.

CHAPTER TWO

"RYAN, I SWEAR, I'm not bailing out. I've *got* to work late tonight. I can't meet up with your future sister-in-law."

Although he knew Ryan would be skeptical, considering Lex's aversions to nice girls and blind dates, he was being entirely truthful. He'd been thrilled to get an interview with a popular, and tough, professional goalie, who'd spoken out in support of gay players in the NHL. The media had been all over the guy but he hadn't given any exclusives...until now. The goalie's agent had given Lex a half hour of the star's time for an interview, and he intended to make good use of it.

Ryan huffed into the phone. "Is that the best you've got?"

"I'm not kidding."

"Lex, you *have* to go on this date. Believe me, you will *hate* yourself if you don't."

That seemed dramatic, but then Ryan was in love with his blind date's sister. "My interview is with Pete Whitecastle, man."

Ryan, a big hockey fan, whistled. "You're not kidding?"

"Not about this."

"An exclusive?"

"Yeah."

"How'd you get it?"

Lex thought about the agent's surprising call to him earlier. "Whitecastle actually pays attention to Twitter. He saw my supportive tweet after his public statement, made a mental note of my name and decided to give me the exclusive."

"Think he's gonna come out himself?"

"I have no idea. But I wouldn't miss this interview even if I was supposed to go on a date with Angelina Jolie."

Ryan was silent for a moment, then he sighed. "I guess I can accept that. When's the interview?"

Lex glanced at his watch. "I'm meeting him at his lawyer's office downtown at four. There's no way I can be in Georgetown to meet with your fiancée's sister for drinks at five."

"So could you make it at seven?"

Grabbing his jacket, Lex said, "Besides the fact that seven sounds like dinner, not drinks, I still don't think I can."

"Eating dinner with a woman does not equate to putting a ring on her finger," Ryan said.

Maybe not. But every blind date handbook said no dinner, just drinks the first time out.

"And I'm telling you, Lex," his friend said, "you *want* to meet this girl. Make it work."

"I've got thirty minutes with Whitecastle, but we both know I'm gonna try for more. Then I have to come back here for editing and promo spots, which could take hours. Would you rather I say I'm coming late and then stand her up altogether?"

"Okay, okay," his friend said, finally giving up. "I'll get a message to her that you can't make it at all tonight, but you *will* get in touch to reschedule. Right?"

"Yeah."

"Swear it, dude. Swear it on Lily Lundgren's red sweater."

Lex laughed, well remembering the teenage goddess who'd had him and all his friends in thrall for so long. Ahh, that red sweater. What any one of them wouldn't have done for a brush of a hand against it.

"I swear. If I don't, may I never see another woman in a red sweater again." Shoving a small notebook into the pocket of his sport coat, he said, "Text me her number."

"I will. And you owe me."

"Want a date with Whitecastle if he comes out?"

"Ha. Ask Dean. But I wouldn't mind an autograph."

"Done."

"And tickets the next time the Flyers are in town."

"Don't push your luck."

Lex ended the call, jogged over to his cameraman and they headed to the lawyer's office. They were brought to Whitecastle right away, who was ready to talk. The hockey star was a lot more eloquent than he'd have expected for a guy who'd had all his teeth knocked out of his head by the age of twenty-five.

Lex pushed his luck, and got seventy-five minutes, during which the goalie explained that his brother was gay and getting married. Lex had always liked Whitecastle, and the way he talked about his family and showed his love for his sibling, bumped Lex's respect for the man up a notch. He'd be a good spokesman for what was a hot-button issue in the world of pro sports. Careers had risen or fallen on such stances, and he had to give Whitecastle props for taking such a public one.

At the end of the interview, as he thanked the man, he remembered Ryan's request. Whitecastle autographed a few photographs, and his agent promised to send Lex tickets to the upcoming Flyers match. That ought to get Lex out of Ryan's doghouse for bailing out on the blind date.

He went back to the station with his crew and they did some editing for the interview, which would air in several segments, starting with tonight's 11:00 p.m. broadcast. Although he usually did the morning, noon and early evening programs, Lex wanted to be on air tonight to set up the piece himself. The producers were already throwing out promo clips for a hot exclusive at eleven. In the meantime, though, he had a few hours to kill.

It was almost eight and DC had descended into a cold January night. He passed few people on the street as he walked from the studio to the nearest Metro station. He wasn't sure of his destination, he just wanted to get to another part of the city where he could find a decent restaurant. It was too late to try to reschedule his blind date. Besides, he didn't even know how to reach the woman—Amelia.

Then, remembering his conversation with Ryan, he checked his phone. True to his word, his friend had texted Lex his future sister-in-law's phone number.

He glanced at the number, thought hard, remembered last week at the club, when he'd made the resolution... and of course remembered the woman he'd met right after making it.

Lia. God, he hadn't been able to get her out of his head. He'd called himself ten kinds of fool for walking out of that bar New Year's Eve. It had been a missed opportunity, two ships passing on a stormy night when neither of them could do much more than wave. Well, at least, *he* couldn't do much more than wave. The sultry promise in the beautiful woman's eyes had said she might have been ready to drop anchor and storm the decks.

"Forget it," he mumbled as he lifted the phone and tapped a text message to Amelia. This is Ryan's frnd. Sorry I bailed 2nite—long story. Rain check?

Dropping the phone into his pocket as he reached the street-level entrance to the underground Metro station, he was surprised to feel it vibrate almost immediately. He pulled it back out of his pocket to read her response.

R u still at the hospital?

Lex stared at the small screen, his brow furrowing as he responded with one character: ?

Another fast reply. Ryan told me what happened. So sorry.

Oh, hell. Ryan had said he was in the hospital? Why would he do that? It wasn't as if Lex didn't have a legitimate excuse for breaking their date on such short notice, at least, an excuse any reasonable woman would consider legit. He had to wonder if the future sis-in-law was some hard-ass who wouldn't believe a guy might actually have to work overtime.

Uh…thanks, he responded, playing it safe.

How long wl yr sister be in the hospital?

His sister. Okay, so it wasn't Lex who'd been injured and hospitalized, it was a phantom relative. "Ryan, I'm really going to kill you," he muttered. I rly don't have much info.

Another message came in, signaled by the slight vibration of the device in his hand.

You'll be a big comfort to her, Alexander...so terrifying!

Good grief, what the hell had Ryan told her? Was his nonexistent sister lying in a hospital bed after a plane crash, or something? And why was Amelia calling him Alexander? Hadn't Ryan even given the woman his nickname?

Although his first instinct was to set her straight, he hesitated. What if that got Ryan in trouble? The bride-to-be might not be pleased if her groom had been yanking her baby sister's chain.

That would probably serve Ryan right. Still, Lex wasn't about to rat his oldest friend out until he knew the whole story. And then, depending on his friend's version of events, Amanda might not be the one putting Ryan on crutches before their wedding day. Lex would.

He tried to play dumb and neutral. He typed, Yeah. Scary.

Instead of descending down into the bowels of the train station, where he knew he would lose his signal, he leaned against a streetlight, waiting for the next response.

It came quickly.

I had no idea prairie dogs carried rabies.

Lex almost dropped the phone. What had Ryan been thinking? Prairie dogs? Rabies? Had his imaginary sis been in the desert? Had she been on a Life Flight home from Africa this afternoon?

Gaping, he managed to punch in, Scuse me?

He hadn't even pressed Send when the next one appeared.

And crazy that the zoo didn't catch it b4 your sstr was attckd. Hope she sues.

Wondering if he was seeing things, he tried to think how to reply. Before he could, the strangest comment yet came in.

Good thing the lion wasn't hungry when your sister fell in his cage while trying to escape.

"Lion?" he muttered. "What the hell…"

Suddenly, the ridiculousness of the conversation hit him. The truth became obvious and he barked a loud laugh that earned him a few glances from passersby heading down to the trains.

She was messing with him. Punishing him, maybe, for breaking their date on short notice. Ryan hadn't convinced her that Lex had backed out of their blind date for a valid reason, or that he genuinely wanted to reschedule it.

Which he did, he suddenly realized. He truly did.

Laughter still on his lips, Lex found himself growing far more intrigued by the stranger at the other end of the string of messages. Certainly he was more interested than he'd been by the craft-store owner whose virtues Ryan had extolled.

He'd never laid eyes on her, but he liked her sassiness, which he'd never expected, given the sweet, gentle, creative and quiet descriptors his buddy had offered about Amelia. Her messages sure didn't seem sweet, gentle and quiet, but they were pretty creative.

Thoroughly engaged now, he leaned against the station wall. It was a tiger, he typed. Ryan musta misunderstood.

A long pause.

Ahh. Unobservant, that Ryan. Can't tell 1 cat frm another.

Chuckling, he replied, Also not a prairie dog. It was a posse. He realized what he'd typed and grunted. A pestle. Wrong again. Groaning in frustration, he tapped so hard his fingers bent. Stupid autocorrect.

Sure. Blame technology.

A poster.

ARGH!

Are you trying to say an opossum?

He gaped. Good Lord, is that how you spell it?

Think so.

Well, that's dumb.

I wont tell Mr Webster you think so.

Thanks. I owe ya one.

He definitely owed her one and wondered if she'd pick up on the opening and slam him for tonight.

Instead, she went back to her future brother-in-law. Ryan didn't mention the opossum.

Trying to spare your delicate sensibilities. Bloody creatures, I hear.

You can spell sensibilities but not opossum?

Sometimes autocorrect is my friend. A pause. But not often.

Don't know if I can go out with u if you're a bad speller.

Look who's talking, U.

Ha.

Ryan wouldn't set you up w/ a bad speller, & he has great taste—Amanda's awesome.

He figured sucking up to her by complimenting her sibling couldn't hurt. Besides, it was true. He didn't know Amanda well, since she and Ryan lived in Baltimore and Lex was down in DC. Still, he liked the woman, and she seemed to adore his oldest friend.

Another pause and then she replied.

Too bad his taste doesn't extend to his friends.

He grabbed a hand and clutched his chest as the

zinger hit home. Now she was going for his throat, zooming in for the kill.

I'm wounded.

Is that why U were rly in the hospital?

He thought about it, confident now that Ryan hadn't made up a story, and called her bluff. Ryan told you the truth. I had to work. It was last-minute, & uberimportant. I swear I'm not a bum.

A long pause. He held his breath.

Did u just say uber?

Damn, the woman wasn't going to let him win. He already liked that about her. Guilty.

Nerd.

Wondering why the question was so important, he asked, So am I forgiven?

Not sure. I went all the way to Gtown b4 I got Ryans msg.

You're kidding!

On the Metro. No cell service underground.

Oh, hell. He really had inconvenienced her. Given the misery of traveling to Georgetown by Metro on a cold Friday night, he'd be surprised if she ever went out with him.

I'm really sorry, Amelia. Let me make it up to you.

A long pause. Several minutes had gone by while he'd stood here having a text conversation with a phantom. In all this time, he could have gone down to the platforms, hopped on the Red Line and gone home to grab dinner. But something was making him stay still, waiting to see what else she'd say.

Finally, a vibration. He didn't realize he'd been holding his breath until he read the word Okay and slowly released it.

Smiling, he glanced at his watch. It was eight fifteen. He had only a couple of hours before he had to go back to the studio, but he couldn't help adding up the number of stops and transfers between here and Georgetown. There were probably too many, and wasn't that a damn shame.

What are you doing now? Still in Gtown?

He calculated the times, adding in Friday night traffic. Even on a cold winter night, the crowds would be heavy in Georgetown. It had probably been a dumb place to meet anyway.

No. Went home. Now out w/ friends at a bar near my shop.

Her shop. Hell, where was that again? He couldn't remember.

He got another message. Call or text me next week.
Maybe I'll give you another chance to not stand me up.

He suspected that was her signal for *Stop texting me,
I'm out with my friends*. And he was a smart enough
man to follow orders.

I promise. G'night.

Lowering his phone, he realized how lucky he was
that she'd agreed to give him another shot. Amelia was
a good sport, and he enjoyed her sense of humor. No,
she probably didn't have gold hair shot with red streaks,
amazing blue eyes, lush lips and a killer body, like the
woman he'd met on New Year's Eve. But Amelia had
wit, and personality, and came with a big thumbs-up
from his oldest friend. She was exactly the woman he'd
told his friends he would date, and he was no longer
worried about that. Because with just a short electronic
conversation, she'd managed to arouse his interest more
than any woman he'd met in ages. Frankly, he was curs-
ing his job for having missed out on meeting her tonight.

He still didn't go down to the trains; instead, he dialed Ryan.

"Dude, did you get the tickets?" his friend asked.

"Got 'em."

"I guess you're forgiven for standing up my baby
sister."

"She's not your sister yet, and I didn't stand her up.
We've been in touch and I'm going to reschedule for
next weekend." He didn't try to keep the interest out of
his voice. "I'm looking forward to it."

"I'll bet. You talked to her, huh? Heard her voice?"

"No, we texted. Why?"

His friend's laughter deepened. "Oh, no reason."

He zoned in on Ryan's amusement. The guy was acting weird. "Does she have a voice like Jessica Rabbit or something?"

"No, though she probably has the curves under the nice-girl dresses she usually wears."

Da-yum. Jessica Rabbit's red dress had titillated him even more than Lily Lundgren's red sweater. "Where is this shop of hers?" he asked, his curiosity eating at him.

"Dupont Circle," Ryan said. "It wasn't far from the bar we went to on New Year's Eve."

"Seriously?" His heart thudded as memories of the woman he'd danced with intruded on his interest in the woman who'd charmed him via text. He shoved both memories away, focusing on the future, not on the past.

"I pointed the shop out to you when we walked by."

Yes, but that had been before Lex had made his resolution, before he'd begun to acknowledge he might be looking for the wrong woman, for the wrong reason. Before he'd begun to think about searching for the right woman. Before his interest had been captured by a girl who'd managed to make a point and put him in his place while also making him laugh. All via text message.

That sounded like a woman he wanted to meet in person. And he didn't really want to wait.

Perhaps it could still be tonight. After all, he had time to get home. He lived close to her shop, and she said she was out with friends in a bar in that area. Maybe instead of going to his place to grab a sandwich, he'd check out the menus at some of the restaurants and bars nearby.

He didn't know what she looked like, but something made him wonder if he'd recognize her anyway. She'd be with a group and dressed conservatively, judging by what Ryan said, probably with her hair pulled back. A brunette, he'd bet. Smiling and laughing, almost certainly. How hard could it be to find her?

"Very hard," he reminded himself, coming back to earth.

It was crazy, she'd be a needle in a haystack. Or a particular needle in an ocean of needles, considering it was Friday night and there were tons of bars in that area.

Lex had never been one to give up easily, however, not when he was intrigued. And he was intrigued by Amelia Jones.

"ARE YOU GOING to put that dumb phone away and join the rest of the world?" Viv asked, grabbing Amelia's phone from her hand and dropping it into her own purse, out of reach.

Amelia extended her palm, not wanting to end her conversation, though she'd essentially ended it by asking her no-show blind date to contact her next week. "Give it back."

"You're being rude."

"You sat there and talked to your ex for twenty minutes," she exclaimed. "And Lulu just got here. I was bored."

Hence the texting. The silly, funny, slightly sharp-and-annoyed-at-being-stood-up texting.

Viv started chattering about her ex. Amelia zoned out.

Honestly, if she'd met this Alexander face-to-face, she probably would never have spoken the way she had via text message. Although she rarely let her inner snark take the reins of a conversation, something about the anonymity of messaging had allowed it to sneak out there tonight. The guy might have been totally serious about having to work, but given her mood and romantic track record lately, Amelia hadn't been ready to give him the benefit of the doubt. It was only after he'd amused her with his messages, and tried to convince her he really did want to meet her, that she'd let her guard down.

His persistence was kinda nice. He might have blown off their first date with little notice, but he was at least quick-witted and friendly, if only in print. He seemed genuine about rescheduling, so maybe she'd take another chance on him.

At the very least, if he stood her up again, she'd have the weekend of the wedding to suitably punish him. The whole bridal party, family and guests were flying up to a ski resort in Vermont for the Valentine's weekend. She was sure she could think up a suitable punishment by then. Like trapping him on a ski lift or luring him into a bear's den or something.

"This place isn't going to get more interesting until we make it that way. Go up there and dance," Viv ordered, snapping her fingers in front of Amelia's face to gain her attention.

Amelia glanced from her friend toward the empty dance floor. The crowd was quiet and laid-back, enjoying drinks that warmed and music that relaxed on this cold night. "Nobody dances here."

"You can start a trend."

"Not happening."

It had been one thing to get up and shake her groove thing at Shady Jo's on New Year's Eve. She'd set out that night to have an adventure, and maybe meet someone sexy and exciting. This place was quieter and easygoing, while Shady Jo's was known for live music and dancing. Oh, and hookups.

"We should've gone to Shady Jo's," Viv said, bored.

Hooking up was one of Viv's favorite activities.

"I like it here," said Lulu, now happily committed and not looking for a man. "We can actually talk and hear each other."

Viv glared at her. "We can talk when we go to the movies."

Amelia exchanged a puzzled look with Lulu. Why the movies would be a better place to have a conversation than here, she truly didn't know. Sometimes, it was best not to ask.

Viv ignored their questioning glances. "When I go to this much effort to dress up, I want the prospect of getting lucky."

Not Amelia. She'd intentionally steered clear of Shady Jo's because if she went there, she'd be keeping an eye on the door to see if Lex showed up. Logically, she knew he wouldn't, not after he'd walked out on her. Still, her heart—and her libido—would make her study the face of every man who entered. Frankly, she wasn't sure she was ever going back.

Still, she wasn't exactly dressed for a quiet-night-with-girlfriends evening, either. She didn't even understand her own impulse, but after being stood up, she'd called her two best friends and asked for an impromptu girls' night out. She'd donned her second most risqué outfit and had done her hair and makeup in the same I'm-on-the-prowl way. Funny, considering the only prowling she'd done lately was through her stockroom, in search of an elusive pattern she'd bought and misplaced.

Viv wasn't done kvetching. "It's only fair that if you two got a ride on the lucky bar stool that I get one, too."

"That sounded really suggestive," Lulu said with a grin.

"It didn't work out so well for me," Amelia reminded her.

"It did for me," said Lulu, eyeing her engagement ring.

"So I've got a fifty-fifty shot of romance if I sit on that corner stool at Shady Jo's," said Viv. "Which is better than the zero percent chance I have in this middle-aged snooze box."

That was an exaggeration. There weren't a lot of twentysomethings here, but the thirtysomethings all seemed to be happy and talkative. Unfortunately, for Viv anyway, none of them appeared single and interested. Well, the interested part was unfortunate. Single wouldn't always stop the man-eater.

"Go start dancing and somebody will join in," Viv urged.

Amelia sipped her wine. "You're the vixen, you go start."

Lulu laughed. "She's got you there, Viv the Vixen."

Viv rolled her eyes and Amelia knew why she didn't want to go out there and dance. Viv always wanted to be noticed, but didn't want to be thought of as desperate.

Remembering what had started the whole conversation, she extended her hand again. "My phone please?"

Viv retrieved it from her purse, but she didn't hand it over right away, instead swiping her finger across the screen. With a Cheshire cat smile that made her eyes gleam in the semidarkness, she asked, "So, who's Alexander?"

Realizing her friend was reading the messages, Amelia tried to snatch the device away. "None of your business."

"Seriously?" Viv asked, her eyebrows high. "We were second best? You came tonight because your blind date bailed on you?"

Lulu squealed. "Oooh, blind date? Why didn't you tell us?"

"Because I felt stupid for saying yes to the date to begin with. I knew he'd stand me up," she said sourly. Of course, her mood had improved after texting with him, half believing his work excuse, but she wasn't ready to admit that aloud yet.

"Who fixed you up?" asked Viv as she sipped her frothy big pink chick-drink, still not delivering the phone.

"Amanda's fiancé. Alexander is Ryan's best friend from childhood, and he'll be in the wedding on Valentine's Day."

"Perfect, a groomsman all picked out," said Viv. "You don't have to wait until the wedding to claim him for the night."

It was Amelia's turn to roll her eyes. "That's so cliché."

"Clichés exist for a reason," Viv pointed out. "Bridesmaids gettin' frisky with groomsmen, well, that's about as traditional as hot dogs and apple pie on the Fourth of July."

Maybe for some women. Amelia wasn't one of them. Tonight's date with Alexander wasn't supposed to be about getting frisky. When he'd told her about his buddy last weekend, Ryan had sworn Alexander was a nice guy, responsible, reliable. His description had been enough to get her to take a chance.

Maybe she'd even stop regretting it, if he followed through on his promise to reschedule. In any case, he'd almost been enough to distract her from the guy she'd spent the past eight days thinking about.

Lex. Her midnight phantom, who'd seduced her senses and then disappeared like a kissing bandit on New Year's Eve.

Lex. The man with whom she'd shared a sultry dance and a steamy kiss, and who'd been the star of her vivid dreams every night since.

Lex. Who was walking into the bar right this very minute.

"Oh, my God," she whispered, seeing that tall, powerful form stepping in and shrugging off his coat. She blinked, telling herself her mind had conjured him up. But a closer look confirmed it. The dark hair, firm jaw, great smile…no mistake. It was him. The guy of her dreams.

"What's wrong?" asked Viv. Following Amelia's stare, she almost purred. Wait, make that did purr. "Meow."

"Mine," Amelia snapped, not knowing where she got the nerve or the confidence to be so territorial.

"Excuse me?"

"I saw him first. He's bar-stool man."

Viv studied him, letting out a petulant sigh. "Crap."

It didn't mean a lot to Viv if a man was committed to another woman, but with her friends' partners, she was pretty respectful. Even if bar-stool man, er, Lex, hadn't stuck around after that one amazing kiss, he had obviously seemed interested. Viv, Lulu and their other friends had all teased Amelia mercilessly when she'd rejoined them on New Year's Eve.

Amelia grabbed her phone from Viv and dropped it into her purse. Funny, she felt a hint of disloyalty for being so interested in this stranger who'd walked out of her life last week, when she'd begun to feel some sort of connection to Alexander. Still, she and Alexander hadn't met in person yet. She might not even be attracted to the man. But oh, she was to this one.

Holding her breath, she watched as Lex stepped farther inside, out of the way of the door, to allow another couple to enter. Bitter air whooshed in, but he stayed near the entrance, as if unsure he would stay. She licked her lips, waiting for him to notice her.

His green eyes searched the room, his attention not zeroing in on any of the attractive women here, though some of them gave him looks that said they wouldn't have minded. But he kept scanning…right up until he saw her face.

And he stopped. And he stared. And she stared right back.

He didn't move for a long moment. Their gazes locked.

After a long, heady pause, a smile curled his sexy lips upward and he offered her a look that was warm and friendly, but also…what was it? Accepting? As if he maybe shouldn't be glad to see her, considering what he'd said last week. Yet when he'd spotted her face in the crowd, as if fate had brought them both here, something in him had leaped for joy? Well, maybe that was her inner self leaping for joy. Or at least hopping.

The leaping commenced when he walked right to her table.

"Are you stalking me?" she asked as he reached her side.

His mouth fell open. "Stalking? God, no, honestly, I..."

"I'm kidding. I guess fate brought you here."

She maintained the joking tone but also wondered if her words were true. This wasn't the bar where they'd met last week, where she'd told him she sometimes hung out. But he'd found her anyway. It had to mean something, if only that her romantic luck might have turned around.

"I came in to grab a quick bite to eat," he admitted.

"Oh, perfect," said Viv, standing up and slipping her coat on. "We were just leaving—hello and goodbye."

Amelia gaped, watching her friends launch themselves out of their chairs to get out of the way of her possible romantic conquest. Nice of them, but talk about abandonment. She only hoped Lex wasn't some serial killer because, boy, would they feel bad if her skinned corpse turned up in a ditch somewhere.

Although she appreciated their discretion, part of her immediately panicked, and it wasn't just standard serial killer worries. She'd had hours to work herself into siren mode on New Year's Eve, physically and mentally. She may look the same, but mentally, she wasn't ready for this tonight.

"Bye, honey," said Lulu, shoving her arms into her coat.

Viv swung a cape over her shoulders, licking her lips as she smiled at Lex. "Don't do anything I wouldn't do."

Sitting down across from her, Lex murmured, "Is there anything she wouldn't do?"

Amelia laughed softly. "I doubt it."

They eyed each other across the table. Amelia tried to find the woman she'd been last week—the woman he'd met—but was having trouble pinning her down. Or even catching a glimpse of her.

"So, Lia, what kind of odds do you suppose there were on me showing up here tonight, and you—who I haven't been able to get out of my mind—being here, too?" he asked.

She licked her lips and reached for her wine, telling herself to remain relaxed. "I wouldn't know. I'm not a gambler."

"I've never been one, either," he said. "But I'm thinking I might be experiencing a lucky streak."

"Really? I had the impression you weren't interested." She couldn't pretend the way he'd left last week hadn't stung.

His jaw tightened. "I was interested."

"Was?"

"Until midnight."

"I remember that part."

Visibly considering what to say, he finally admitted, "I made a resolution. After midnight, I was determined to stick to it." He shrugged and offered her a boyish grin. "But I'm not breaking it if I run into you completely by chance, right?"

"That depends. What's the resolution?"

"I'd rather not say." The coyness didn't suit him. But his expression said he was serious.

"A resolution is not like a wish on a birthday cake," she said. "Telling it doesn't mean it won't come true."

"Let's say it was a guy thing, among my buddies."

She licked her lips, trying to channel the inner-Viv she'd found last week. Tracing the tip of her finger around the rim of her wineglass, she half lowered her eyes, letting her lashes flutter. She lowered her voice, too, going for sultry and mysterious, and hoping her voice didn't crack as she attempted pure come-hither flirtation. "I can keep a secret," she said, leaning closer, letting her leg brush his under the table.

"So can I," he said, his eyes twinkling.

Laughing softly, she murmured, "Touché. I'm sorry, that was nosy of me." It had been, and that wasn't like her. She'd apparently taken the bad-girl thing to an extreme and exhibited some really bad manners.

"It's okay. Have you ordered?"

"I've already eaten, but you go ahead," she said.

He waved at a server and ordered a sandwich. So, apparently he really had been coming in here to eat, and not to search for a sexy temptress he couldn't get out of his mind from last week. Or, well, an ordinary woman pretending to be a sexy temptress.

"I don't mean to be rude and eat in front of you," he said. "But I have to be back at work in an hour."

Great. Her friends had left, and he would be leaving soon, too. Looked as if she had another date with Netflix.

Still, he had some time, and she didn't want to waste the opportunity. So while they waited for his dinner, she did her best Viv impersonation—she acted flirtatious, a bit helpless, ditzy even. She'd seen friend after friend land a guy by behaving in exactly the same way.

This guy wouldn't land.

Oh, he was nice enough, funny and charming, and he

flirted back when she brought up their New Year's kiss. But something was missing. The spark wasn't there. The sexy playboy she'd met at Shady Jo's wasn't picking up on any of her innuendos, much less tossing them back at her. He was respectful, friendly and that was all.

Part of her was glad. She liked him, actually enjoyed talking to him, and she found herself forgetting to act like va-va-voom-Viv. But another part couldn't help wondering if he'd seen through her masquerade and had merely lost interest. Not just on New Year's, but now, during her second time at bat.

The boring good girl swings and misses again.

Heck, who was she kidding? He wasn't even pitching.

And when he finished his meal and picked up the check, thanking her for keeping him company and apologizing for eating and running, he didn't ask for her number, or say anything about running into her again.

Meaning, she hadn't merely missed her chance and struck out, she'd lost the game entirely.

CHAPTER THREE

LEX HADN'T PLANNED so carefully for a date in a long time.

Having gotten Amelia to give him another chance, he wasn't about to screw things up. Nor was he playing by his own rule book and going for a happy hour meet-up. No, after the weeklong text conversation he'd had with the woman, during which she'd provoked him, intrigued him and cracked him up more than once, he fully intended to make their first date something special, something she'd long remember.

He wasn't sure why neither of them had picked up the phone so they could have a voice conversation. Maybe because that playful zing of their first interaction last Friday had been so memorable, neither had wanted to jinx it. He just knew his heart was racing as he prepared to meet her in person for the first time.

Having worked in journalism in DC for a few years now, he'd made a lot of connections. He'd called in a favor with one of them, and the guy had really come through, which was why he was currently standing near the top of the escalator at the Woodley Park Zoo/Adams Morgan Metro station. The one closest to the National Zoo.

It was late afternoon on Saturday, sunny and cold, not outdoor weather. But they wouldn't be outdoors for long. She'd said she would meet him at four, and would be wearing a yellow coat. So when he caught a flash of yellow from far below, down on the bottom of the escalator, his breath caught.

He crossed his arms over his chest, and leaned against a cement barrier, feigning a nonchalance he didn't feel. It was crazy how into this girl he already was, especially since he'd never considered getting involved with somebody like her before. But even before she was halfway up the escalator, he suspected she was going to turn out to be special.

An older couple stepped off the escalator and walked down the street. They were followed by a family with a couple of kids—probably heading for the zoo, despite the cold weather.

And then there she was, in her yellow coat.

"What the hell?" he mumbled, shocked as he met the equally confused stare of the woman in yellow.

The woman with the gold-and-red hair. The woman with those beautiful blue eyes that had haunted him since the night he'd kissed her to welcome in the New Year.

Lia. His blind date, the nice girl, the craft-store owner, the funny texter—Amelia Jones—was Lia. She was the "bad girl" he hadn't allowed himself to get to know, though he'd wanted to, especially after their impromptu dinner last weekend.

"It's you," he said softly, a crooked smile tugging at his mouth as she walked up to him and stared into his face.

She looked just as stunned. Her brow was furrowed, and she shook her head in sheer confusion.

"It's me," she finally replied, still staring searchingly up at him. He hadn't realized how petite she was—she'd been wearing spiked heels the previous times he'd met her. Now, in her flat brown boots, casual pants and canary-yellow coat, she looked not one bit like the hot bar chick he'd met, and every inch the pretty shop owner his friend had described.

Right at this moment, he couldn't have said which appealed to him more. Frankly, they both did. And as the sexy siren he'd run into twice began to merge with the funny girl-next-door he'd been texting with all week, he found his smile growing even broader. "Ame*lia*."

She sighed. "A*lex*ander."

"I go by Lex."

"I go by Amelia."

He laughed out loud. "Except when you're trying to pick up a guy on New Year's Eve?"

Shuddering, she threw both her hands over her face and groaned. Regretting teasing her, he covered them with his own and gently pulled them away. "Don't be embarrassed."

She nibbled her lip, her face growing pinker than the windy day warranted. "I feel like such an idiot."

"You? God, I've been mad as hell at myself for not being able to get the sultry Lia off my mind, since I was becoming so fascinated by the sweet and funny Amelia."

Her lips quirked the tiniest bit. "Fascinated?"

Yeah, he was. By all aspects of her. "Definitely."

Her long lashes shifted down to shield her eyes, and he suspected she didn't want him to see the pleasure there.

"Do you think Ryan knew?"

"Of course he knew, the jerk," she said. "He was there when I told Amanda about meeting you. He never mentioned he was at Shady Jo's that night. After hearing my conversation with Amanda, he questioned me about the guy I'd danced with. The one who left like Cinderella, racing to get home before his carriage turned back into a pumpkin."

He'd never been compared to a fairy-tale princess before, but he skipped over that. "Jerk," he agreed. "He must have missed you by minutes. He left right before we met."

"I'll bet it's been killing him not to say anything."

"I wouldn't take that bet."

No wonder Ryan had been so insistent that Lex reschedule the date. He was seriously tempted to keep the Flyers tickets.

Then he looked into her eyes, saw the spark of both humor and intelligence there, and figured he owed his old friend more than tickets to a hockey match. A lot more.

"I can't believe my sister didn't tell me," Amelia said. "Matchmaking?"

"I guess. Ever since she got engaged, she's been pushing me to get out more, meet people."

"And I happened to be the lucky guy you met."

They fell silent for a moment, staring at each other. He read the uncertainty on her face, and knew she was probably replaying everything she'd said or done during their previous encounters. He half wondered if she would change her mind and go right back down the escalator.

But she surprised him. "So, what was your resolution?"

"Huh?"

"On New Year's Eve. You said you left because you made a resolution. And you stuck to it last Friday."

He wasn't sure how to word his resolution so she wouldn't find it insulting. If he hadn't gotten to know her so well through her sharp and chatty texts, he might have softened it, but something told him the real Amelia—who was someone in-between the wild child and the sweet crafter—could take it.

"I swore off bad girls."

She sucked in a shocked gasp, then laughter spilled from that pretty pink-tinged mouth. "Wait, and you thought I was a bad girl?"

"You were doing a pretty good impersonation of one on New Year's. And last Friday," he said, daring her to deny it.

She appeared pleased by the comment. "Why, thank you."

"That was the goal?"

"Yep. I was sick of being nice, sweet Amelia and decided to let loose for once."

"On the very night I promised myself—and my friends—that I wouldn't be picking up any girls who were too, er, loose."

"Meaning you would have tried to pick me up if not for the resolution?"

He slowly shook his head, but explained when he saw the flash of disappointment on her face. "There is no try. There is only do or do not."

It took her a second, then she snorted. "Okay, Yoda. You're that confident you would have succeeded, huh?"

He lifted a hand and brushed back a strand of hair that had blown across her cheek. As expected, it was silky soft, as was her skin. Soft and feminine and beautiful.

"I *would* have succeeded, Amelia."

She didn't even try to deny it, she just nodded slowly.

Their stares met, both of them silently asking and answering questions about that night, and the days and weeks that had followed. He wondered if her dreams had been as intense as his, and if he'd had a starring role in them.

"We came close to never knowing the truth," she said. "I guess we're lucky Ryan decided to play matchmaker."

Hearing what she wasn't saying, he asked, "Does that mean you still want to go out with me?"

Thinking about it, she took a deep, audible breath. Lex's heart pounded as he waited for her answer. He knew that, despite her joking, she was embarrassed about what had happened New Year's Eve. It had apparently been quite out of character for her. But Lex would never regret that night because it had shown him that there were many facets to this lovely woman, facets he might not otherwise have seen.

She was daring, she was sexy and she was sultry. But she was also smart, funny and a very good sport.

God, he hoped she didn't turn him down.

Finally, she put him out of his misery and gave him her answer. Sort of.

Sticking out her hand, she smiled at him and said, "Hi, I'm Amelia Jones. I'm so glad we finally got the chance to meet. Ryan's told me almost nothing about you."

Starting over from square one. He could do that. Most definitely. So he put out his hand to shake hers, and replied, "I'm Lex. And it's nice to meet you, too, Amelia."

ALTHOUGH AMELIA HAD known from the moment she met him that Lex was a unique man, she'd had no idea how unique he was until he led her to their destination. No, the National Zoo wasn't the usual choice for a day as cold as this one, but she did love animals and was always up for a visit with them. She liked that he'd put some thought into their date and gone back to their first text exchange.

He confirmed it when he said, "Don't get too close to the tiger cage, you don't want to fall in." His voice was solemn, though his eyes twinkled.

She snickered. "Okay, and if I see a sign for the opossums, I'll be sure to point it out so you can learn how to spell it."

"Well, now at least I'll remember it starts with an *O*."

"Meaning when I get a text from you saying you just saw an opposite or an operation, I should assume your autocorrect is on the job again?"

"Smart-ass."

She didn't let up. "Ryan said you were a journalist. How'd you get a degree in journalism if you can't spell?"

He snorted. "I can spell, Miss Jones. I happen to be dyslexic, and putting an *O* in front of a word that sounds like it should start with a *P* makes my brain misfire. I've been working against that sort of thing all my life."

His tone was light, teasing, but she found his comment interesting. "That must have been challenging— studying journalism in college with that kind of reading issue?"

Shrugging, he said, "One of my stepmothers was dyslexic. She recognized the trouble I was having when I was in fourth grade and I had private tutors and stuff to get me through it."

More interesting. *One* of his stepmothers? She certainly wasn't going to ask him to explain. Despite how nosy she had probably sounded last Friday, Amelia really wasn't the type to pry. Still, she couldn't deny she was curious. The more time she spent with Lex, the more she wanted to know about him.

"By the way, I'm not a writer," he explained. "I'm a sports telecaster on channel eight." He looked at her, as if expecting her to say she'd seen him before. When he didn't get a reaction, he asked, "Seriously? You don't watch the morning or noon news? Ever?"

Nibbling her lip, she admitted, "Not on that channel."

Barking a laugh, he said, "Well, at least you're honest."

"I try to be."

"Except when you're pretending to be someone you're not."

She knew he was teasing her, and swatted his upper arm. "It's not nice to remind me of that. I'd almost forgotten what a fool I made of myself in front of you."

Lex stopped walking and turned to face her. Dropping his hands onto her shoulders, he held her tightly until she met his gaze. "You were in no way a fool," he said, his voice thick with intensity. "You were—you are—beautiful, and desirable, and from the moment I laid eyes on you until this moment right now, I've wanted to kiss you."

Something inside her softened and melted, not just at his words but at the tenderness with which he said them. Not even channeling Viv this time, she licked her lips, silently inviting his kiss, quivering when he bent toward her. When his lips brushed against hers, then returned for a deeper taste, she sighed into his mouth, loving the feel of him and the way he lifted a hand to gently cup her cheek.

This was nothing like the kiss they'd exchanged on New Year's Eve. That had been all heat and excitement, while this was sweet and soft. Yet it was every bit as earthshaking, and she wobbled on her feet, having to lean against him for balance.

As their bodies pressed together, he groaned softly. He deepened the kiss so they could thoroughly taste each other—but only briefly, swiftly, as he ended things and stepped back.

Still close to him, feeling his hand on her cheek, the other on her shoulder, Amelia swallowed hard and glanced around. A family stood nearby. The parents of a pair of young children eyed them in disapproval. Closing her eyes, she grimaced, more embarrassed than she had been on New Year's Eve when they'd had their tongues down each other's throats. "I think we're drawing more attention than the exhibits."

He glanced at the family, unconcerned. "I suspect they didn't have those kids by waving at each other from across the room. Come on," he said, turning her and sliding an arm around her waist, as naturally and easily as if they'd known each other for years.

She fell into step beside him. "Where are we going?" she asked when she realized Lex wasn't leading her toward the public area of the zoo and the exhibits.

"You'll see."

Wherever it was, she hoped it took a while to get there because she was enjoying the possessive way he kept his arm around her, and the brush of his leg against hers as they walked.

He led her toward a building marked Employees

Only. When they reached it, he made a quick call on his cell phone.

"Are you friends with someone who works here?"

"I know a guy who knows a guy."

"That sounded mobster-ish."

"I didn't say I know a guy who knows a guy who'll bust some kneecaps."

"That's good, I like my kneecaps."

"I liked them, too…wow, those legs. If it weren't so cold, I'd be wishing you'd worn that sexy green dress you were wearing the night I met you."

"It's not just the cold that kept me from wearing that dress. This isn't exactly a bar on New Year's Eve," she said, glancing away so he wouldn't see the pleasure in her eyes. She liked how he flirted with her, and liked that his flirtation always sounded relaxed, never forced. He didn't seem to have any agenda other than making her smile.

Before he could reply, the locked door swung open. A uniformed zoo employee ushered them in. He and Lex exchanged greetings and shook hands, and then the employee, named Dave, said, "Remember, no waving, no tapping on the glass, no trying to get their attention, okay?"

Her excitement building as she realized they were going to be shown something not usually seen by the public, she grabbed Lex's hand and squeezed. He squeezed back, smiling down at her as they followed Dave through the cement-floored hallways of the huge building.

"Oh, my God, I've watched this on the zoo cam," she exclaimed as they reached the nursery area, which was usually only accessible to the public via a video feed the zoo had on their website. The nursery's quiet enclosure was shielded from noise and distraction by thick Plexiglas. When she spied the mother panda, with her cub tucked against her big belly, tears actually filled her eyes.

"They're so beautiful."

Dave nodded, smiling. "She's a good mommy. Baby's healthy and happy. He should be able to go outside with his folks in March or April, once it warms up."

She couldn't say a word, fascinated by the tender scene taking place below them. The mother panda, her fur thick and lush, never took her big brown eyes off her cub, who tried to roll and scramble away, like any toddler anxious to explore. Careful not to touch the glass, or move too much, she slid closer, feeling Lex do the same. They were both enraptured by the scene.

"That is amazing," Lex whispered as if worried he might disturb the animals.

They stood there, watching the pandas, smiling at the baby's antics and the mother's patience, for a good fifteen minutes. Finally, noticing Dave shifting from foot to foot, Amelia realized they were probably keeping him from his work.

Turning regretfully away from the window, she said, "Thank you so much, this was an unforgettable experience."

The zoo worker smiled. "No problem. Mr. Rollins here really helped out by showing up at that fund-raiser for my nephew's Pop Warner football team."

Eyeing Lex in surprise, she smiled up at him. She was learning more about him by the minute. He wasn't just the smooth, sexy, great dancer and fabulous kisser she'd first met. Arranging this visit today had been incredibly thoughtful, a wonderful gesture. As was appearing at a fund-raiser for a youth football team. There was obviously much more to the man than met the eye, and she was glad he was opening her eyes to him.

After they left the nursery, they explored the zoo. The chill in the air and the oncoming darkness kept the animals from coming out, so Lex and Amelia didn't stay long. Grabbing some hot chocolate from a stand, they left the zoo, sipping as they walked.

As they headed back to the Metro station, Amelia said, "I will never forget this afternoon, Lex. I'm so very grateful to you for arranging it."

"It was as fun for me as for you," he insisted, shrugging off the thanks. "I'm a sucker for fur babies."

"Do you have any of your own?"

"A big slobbery mutt who keeps me on a tight leash." He grinned. "He'll be texting me anytime now to let me know he's eaten another pair of my shoes."

"Talented dog."

"Not really. Lots of dogs eat shoes," he said, the streetlights above revealing the twinkle in his eyes.

"You really are a nerd."

"Shh. Don't tell anyone."

A gust of wind whipped up Connecticut Avenue, and she wrapped her coat more tightly around her body. Lex stepped closer, dropping an arm over her shoulder and tugging her close, sharing his warmth. By the time they reached the Metro station and started down the escalator, she was greedily soaking up what he offered, not just appreciating the heat of him, but loving the way he felt pressed up against her. There was nothing sexual in the embrace. But the strength of him, the brush of her cheek against his leather jacket, the faint whiff of his aftershave, the smooth rumble of his deep voice, had all her senses on alert.

Halfway to the bottom of the long escalator, standing hip to hip on a narrow step, he took one step down and turned to look up at her. Eye to eye now, he smiled as he stared at her face. "You are so beautiful."

This time, she didn't have to rise on her tiptoes, didn't have to tug him down; she had him at her level and was determined to take advantage. Wrapping her arms around his neck and twining her fingers in his hair, she pressed her mouth to his in a kiss that was somewhere between their first and the one they'd shared earlier today in heat level. Not graphically sexual, not sweet, either. It was warm, hungry, giving pleasure for pleasure's sake, not just a box to check off on the road to another destination. With a man who kissed like this one, the journey would be as amazing as the arrival.

He wrapped his arms around her waist, holding her close. The kiss lasted throughout their descent, and when they reached the bottom of the moving stairway, he stepped effortlessly backward, pulling her with him, his mouth never leaving hers.

Of course, he collided with a Metro cop, which sort of ended the moment.

"Watch it, you two," the gray-haired man said, though he sounded amused.

Immediately pulling apart, Amelia and Lex offered the officer matching sheepish apologies.

"You're lucky he didn't arrest you," she mumbled as they inserted their fare cards and walked through the turnstiles.

"It would've been worth it."

The certainty in his tone warmed her, and she couldn't

keep a smile off her face. It remained there during their ride back to Dupont Circle, during the dinner they shared afterward and during the walk from the restaurant to her place. It lasted through their good-night kiss at her door, and didn't fade even as she watched him turn and walk off down the street.

He hadn't asked if he could come in, and she hadn't invited him. It was as if, having gotten past the charade of their first meeting—when she'd been pretending to be something she wasn't—they were both willing to take a step back and let this develop the right away.

Honestly, she wasn't sure where they were heading, or what would happen. She couldn't say whether her plain old self would be enough to hold the interest of a man who admitted he had a track record with a lot of women. Or even if she wanted that kind of man long-term. Despite her bad-girl persona, Lex had quickly ferreted out the true Amelia, and he undoubtedly already realized she was the type who would, eventually, want the white picket fence, kids, the whole deal. Despite his New Year's resolution, though…would he want all that?

She honestly didn't know. And right now, she was a little afraid of getting hurt. If they took this further and he turned out to be the kind of guy who cut and ran when things got serious, she could end up with a broken heart.

Still, life was all about taking risks, wasn't it? The new Amelia, the one who'd been so bold and daring on New Year's Eve, was ready to take even more risks. Including, perhaps, taking a chance on real love with a guy who, she suspected, wasn't even sure he was capable of it.

CHAPTER FOUR

ALTHOUGH HE THOUGHT about her every day, Lex's work schedule made it difficult to see much of Amelia during the next week. His interview with Whitecastle had, as expected, caused a sensation, and he'd become the subject of media attention. Being the guy who'd landed the interview—even though it had been totally by chance and a well-worded tweet—had apparently upped his standing in the TV sportscaster world. Lex wasn't looking for a new job, he liked where he was, even if it wasn't a national gig. But it was kind of nice to feel he could probably get one if he tried.

He and Amelia had managed to grab a quick dinner on Tuesday night, plus they'd met for coffee one morning when he was between newscasts and her shop was closed. It wasn't enough, though, not nearly enough. She was all he could think about, despite the calls from *Sports Illustrated* and ESPN.

A whole week went by before they were able to go out for an evening again. This time, he hadn't planned a zoo trip, instead copping tickets to a touring opera. He'd never been to the opera, though it was one of those things he'd planned to do...someday. Wings, beer and a football game were much more his thing. But a night at the opera sounded like the kind of date a non-bad-girl-seeking guy would plan. And how rough could it be? A couple of hours of singing never killed anybody. He hoped.

"Seriously? Opera?" she asked, her tone skeptical. He'd kept their destination a surprise and hadn't told her where they were going until they'd arrived at the Kennedy Center.

"I hear it's amazing."

The arts reporter at work, who'd gotten him the tickets, had raved about the production. She'd looked pleased that Lex wasn't quite the plebeian she'd always thought him to be.

"You should have warned me this was formal," she said, gesturing toward her pretty but short dress, and then to the gowns and tuxes of DC's jet set. He spied a congressman and his wife.

Lex glanced down at his own suit, and said, "Yeah, maybe I should have worn a tux." Taking her arm, he said, "But what the hell. We're here."

Putting on a game face, she let him lead her into the opera house. She gazed around, wide-eyed, as the seats filled and the subscribers greeted each other. They were obviously a cliquey group. Lex didn't get one sports comment from a single guy who recognized him, which was a rarity in this city where everybody had a favorite team and an opinion.

He did note that Amelia drew more than a few appreciative glances, and he draped his arm across the back of her chair. It was a little caveman, claiming her like that, but she didn't seem to notice. She sighed softly when he brushed his fingertips across the nape of her neck and fingered a silky strand of her hair. Though it pained him, he had to move his hand away. He was dying to touch her, but he knew the time and place were all wrong.

Thirty minutes into the performance, Lex kind of suspected he might understand what was going on. The gray-haired guy was in love with the woman in red, who wanted the old guy's son, and somebody was about to get stabbed.

Or they were all going to Disneyland together. It could be that. He truly had no idea. And honestly, that would have made about as much sense to him as anything else.

Figuring his confusion was abnormal, since most of the people around him seemed enraptured by the performance, he glanced over to see how Amelia was reacting.

Her eyes were closed. Hmm. She was either also enraptured by the soprano voice of the…Mother? Aunt? Goddess? Queen? Minnie Mouse? Or she was…

She let out a tiny snore and leaned closer to tuck her head against Lex's shoulder.

He laughed silently, trying not to let his shaking shoulders disturb her. Of course, he doubted much could wake her. Not even the simulated cannon explosions—which he really didn't think were supposed to be from the Pirates of the Caribbean ride—were enough.

She stayed there, leaning against him, sleeping peacefully, throughout the first act. At intermission, when the lights went up, he whispered, "Ready to go?"

She blinked slowly, then yawned. "Is it over?"

"Act one is."

"Oh, too bad," she said, sitting up straight. Color rushed into her face as she realized she'd slept so soundly. "I mean…it's wonderful."

"I have no idea what the hell is going on," he admitted.

"Me, neither," she said with an impish smile. She quickly added, "Though the singing is lovely."

He merely shrugged. He wouldn't know lovely opera singing from bad, he just knew he'd prefer to be sitting at the Verizon Center at a Green Day concert. "I'm starving. Chinatown's a train ride away. Do you like Chinese food?"

"Oh, yum," she said, her eyes sparkling. "It's my favorite."

"Whew. I mean, I can tolerate you sleeping through my opera, but I'm afraid we'd have to end this here and now if you said you hated fried rice."

"Your opera?" She playfully punched his arm, knowing she wasn't the only one who'd been tempted to fall asleep.

By silent agreement, they got up and headed out of the center, hand in hand. He was pleased to notice a few of the more well-heeled audience members were slipping out, as well. So maybe they weren't the only plebeians in DC.

Once they were outside, Lex took a deep breath. The icy January wind was bracing after the stuffy air in the theater.

"I'm really sorry I fell asleep," she said. "I appreciate you going to the effort to get the tickets."

"It wasn't a problem. I've always wanted to go… once."

She laughed with him. "You can check that off your bucket list, then."

"Does it count if I only stayed until intermission?"

"I'll never tell."

"Then consider it checked."

They talked about the production, and then about music in general—she was a Green Day fan, too—as they made their way onto the Metro and across the city. Arriving at their stop, Lex headed toward his favorite restaurant, looking forward to introducing her to the best damn Chinese around. They walked in the door, however, and the doorman greeted Amelia by name. He could only stare.

"What?" she asked, her eyes twinkling. "I told you I love Chinese food."

"But I didn't expect you to be Norm from *Cheers*."

Her expression was blank.

"The old TV show," he explained.

Still nothing.

"Seriously? You've never heard of it?"

She merely shrugged.

He slapped a hand against his forehead. "How old are you?"

"Three years younger than you, if you're the same age as Ryan. I apparently watched more *Teletubbies* and fewer sitcoms." Her lips twitching the tiniest bit, she added, "Besides, it's not like *everybody* knows my name."

He realized she was messing with him, and barked a laugh. God, this woman kept him on his toes. She was so good at playing it straight—that sweet, innocent face disguised a deep mischievous streak. He wondered how many men had been fooled by the demure smile, the quiet voice, the job, the clothes, the demeanor and never saw the sexy, witty woman underneath. And he wondered if she'd ever have let him see that woman, either, if he hadn't met her the way he had on New Year's Eve.

God, what a crime against nature *that* would have been. He only hoped he wouldn't have been stupid enough to overlook quiet, understated Amelia. He'd like to think he wasn't shallow, but given his track record, if she hadn't been wearing the vamp getup, he might have blown it right out of the gate.

"I was too young to watch that show in prime time," she said. "But come on, is there a kid who grew up in the '90s who didn't have TVLand speed-dialed on his TV remote?"

"Your remote had speed dial? Damn, I'm jealous. But you're right, I guess I was a TV junkie for a while, too. At least, when we had one."

She raised a curious brow as they were led to their seat by a server. "What do you mean?" she asked when they were alone.

"Well, there were no TVs in my house until I was five. And then for a few years we had one in every room. Then none again for three years. Followed by a big-screen declaration of independence by my dad, which continues to this day."

"I'm so not following any of this," she said as she lifted a glass of water the server had deposited by her plate.

He shrugged, reaching for his own. "My mother was an anti-TV crusader. Rots the brain and all that."

She nodded, understanding.

"After she left, my father remarried four times."

She managed to hide her shocked reaction, and he continued.

"Stepmother number one was a soap junkie. She had cable hooked up in every room in the house, including the bathrooms. When she left, I knew the intimate details of every relationship on *The Young and the Restless*, and could reenact entire scenes from *General Hospital*."

Lifting a brow, she said, "Hopefully not all the scenes."

He chuckled. "Not those scenes. More like, 'Nurse, this man needs a central line, stat!' I have no idea what that means, but I was damned convincing when I said it. They'd roll me out for party tricks."

"I guess it could have been worse. She could have been a reality-show junkie."

"That was stepmother number three," he said with an intentional eyebrow wag. "Did Ryan ever tell you about the *Survivor* game I organized in our neighborhood? He broke his arm when he fell off a roof during a challenge."

She was laughing out loud, obviously not believing him. When she saw he wasn't laughing, she tsked. "Did he get voted off the island?"

"No, but I was voted off the property by his mom who didn't let us play together for a month."

She looked indignant. "It was just as much his fault, it wasn't as if you made him do it."

"That's exactly what I said," he replied, liking that she immediately stood up for him. Even if he had been a bossy son of a bitch and probably had browbeaten Ryan into playing.

"He should have gotten the 'If everybody jumps off a bridge, would you do it?' speech."

"I think he was tired of hearing it by that point." He shrugged helplessly. "I was kind of a bad influence."

Understatement. After years of never knowing if there would be a mother at home, or if his father would be drowning his sorrows, he'd been out of control by the age of twelve. Christ, it was a miracle he'd made it to adulthood without an arrest or an addiction. If not for his aunt—his dad's sister, who'd moved in with them when Lex was fifteen—he might not have. She'd been the one who'd finally provided some kind of stable home life for him, enough that he'd been able to make it through high school and go off to college anyway.

"So what about stepmother number two? You skipped her."

Thinking of his second stepmother, he couldn't help but smile. "She was a hippie and the one who diagnosed my dyslexia. She was only around for about a year, but during those months, we lived on sprouts and tofu and weren't allowed to be near a TV because of all the radiation."

"You are totally making this up!"

He lifted his hand. "Swear to God."

"And number four?"

He fell silent for a moment, his smile fading. Dropping his gaze to his glass, he moistened his fingertips with the condensation from the cup, his eyes welling up with the same emotion he always felt about this subject. "She died when I was fifteen. Cancer. My dad had finally found somebody who was good for him. Us. And she died."

Amelia reached across the table and covered her hand with his. "I'm so sorry, Lex."

"Yeah, me, too. Dad never really got over it, though at least he stopped playing here-we-go-round-the-marrying-bush every couple of years."

"Is he single still?"

"He was for a long time. But he's apparently dating someone now. Sounds like it might be serious."

"Oh."

He didn't elaborate, considering that he hadn't met the future-ex-Mrs. Rollins. He didn't feel up to commenting.

He immediately gave himself a mental slap. His old man had made some bad choices, sure, but at least he hadn't remarried for a decade. If he'd finally decided to give it another shot, hopefully he'd chosen somebody who'd be there for the long haul this time. She wouldn't fly off to the third world, or join a commune, or cheat on him, or die on him. That wasn't too much to ask… God, he hoped it wasn't.

Although she'd fallen silent, he did sense her curiosity. There was a question she hadn't voiced, and he was grateful. He didn't like talking about his biological mother, who was now living in India, bathing in the Ganges, basking in the admiration and adoration of people who thought she was the most selfless person on the planet. So good, so kind, so noble, so perfect.

So gone.

Whatever. It was ancient history.

Lex was in the now, maybe slightly in the future— with Amelia. He'd never really envisioned a future with previous girlfriends. He'd somehow always waited for the other shoe to drop, knowing something would happen to screw the relationship up. An ex had once accused him of practically inviting her to cheat on him because he had such a low expectation of the relationship. Hell, maybe she'd been right.

Not with Amelia, though.

He wasn't sure what was so different about her. He

knew only that, for the first time in forever, he wasn't already wondering what, exactly, was going to go wrong. He was focused only on what was going so very right.

SIX DATES. THAT WAS Amelia's rule, six dates before sex.

Tonight was their sixth date.

Okay, well, that was only true if you counted New Year's Eve and the following weekend when they'd run into each other at the bar and he'd eaten dinner. Oh, and their coffee date, which had lasted only forty-five minutes. But she *was* counting them.

When she made the realization during their meal, she almost dropped her chopsticks. Lowering her gaze to focus on the table, she prayed color hadn't flooded her cheeks as a slew of mental pictures danced in her head. Not exactly wild, X-rated ones, but definitely R-rated. Judging by the kisses they had shared, she suspected Lex would be a magical lover, and she wanted those strong hands of his on every inch of her body.

"Is it hot in here?" She lowered her chopsticks and fanned her face with her napkin.

"Not really," he replied, sounding confused.

By the time she drew in a few deep breaths, calmed herself and glanced up at him again, he was eyeing her with curiosity and concern.

"Are you okay?"

"Oh, sure."

"You had the strangest expression on your face."

Strange? Ha. Probably a cross between overjoyed and constipated. Because part of her—the part that looked at him and saw the most handsome man she'd ever known—was dying to take him home and find out if their amazing kisses led to amazing…other stuff.

While another part—the part that looked at him and saw the most handsome man she'd ever known—was wondering why on earth he was with her, and whether he'd laugh in her face if she tried to seduce him.

"Just enjoying my dinner," she mumbled.

"That didn't look like enjoyment, it looked like terror."

Surprised, she jerked her head up and stared at him. "I'm not terrified."

Not of him. She wasn't the least bit afraid of Lex. She was, perhaps, afraid of being rejected by him, though. Maybe of being tested and found wanting. Well, any woman with as little experience as she had would be terrified, she supposed.

Lex, on the other hand, had a lot of experience with women. Their previous conversations had made that clear. Plus, his best friends had felt it necessary to convince him to give up bad girls. Her sister had also dropped a warning in her ear. Amanda had admitted she liked Lex a lot, but that Ryan had told her about some of Lex's antics with women over the years, warning Amelia to be cautious.

Hearing him talk about his childhood, about the revolving door of adult females in his life and the lousy example set by his father, she could certainly see what drove Lex to be something of a playboy. But Amelia had never been the type to go for a playboy. During every one of their dates, she'd wondered at least once when he would open his eyes wider and realize that nice girls weren't terribly exciting or desirable.

Stop it. She wasn't being fair to him, or to herself. She wasn't unattractive, and he wasn't a jerk. The sizzling tension between them had been obvious from their first meeting, even if she hadn't been the kind of girl he'd thought her to be. Her clothes might have changed, but she was still Amelia, still even partly Lia. He saw that, she'd lay money on it.

Yet a lifetime of being the girl-next-door was hard to overcome.

"I'm glad you're not afraid." His smile was tender, teasing. "But just in case—I assure you that fried rice isn't going to bite you back."

No, but you might. The thought was instinctive and naughty and a shiver rolled through her at the idea of him nibbling on all her most sensitive places.

"Whoa, now I've gotta know what you're thinking," he said, sitting back in his chair and eyeing her. "That expression was entirely different."

"Are you a face reader or something?"

"Not professionally, but it helps in my line of work."

Amelia licked her lips, stalling, wondering what to tell him. She could just bring the subject of sex up, throw the whole thing on the table right between the egg drop soup and the kung pao chicken, and see what he said. That would be the confident, strong woman way to do it. Or she could keep staring at her egg roll as if something was going to crawl out of it and hope he finally changed the subject.

He didn't give up. Reaching across the table, he grabbed her hand and squeezed lightly. "You can tell me what's on your mind."

"Sex," she said, the word slipping from between her lips before she could bite down on it.

She kept her stare focused on their entwined hands. His tightened reflexively. "Oh."

Yeah. Oh. She waited for him to say something else.

When he didn't, she looked up at him and found his expression serious, his eyes…hungry? Was that desire she saw there? Did the tightness of his jaw hint that he was suffering from a few mental pictures of his own? And was affected by them more than he'd like to be, given their public location?

Their stares locked, and she was torn between confusion, want and embarrassment. His expression said she shouldn't be embarrassed or confused. She thought it also said she wasn't alone in her want.

"I should confess, it's been on my mind, too."

"In a generic, here's-how-we-perpetuate-the-species way? Or something more specific?"

He didn't laugh. "Definitely more specific."

The desire in his voice made her hot again. All over. Amelia drew a few slow, easy breaths, wishing her mind would stop giving her gifts that were totally inappropriate for the setting. And wishing those gifts didn't leave her body so prickly and aware, tense and anticipatory.

"I want you."

She gave up wishing her mind would stop drawing such erotic pictures because that was so not gonna happen now. Lord, hearing those three words made every part of her that wasn't already soft and sensitive get that way on the double.

"I've wanted you since we kissed on New Year's Eve," he added.

She let out a shaky sigh, her tiny groan undoubtedly telling him she felt the same way. But he wasn't finished.

"I wanted you even more after our first text exchange."

"Even not knowing you were texting the same girl you'd met New Year's Eve?"

"Even not knowing. I thought about you a lot after the night we met, but I was also drawn to the woman behind the texts. Seeing you come up the escalator in that yellow coat, recognizing that you were one and the same person, was one of the best moments of my life. I couldn't believe my luck."

She heard it in his voice. There was a but.

He confirmed it. "But it's okay, we don't have to rush things. I'd never ask you to do anything you're not ready to do."

How gentlemanly. How thoughtful.

How frustrating.

God, she needed to get him to see past the good girl label he'd slapped on her. She wasn't entirely sure how to get him to do that without coming across like a very bad one, unfortunately.

"I don't want to ruin this," he added. "You and me."

Her jaw dropped. "And sex would ruin it?" She had a horrible thought. "Are you bad in bed?"

That did make him laugh, and he squeezed her hand again. "I've never had any complaints."

I'll bet you haven't.

"This is different for me, though. You're different."

Huh? "Are you saying I'm too nice to sleep with?"

He let go of her hand and reached up to brush his fingers over her cheek, his thumb rubbing against her bottom lip. Unable to resist, she flicked her tongue out, tasting his warm skin.

"No, not too nice," he said, his voice husky. He wasn't at all unaffected by her. "In fact, you're not nearly as nice as people think you are. You have a wicked streak, Amelia Jones, whether you let anyone see it or not."

Oh, she was so glad he recognized that. It got so

tiring, sometimes, to fill the role of nice sister, sweet daughter, crafty friend, down-to-earth business owner. Lex brought out something else in her—something she rarely, as he'd said, let people glimpse. He'd seen it from the first night, though, and it appeared he liked her all the more for it.

"What I'm trying to say is, I don't mind going slow. I haven't done this whole romance thing in…well, ever."

No, she suspected with his looks, charm and charisma, he did the fall-into-bed-and-find-out-last-names-in-the-morning thing.

"I'm enjoying this," he continued. "I don't want you to feel pressured."

Hmm. She could tell him that her desire for him was causing her more pressure than anything else, at least in certain parts of her body. But that was a wee bit too…blunt.

"Thanks," she murmured, half meaning it. Because while the idea of going to bed with Lex thrilled her, she couldn't deny a nub of insecurity that made her happy to put it off. If she didn't know his history, wasn't aware that he'd played the field—a lot—she might not feel as anxious about it. But for a woman as inexperienced as she was, it would be hard to not think about the things other women might have done better.

Hopefully, though, they wouldn't wait too long. And, she decided as he took her home, just because they weren't going to sleep together right away didn't mean they couldn't put an end to at least some of this tension. Which was why, when they arrived at her apartment, she didn't kiss him and say goodbye. She instead unlocked the door and said, "Want to come in?"

He met her gaze, visibly questioning. She kept her

expression friendly and unexpectant. "For coffee or something."

Something like...me, perhaps?

"Sounds good," he said, following her inside.

For a moment, she felt like chuckling evilly, rubbing her hands together, and whispering, "Step into my parlor, said the spider to the fly." Only, she wasn't a spider, and he sure wasn't a fly. And it was sort of ridiculous to think she could initiate any seduction when he'd made it clear he wanted to slow things down.

Kissing, though...well, that she felt fully capable of initiating.

They drank coffee in her living room, sitting together on the overstuffed sofa that was draped with one of the blankets she'd made. He commented on it, admiring the softness and the colors, and appeared impressed when he heard she'd knitted it.

Talking about nothing more significant than her shop, their dinner and the weather, Amelia found herself losing her nerve minute by minute. It was one thing to tell herself she'd go ahead and kiss the taste buds out of his mouth, it was another to do it.

Fortunately, she wasn't the only one thinking about it.

"If you don't stop staring at my mouth, I'm going to have to insist you let me use it on you."

She gasped, hearing the heat in his voice. "I wasn't... I mean, I was, but you see..." How to explain that she'd only intended to seduce him part of the way.

She licked her lips, her thoughts scrambling.

"God help me," he muttered.

He lifted her by the hips and hauled her onto his

lap, facing him. Amelia parted her legs and straddled his thighs.

Sliding his hands into her hair, he pulled her face toward his. Amelia sighed with pleasure and met him halfway, their mouths coming together and opening hungrily.

Lex tasted sweet and hot, his kiss sending slow waves of pleasure through every inch of her. She tilted her head to one side, wanting him deeper, and their tongues thrust together in a steamy, sultry dance. She loved the way he cupped her cheeks, possessive but tender. Gripping his shoulders, she stroked the powerful muscles, dying to know what all that smooth, male skin under his dress shirt would feel like beneath her hands.

Not asking permission, she reached down and began to work his tie out of its knot as their kiss went on and on. She unbuttoned the top button of his shirt, and then the next, sliding her hand against his chest and tangling her fingers in the sparse, wiry hair.

As if unable to help himself, he groaned, dropped his hands to her hips and pulled her more tightly against his groin. Amelia whimpered when she felt his arousal surging between her thighs, and actually cried out when his mouth left hers and he kissed his way down her throat. His hands slid sinuously up the front of her silky dress. She arched toward his touch, quivering with pleasure as his palms scraped across her sensitive nipples. He bent lower, kissing a path down the deep V-neck, licking her cleavage until she began to shake.

Lex was strong and sexy, but the way his hands shook as he touched her said he was every bit as affected as she was. And that this wasn't merely another interlude for him, that perhaps it meant something more.

It did mean something more to her. She was falling head over heels for this guy, and her emotions were singing at the seriousness with which he was handling this kiss. But she also wanted him to rip her damn dress off and take her. Her inhibitions and self-doubt were melting away as he introduced her to all the delights they could share.

"Yes, Lex, please," she whispered as he dipped his tongue low on her breast, teasing her, tempting her.

Rather than giving in to her unvoiced demand, he kissed his way back up her throat and dropped his hands. They came to rest on her outer thighs, stroking lightly, but not quite high enough.

"You drive me crazy," he whispered, looking into her eyes.

"Ditto."

He pressed a soft kiss to her mouth. Then another. A third.

But there was no fourth. Instead, he gently pushed her off his lap and stood up.

"I should go," he said, though his raspy breath made her doubt he wanted to.

"You don't have to."

He thrust a hand through his hair, tousling it even more than her fingers had done moments ago. "Yeah, I do."

Amelia closed her eyes, shattering inside, wondering if he was being noble, sticking to his go-slowly plan, or if he didn't really want her.

As if he'd read her thoughts, he cupped her chin and tilted her head so she was forced to open her eyes and look up at him. Considering she was eye-to-crotch with the most impressive-looking bulge she'd ever seen, she vacillated between sighing in relief—oh, yes, he most certainly did want her—or slapping him for leaving.

"I'm trying to be good here."

"Good boys are overrated," she snapped.

He laughed softly, rubbing her cheek with his thumb. "You know, I made a similar comment not too long ago about good girls. In a few short weeks, you've managed to turn all my beliefs upside down and have me thinking in ways I've never thought before." He bent down and brushed his lips across hers. "Which is why it's time to say good-night."

And he did. With one more soft kiss and a whispered goodbye, he turned and walked out of her apartment.

A few minutes later, after she'd found her breath again, she saw he'd forgotten his coat. She took momentary satisfaction from that, realizing he hadn't been nearly as calm as he'd sounded when he'd left. Walking out of here hadn't been any easier on him than it had been on her.

She thought about calling him to let him know she had his jacket, but figured he had to have realized he'd left it behind the minute he stepped out into the bitter January night. The fact that he hadn't returned for it said he'd rather not risk coming back and starting things all over again.

"Fine, Mr. Noble," she murmured. "Be cold."

As for her, although she far preferred *him*, she was going to wrap herself in his coat, which smelled warm and spicy and totally Lex, and go to bed.

CHAPTER FIVE

FOR THE NEXT two weeks, Lex stuck to his guns and took things with Amelia at a snail's pace. He was the patient, nice-guy boyfriend women were supposed to want. Or, at least, the respectful one a sweet, classy woman like Amelia deserved.

They'd been dating for more than a month now, without sharing much more than supercharged kisses, despite the fact that he went crazy with desire whenever they touched. This relationship was progressing more slowly than any in his life, and he honestly wasn't sure he'd be able to hold out much longer.

Your resolution was to give up bad girls, not give up sex.

The only reason he'd been able to resist her this far was because he'd avoided going back to her apartment, knowing there was no way in hell he'd be able to walk away from her again.

He'd survived. Barely. But he wasn't sure how much longer he could take it.

They saw each other a lot, going to dinner, meeting for coffee, catching a movie. They even went ice-skating once, and he'd managed not to fall and break his ass. He enjoyed each minute he spent in her company. And the ones he spent reading her sassy texts or sharing witty phone calls with her—well, he enjoyed those, too.

The problem was, every time he kissed her good-night, each kiss was more intimate and sexually charged than the last. He was finding it harder and harder to stick to his promise of a gradually developing relationship. He sometimes wished he'd kept his big mouth shut that night at dinner, when he'd told her he wanted to take things slowly. But he couldn't make himself forget that he'd seen a hint of relief in her expression, though she'd tried to hide it. For all her sass, her confidence, her flirtation and her sex appeal, there was still a pretty innocent, inexperienced young woman beneath the shell.

She'd told him she wasn't a virgin. He also knew she'd only ever had one lover, more than two years ago, and that he hadn't been very memorable.

They'd had that revealing conversation after dinner in a restaurant, and he'd gripped his wineglass so hard he almost snapped the stem. Because, more than anything, he'd wanted to whisk her out of the restaurant, take her home and show her what real physical pleasure was all about. If he was absolutely certain Amelia was ready, he'd stop being reserved and romantic and go right into sexual beast mode.

But he wasn't certain about much of anything lately. He wasn't even totally sure he hadn't made a mistake getting involved with someone like her. Amelia inspired thoughts of pretty houses with lawns and swing sets, stuff Lex wasn't cut out for and didn't want.

But, God help him, he wanted *her*.

Was it really possible for him to have it all? For such a long time, he'd believed he wasn't cut out for commitment—marriage, family, all that stuff. God knew growing up, he'd never seen any evidence that things like that really worked. Maybe he'd seen it recently, with some of his buddies, but that didn't mean it had ever happened—or ever would—for Lex.

Despite how much he cared about her, he just didn't know that he would ever have enough to offer someone like Amelia. He was damaged goods when it came to relationships…and she was the most undamaged, kind-hearted, genuine person he had ever known. Honestly, he wasn't sure what the hell she saw in him, unless it was a wounded soul she wanted to heal.

Now, though, wasn't the time to dwell on it. Not when they were about to spend the next few days surrounded by her friends and family.

It was almost Valentine's weekend, and Ryan and Amanda would be married in two days. The bridal party, their family and friends were all meeting up at Reagan National airport to fly up to Vermont for the destination wedding at a ritzy spa-lodge.

"I'm not so sure this was a great idea," Amelia said as they walked through the airport, her steps slowing, then dragging.

"What? Your sister marrying Ryan?"

She rolled her eyes. "Don't be silly. They're perfect. I mean us showing up here together."

He stopped suddenly, and a sea of travelers had to swarm around them. Ignoring their glares and grumbles, he turned to face her. "Why is that a problem?"

She caught her lip between her teeth and sighed heavily. "My family is…overprotective."

"That's how families are supposed to be." Normal families, anyway, not that he'd had much experience with those. "I'm not worried."

Why would he be? He hadn't given them any reason to hate his guts. Hell, he'd been such a gentleman, even her cop uncle shouldn't have anything to complain about.

"They also would like me to settle down with someone." She held up her hand, palm out, stopping him from saying anything. "I'm not making demands on you. I know this isn't serious."

Huh. Well, that was crazy. Hell, he hadn't even seen her naked, but he already cared more about her than any woman he'd ever dated. And she thought he wasn't *serious*? If he hadn't been serious, on some level, about Amelia Jones, he would have slept with her weeks ago.

He stared at her, knowing there was more, waiting for the rest.

"It's just, if they realize we came to the airport together, they might start making assumptions, might think it means something."

Right. And she didn't want any assumptions made about them. Or was it that she feared he didn't? Funny, considering she was the one making assumptions about how he might feel or what he might want. That made him grit his teeth, and he wondered what would lead her to think what they had didn't mean anything.

God, this was so confusing. He'd just been telling himself he didn't deserve her, and was now offended and upset when she commented that what they had was casual.

Not responding right away, he took her arm and led her to a corner of the terminal. He stepped close, asking in a low voice, "Why do you think we're not serious?"

She pushed a strand of hair away from her face, and he noticed her hand was trembling. "Well, we've…"

"We've what?"

"I mean, we *haven't*…"

"Made love?"

A pretty flush colored her cheeks. "Yes, so you see, I know we're just having fun and this isn't anything special. I mean, that I'm not anything special to you…"

He couldn't stand hearing her say such a thing. In fact, it angered him that she might even think it. So, not giving a damn that they were surrounded by travelers, any one of whom might be a relative or family friend, he sunk his hands into her hair and pulled her to him for a hot, hungry kiss.

He plunged his tongue into her mouth, claiming her, demanding she acknowledge that what they had was serious. This waiting to be with her, this patience to make it good for her, had been agonizing. Yet she thought it meant she wasn't *special* to him? Jesus, so much for being the nice guy. Would she have believed he cared for her if he'd jumped her bones the way he'd been dying to every night for weeks?

She didn't resist his kiss. In fact she wrapped her arms around his neck and kissed him back, deeply, hungrily. Time and place melted away, and he lost himself in the taste of her, the feel of her. Amelia was both the cool breeze in his life, and the raging volcano. She relaxed him and inflamed him, and everything in between. He wanted her like he'd never wanted anyone.

Not mean anything? She might as well think the sun didn't mean anything to the earth, or the moon to the tides.

She meant so much to him. More than he'd ever expected.

When the kiss finally ended, he whispered, "You're special to me. And what we have definitely means something."

Her beautiful face was flushed, her lips full, moist, pink and well kissed. She gazed up at him, those blue eyes half-shielded between heavy, lazy lids. She looked aroused and needy, and he cursed himself for not having this conversation at home, where he could have shown her how special to him she was.

"I'm finished being the nice, patient guy," he told her, hearing the snap of want in his voice. "If taking this slowly made you think I didn't want you, you'd better get that idea out of your head right now. Because I'm dying for you, Amelia. I want you in every way a man can have a woman."

She quivered in his arms. "I want you, too," she whispered. "But oh, God, why couldn't you have told me this three hours ago when we had a little privacy?"

He let out a loud laugh. "Three hours? Give me some credit." Lifting a hand to her cheek, he cupped it and stared into her face, memorizing the blue-velvet shade of her eyes, the curve of her jaw, the fullness of her lips. "It'll take a lot more than three hours to do what I want to with you. Three decades might not be enough."

A tiny smile tugged at her lips and her eyes sparkled with sudden mischief. "Well, we can't quite pull off three decades right now, but we are about to have three nights at a romantic, swanky resort."

He got the message, knowing she, too, was ready to put an end to this waiting game. Desire sluiced through him, and he wanted nothing more than to push her up against the wall and cover her mouth with his again, get started now on three nights of utter sin.

Then reality set in, and he wasn't just frustrated by their current public location. He groaned deeply. "Yeah, we'll be at a romantic resort…surrounded by your friends and family."

She didn't appear fazed. Rising on tiptoe, she brushed

her lips against his jaw. "I don't have a roommate. Do you?"

God, she was tempting. "No. But what if your cop uncle's room is on the same floor?"

"He's a very sound sleeper." She laughed lightly. "In fact, I can wait for everyone else in the hotel to fall asleep."

"I won't fall asleep," he promised her. "I'll wait as long as it takes."

Their stares locked, promises made and accepted. It might be a long day, they'd be surrounded by nosy family members, unable to have a moment's privacy. But everything would be totally worthwhile come the night.

"All right, then," she said, her voice almost a purr. "I'll see you in your room tonight."

SHE DIDN'T SEE Lex in his room that night.

Due to a mix-up with the hotel reservations, she ended up having to share her room with her cousin, Janice, another bridesmaid. Janice's room would be ready tomorrow, but for tonight, Amelia was well chaperoned. She had to lie there in the dark, listening to her cousin gossip for hours about the wedding. It was after two by the time her whispers finally descended into soft snores.

Unfortunately, Janice was a light sleeper. When Amelia tried to get up, if only to text Lex and see if he was still awake, her cousin jerked up in bed and asked what she was doing.

Amelia was ready to scream with frustration. After weeks of foreplay, she'd finally made plans to have the night of her life with the man of her dreams, and a stupid hotel mix-up had ruined everything. It wasn't fair.

The next day, Friday, was full of wedding preparations, a bridal luncheon, a groomsmen ski outing and the rehearsal. Amelia had seen Lex at breakfast, but didn't even have a chance to whisper an apology before they were swept apart by the day's events.

They were, fortunately, paired for the rehearsal, as she was the maid of honor and Lex was the best man. So as they stood together at the altar, pretending to listen to the minister who was running quickly through the ceremony, she mumbled, "I'm so sorry."

He nodded and whispered, "I hear you shared your room with a loud, talkative brunette last night."

"Yes, but you better not have," she shot back with a grin.

"I prefer strawberry blondes."

"Did you have a question, young man?" the minister asked, turning to Lex with a frown.

Amelia sucked her lips into her mouth and clamped down on them, determined not to laugh.

Lex apologized, adding, "Please, go on," even as he reached around and pinched her butt.

She hid a squeal, her flashing eyes promising retribution on him later.

Tonight. Oh, God, please tonight.

She didn't think she would be able to take it if something happened to ruin their plans again. After weeks of delicious kisses and over-too-soon embraces, she wanted nothing more than to be in his arms for hours, indulging in the kind of pleasure she'd only ever fantasized about.

Fortunately, the hotel and fate were kind. Janice got her own room. Most of the family had too much to drink at the rehearsal dinner and went to bed early. Nearly all their rooms were on the same floor, but she felt sure that with the way the alcohol had been flowing and with the whirlwind of the day, everybody would be asleep an hour after parting.

After sixty-one minutes, she left her room, walking quietly down the corridor toward Lex's. She scanned the corridor, an eye on the elevator, watching for any familiar faces, and breathed a sigh of relief when she saw none. Reaching his room, she lifted her hand to knock softly, but he pulled the door open before her knuckles made contact.

"Get in here, you," he said, wrapping his arms around her waist and drawing her inside.

The moment the door clicked shut, he was kissing her, his mouth hot and demanding, delicious.

Pushing her against the wall, he lifted her to bring their bodies into more perfect alignment. She wrapped her thighs around his hips and her arms around his neck, kissing him back, frantic with need and desire. Their tongues tangled and thrust, their breaths turning into gasps, sighs becoming moans. The kiss went on and on, not even ending when he carried her across the room to the bed, placing her on it and following her down.

"That was the longest hour of my life," he told her when they finally drew apart and looked at each other.

"Mine, too. I was terrified somebody would come and ask if they could share my room."

"They can have yours," he said, kissing his way down her throat. "You're staying here."

Sharing his bed sounded wonderful, though she knew she'd have to slip out before dawn if she didn't want to answer a lot of uncomfortable questions tomorrow. They might, indeed, be involved in something very special; that didn't mean she wanted to explain it to anyone.

"Do you know how long I've been dying to kiss you

like this?" he asked as he moved his mouth down, until he was sliding open the top button of her blouse with his teeth and tongue.

"About as long as I've been praying you would?"

Another button slipped free. And another. Lex sampled every inch of her as it was revealed, pressing warm, sultry kisses on the curves of her breasts and straight down her middle. She felt his every exhalation, the breaths flowing across her skin, sensitizing her nipples. But he didn't detour, didn't stop unbuttoning her, not until he reached the bottom button and then pulled her blouse free from the waistband of her skirt.

"Beautiful," he whispered, studying her bare midriff.

"Maybe it's just as well I couldn't come last night. Amanda gave all her bridesmaids some rather frilly gifts today."

He lifted his head, a brow arching over one eye. "Oh?"

She nodded primly. "I think she was paying everyone back for the naughty shower we threw for her."

"That's one bridal shower a guy wouldn't mind attending."

"You don't have to wait for a shower," she told him, almost purring. "My presents are right here. Under my skirt."

He rubbed a hand on his jaw. "Is that an invitation?"

"More like an order."

"I always follow orders from beautiful women."

He reached around her, and she arched up, allowing him access to the back zipper. Amelia held her breath as he drew it down. His fingers scraped across her bottom, caressing her gently, and she shivered at the sensation of strong, masculine fingers on soft, vulnerable curves.

When he pulled the skirt lower and saw the sinfully

sexy lacy panties she wore underneath, he sucked in an audible breath. And when the skirt descended farther, and he noted the thigh-high stockings, he groaned.

"Do you approve?"

"Most definitely."

She didn't doubt it. Hunger dripped from him. He stared at her as if she was the most desirable woman he'd ever seen, as if he'd die if he couldn't have her. Amelia had never before felt so powerful in her femininity.

"You steal my breath," he told her as he pulled the skirt the rest of the way off and tossed it away.

She couldn't reply, not when he moved his mouth down her hip, to the bare inches of thigh revealed above one stocking. He kissed her, tasting his way along the elastic seam, then moving across to the other leg and exploring just as thoroughly. She felt the scrape of his slightly grizzled cheek against the silkiness of the stocking, and each touch made her quiver.

Amelia hadn't experienced too many intimacies in her life, and he was verging on one that had always sounded shocking but oh, so erotic. When he moved his mouth over the front of her panties and scraped his lips across her, breathing hotly onto her most sensitive places, she cried out, her hips thrusting reflexively. But she also stiffened, nervous about this.

Lex took hold of her hips, steadying her. As if knowing she wasn't sure whether she wanted to beg him to continue or order him to stop, he began to move back up her body. He wouldn't push her for more than she was ready to give. It was enough to hint at what delights awaited her later…when she was more relaxed and ready to accept them.

Lex continued to kiss his way up her body, until he

reached the front clasp of her bra. He unfastened it, watched the material fall open, and then stared at her breasts as they were revealed. "God, you are stunning," he said, sounding almost awed.

He reached for one breast, gently squeezing, stroking, tweaking the tip until she started to shake. When he moved his mouth to her other breast, she whimpered, desperate for more. He gave it to her, licking her gently, then sucking her puckered nipple between his lips.

"Oh, yes," she groaned, loving the hot, strong pull of his mouth, feeling claimed and worshipped all at the same time.

He toyed with her, pleasured her, pushing her blouse and bra off her so he could pay close attention to both breasts. She loved it, but she wanted more.

"Let me see you," she begged.

He rose to his knees and began to strip out of his clothes. Amelia had never watched a man pull off his tie, unfasten his cuffs, unbutton his shirt. It was incredibly masculine and so damned sexy. She held her breath as he pulled the shirt off, revealing broad shoulders, a strong chest and thick arms.

"You're the one who's stunning," she whispered, noting the flex and play of all those muscles. He looked as if he should be carved out of marble, every inch of him was so perfectly designed.

He laughed softly, standing up beside the bed so he could strip out of the rest of his clothes. Amelia held her breath, suddenly unsure. She'd had, after all, only one lover, a college boy. Lex was all man. All powerful, hot man.

And when he pushed his pants and boxer briefs down, she understood what the word *man* really meant.

"Oh, God," she groaned as liquid heat surged through her. She was hungry for him, desperate, wanting everything, but mostly wanting him inside her.

She reached for him, trying to draw him down.

"We have all night," he whispered.

"And we'll use every minute of it, I swear. Right now, though…oh, please, Lex, please be in me."

Looking as though he'd never received a better invitation, he reached for her silky panties and drew them down her legs. His eyes darkened to jade as he revealed her, staring at her as though he'd never seen anything more perfect, and she didn't have to beg him any longer. Grabbing a condom from the bedside table, he pulled it on and knelt between her thighs.

She spread her legs wantonly, urging him on, rewarded by his groan of pure masculine need. And then he came to her, the heat of him thick and heavy as he entered her wet, willing body.

Amelia cried out as he began to claim her, making himself a place inside her that she never wanted him to leave. She arched up to meet him, wanting all he had to give, but he was patient, drawing out the pleasure for both of them, sinking into her ever-so-slowly, with such restraint.

Wrapping her arms around his neck, she drew his mouth to hers for a long, deep kiss. Deeper, and deeper, and soon they were both panting, the tension unbelievable.

"Please," she whispered, "please, Lex, don't make me wait anymore."

He gave in to her plea, thrusting hard, filling her until she let out a cry of satisfaction. She felt broken in half and put together again, all at the same time, and wave after wave of pleasure rose within her, surging and as insistent as the tides. She hadn't known it could be like this, so wonderful, so intimate, so powerful. He wasn't merely making love to her, he was possessing her.

They thrust and stroked, and the tension built inside her. She was on alert, aware, tense, ready for something amazing to happen. Something she'd never experienced with anyone else.

He thrust harder, faster, and she met him stroke for stroke.

"Yes, Lex," she urged, knowing he was close to exploding.

"Not without you," he insisted, reaching down to find her sweetest spot and stroke it. A few brushes of his fingers and she was spinning apart, all the sensations gathering tightly inside and then bursting out to flood her entire body with pulsating heat. She closed her eyes and let herself go with it, let it fill her with energy and happiness, let her mind savor the fact that Lex had given her something nobody else ever could.

And she could only smile.

Lex saw the smile and kissed her. "This *means* something, Amelia," he told her as he thrust harder, rising toward his own climax, groaning with pleasure.

"Yes, it does," she whispered against his lips. "Because I love you, Lex."

He stiffened slightly. Amelia assumed it was his body's reaction to his powerful climax, and she held on tight, wrapping herself around him, never wanting this moment to end. Never wanting this night to end.

Never wanting *them* to end.

CHAPTER SIX

SHE LOVED HIM.

Amelia loved him, or so she'd said.

Lex couldn't stop thinking about her whispered declaration. It had echoed in his head all night long, throughout the erotic hours they'd shared. The three words had imprinted themselves on his psyche like a determined seed, burrowing deep, finding fertile ground in a part of his brain that wanted to believe them, and sprouting.

But he wasn't sure what to think, or how to feel. She was special to him, and their relationship had meaning. She was different than anyone else he'd ever been with.

But did he love her? Honestly, he'd never fully considered himself capable of the emotion.

Could he love her? He didn't know.

That was a crazy position to be in hours before your best friend's wedding, which also happened to be on Valentine's Day. He had to put aside his own misgivings—the fact that Amelia had shaken him to his core with her sweetly whispered declaration—and focus on Ryan and Amanda.

The wedding was scheduled for four o'clock. Most of the guests were already here, as they were either family or part of the wedding party, but there were a few guests coming in today for just the one night. Among those was his father, who'd watched Ryan grow up and had been pleased to get an invite.

He'd RSVP'd for two.

Lex hadn't been sure what to expect of his possible new stepmother-to-be. But when he walked down the corridor toward the chapel and saw his old man standing beside a blonde with more curves than a racetrack, his heart fell. She was wearing a leopard-print dress and was probably no more than twenty-five.

But then he drew closer and saw the look on her face. Her familiar face.

Her eyes were wide, her mouth gaping open. Shock had made her immobile, and she clung to his father's arm, looking wary and nervous.

That was when he placed her. Not her name, just her face. And her body.

Oh, God. This couldn't be happening. Not here, not today, not the morning after a perfect, sweet, wonderful woman had said she loved him for the first time.

But it was true. Even if he hadn't recognized the blonde, her expression would have made it clear that they had a history.

Lex had picked her up in a bar during a trip home for the holidays a few years ago.

He'd had a one-night stand with his father's new girlfriend.

"Lex!" his old man exclaimed, gesturing him forward. "Get over here and give me a hug, kiddo."

Silent, feeling sick and trapped, Lex let himself be drawn into a bear hug, during which he smelled the remnants of his father's liquid lunch on his breath. His dad wasn't lurching, but the loud voice and the suspiciously bright eyes hinted that he'd been celebrating for hours already. The lurching would come later. Probably some tears, too. He usually cried at some point during every father-son reunion.

Jesus, how was Lex gonna make it through this day?

Somehow, he managed to maintain a calm facade as his father introduced him to Brittani, who kept a forced smile on her face. She couldn't take her eyes off Lex, as if waiting to see what he would do, scared he would reveal the truth about her.

Hell, how was he supposed to react? He barely remembered that night. He'd come home for the holidays, read a stupid let-there-be-peace-on-earth note from his mother on her international blog, fought with his father about it and gone out, looking for company.

He'd found it. As had his father, apparently, a few years later.

What did one say in such a situation? He didn't want to shame his father, to embarrass Brittani, to freaking humiliate himself. So what was he supposed to do?

In the end, he did nothing. He pretended not to recognize her, and excused himself to go get Ryan ready for the altar. Promising his father they'd talk later, he headed for the groom's suite.

From then on, he was on duty, with no time to think about the twist of fate that had slapped him in the face with a visceral reminder of the man he'd always been. The man he still was, despite what sweet, beautiful Amelia Jones might believe. Because six weeks of romance with a wonderful, unique, nice woman couldn't possibly erase a lifetime of bad choices and shallow decisions. Those choices defined him, they told the truth about who he really was.

He was the guy who hooked up with equally jaded women who would never expect much from him.

He was the guy who pursued—but never fell in love with—women who were destined to cheat on him, rob him or abandon him. Because he fully expected to be cheated on, robbed, abandoned.

Talk about low expectations for yourself. Lord, it was a wonder he'd never hooked up with a female serial killer.

One thing was clear—he was not the man Amelia wanted him to be. He'd been playing the role of nice-guy-seeking-nice-girl-for-nice-relationship. Opera dates, ice skating, waiting a long time to build up to sex…who the hell was he kidding? That wasn't him, not really. He'd been playing a part inspired by ancient history and some bad breakups and a stupid New Year's resolution.

So how could she really love him?

Answer: she couldn't. Because there wasn't anything worth loving, not for a woman like her.

Funny, though. Seeing everything so clearly, as he was now, also allowed him to see his emotions for the first time. And while he knew she couldn't *really* be in love with him, the truth was, he *had* fallen in love with her.

It was unexpected and shocking, but entirely true. He loved Amelia, for all the good it would do him. He wasn't even happy about it, which made him realize all the more how little he deserved her.

Somehow, Lex managed to get through his best man duties without throwing his head back and screaming, or throwing up. It was hell, though. Standing at the altar beside Ryan and his bride, the love between them filling the room, made him feel small. Spying his father and the woman on his arm among the guests, even smaller.

But it was when he spotted Amelia across the chapel, stunning in a bridesmaid's dress of pale gold, that he was sure he was the lowest creature on earth.

He shouldn't have slept with her. Ending this would be a lot harder now that they'd made love. But because he was such a selfish asshole, he couldn't regret it. The memories of last night would live on in his mind forever.

During the reception, he tried hard to paint on a smile. Although he'd soon have to deal with his father's situation, and with his relationship with Amelia, it wouldn't be tonight, not on his friend's special day.

But Amelia pulled him into a slow dance while everyone around them was indulging in champagne and happy toasts, and he realized he hadn't done a good job of hiding his mood.

"What's wrong?" she asked.

He mumbled something noncommittal and tightened his arm around her waist, wondering how long he could keep up this charade.

"Lex, talk to me," she insisted.

"It's nothing."

"I don't believe that."

Not giving him another chance to deny anything, she stepped out of his arms, took his hand and pulled him out of the ballroom. She didn't stop until they'd reached a lounge area off the lobby of the hotel, which was abandoned. Lowering herself onto a leather sofa, she pulled him down beside her.

"Please talk to me."

He studied her face, those blue eyes, that vulnerable mouth, and wondered what to say. Part of him wanted to keep pretending that nothing was wrong, that the fairy-tale, nice-guy romantic hero she had fallen in love with was real. Another part wanted to cut his losses and get out of here, before he dragged her any deeper into his screwed-up life.

"You can be honest with me," she said, her throat quivering as she swallowed, as if she'd realized this was serious and she might not like his answer. "I'm a big girl, and I can take it."

He rubbed a weary hand over his face, remaining silent.

"You regret last night."

Sighing deeply, he admitted, "Yeah."

She sucked in an audible breath. He turned to look at her, seeing the hurt that said she wasn't such a big girl, and she really couldn't take it. She'd obviously expected him to answer differently. "Oh," she whispered.

"Last night was amazing, and I loved every minute of it. But that doesn't mean it wasn't the right thing for us to do. For *you* to do."

She cleared her throat. "It's because of what I said, isn't it?"

"You don't love me, Amelia."

Her eyes flashed fire. "Don't tell me what I do or don't feel."

He wanted to pull her into his arms and beg her to forgive him, to let him make it up to her and convince both of them it would be okay. But despite the fact that he might be a jaded ass, he wasn't a liar. "You can't love me. You don't even know the real me."

"That's ridiculous."

"Is it?"

"I know you, Lex. I know you're funny and charming, and tender. You're smart, you're a good man—the fact that you took this slowly and never pushed me proved that."

"It proved I was capable of playing a role, acting the part of nice guy who deserves the nice girl. The truth is, I'm not in any way, shape or form a nice guy."

"I don't believe that."

He rose from the sofa and crossed to the large fireplace, its embers low, casting shadows throughout the small room. "You should believe it. I'm an asshole who can't trust anybody, who always expects the worst of any woman I'm involved with."

Until her. Not that he said that.

She leaped off the couch, reaching for him. "Lex, that's not true."

He stepped away from her hand, not wanting her to touch him, not until he'd said what he needed to say. "It's completely true, Amelia. I've been fooling myself and fooling you over the past six weeks. The truth is, a leopard doesn't change its spots. I'm not a good guy, and I'm definitely not a good enough guy for you."

She reached for him again, trying to cup his cheek. He gave himself a few seconds to memorize the feel of her hand, and then ducked away.

"We should get back," he told her, straightening his tux jacket, hardening himself against the grief in her eyes. "We don't want to leave everybody wondering where we are."

She nodded, realizing he was ending the conversation now, before he had to say more. Before he had to hurt her by informing her it was over.

Honestly, it hurt him just to think it. He wasn't sure he had the strength to say the words out loud tonight.

"You go ahead," she urged him, wrapping her arms around herself as if chilled. "It might be better if we don't walk back in together." A bitter laugh spilled from that beautiful mouth. "We wouldn't want anybody getting the wrong idea about us."

"Amelia…"

She put a hand up, stopping him from saying another word. "Go, Lex. Please, just go. I'd like to be alone."

He wanted to pull her close, to hold her, to tell her he loved her, even if he didn't really believe she loved him—the *real* him—too. But it was kinder to stop dragging out the inevitable, so he merely nodded and walked away, leaving her standing there by the fireplace, seeking warmth in a room that had grown icy cold.

AMELIA MANAGED TO make it through the rest of the reception with something resembling a smile on her face. She danced, she hugged family members, she laughed, she ate cake. A lot of cake.

She avoided making eye contact with Lex, wondering what on earth had happened between this morning and tonight to make him change his mind about them. Because, last night, he'd seemed anything but cold, and while he hadn't said the words, she would have bet money that he had feelings for her, too.

She refused to believe that he simply wasn't interested in her now that he'd gotten what he wanted. If that was the case, he could have slept with her weeks ago and saved himself some trouble. So what could the problem be?

"Care to dance, young lady?" an older male voice said.

Amelia looked up and saw Lex's father standing in

front of her. It was late, the reception was drawing to a close and Lex had disappeared without saying good-bye about a half hour ago. Unable to resist the chance to talk to his father and learn more about the man who had her racked with confusion, she nodded and stepped into the handsome older gentleman's arm.

"We met earlier. You're Amelia, sister of the bride."

"And you're Mr. Rollins."

"Alex, please."

Of course. That's why Lex had his unusual nick-name, to distinguish him from his father.

"I noticed the way you and my son were looking at each other earlier."

The man was blunt, she'd give him that. "I don't know what you mean."

His husky laughter reminded her of Lex's. "Of course you do. I also noticed that something went wrong be-tween you and you avoided each other half the night. Let me just say, if it had anything to do with Brittani, there's no reason for you to be upset. Their relationship was over a long time ago."

Her jaw dropped, and she stared at him in confu-sion. "Huh?"

"My date," he said, nodding toward a tall, sexy blonde standing near the deejay. "It seems she and Lex had a fling a few years ago."

Amelia glanced over at Brittani, disliking the woman on principle for having had Lex first.

"She recognized him and told me about it tonight. He must have been pretty shocked when I introduced her." Mr. Rollins shrugged. "But it's no big deal."

No big deal? What? The man had learned that a woman he was considering marrying, at least according to Lex, had slept with his son, and it was no big deal? "I'm not sure you should be telling me this."

"It isn't a problem. I knew Brittani was too good to be true, and I'm not heartbroken. At least we hadn't gotten married—gosh, that would've been awful."

There was an understatement.

He went on. "It's not as if I really expected things to work out anyway."

"I'm glad," she murmured, wondering what one was supposed to say in this situation. Because, truthfully, while she was glad the older man wasn't heartbroken, she wasn't glad to hear about his low expectations of relationships. It sounded far too much like something Lex had said to her earlier tonight.

"Let my son know that, would you, if you see him, that I'm okay? He got out of here so fast, I didn't have a chance to reassure him." He sighed softly. "Though he should know me well enough not to worry."

She heard sadness in his voice that belied his light, unconcerned tone. Her curiosity digging at her, she asked, "Do you mean, you don't care?"

"I mean, something always screws up a relationship. We Rollins men aren't lucky in love." He smiled down at her. "But who knows, maybe you'll break the cycle for Lex. Maybe you'll be the one who actually sticks around for him, unlike all the other women in our lives."

Her heart twisted in her chest, and her breath froze in her lungs. Was this why Lex believed he wasn't worth loving, because so many women had walked out of his life? She'd realized ever since he'd told her about his childhood that he had to bear some pretty deep scars. He'd never said much about his mother, but she knew the woman had moved away and given up custody of him, and so many other women had followed suit. How had that affected him? A better question—how had it not?

"He thinks he's not worthy, you understand that, right? Thinks everyone has left him—from his mother to his last girlfriend—because there's something wrong with him."

"There's not," she exclaimed.

"Of course there's not. The problem was me and my bad choices. Unfortunately, by the time I'd figured that out, Lex had already shouldered some of the blame and inherited some of my attitudes."

"That's a shame."

"Yes, it is." The music ended and Alex stepped away. Before he left the dance floor to return to his—she suspected—soon-to-be ex-girlfriend, he added one more thing. "It's not too late for Lex, though. Maybe he just needs the right woman to show him that."

Then, with an almost courtly bow, he walked away.

Amelia sleepwalked through the rest of the reception, saying her good-nights by rote, not paying attention to anything except the thoughts in her head.

Everything made sense now. Lex's resolution with his friends to stop seeking out casual, destructive relationships that he knew would end in failure because they always had in the past. His inability to see himself as a nice guy, as deserving of real love. His self-protective instinct to play the callous playboy rather than let a woman get close enough to really hurt him again.

He'd let down his guard with her. He'd let her close. He'd let her in. He'd even heard her whisper that she loved him last night.

Only to be confronted with the demons of his past the minute he saw his father this afternoon.

"Poor, sweet Lex," she mumbled as she rode up in the elevator that night.

By the time it reached her floor, she knew what she was going to do. Lex might have put up a shield around his heart for his own self-protection—and for hers—but she wasn't letting him go without taking at least one shot at knocking it down.

Not even caring if a member of her family was nearby, she stalked off the elevator and marched down the hall to his room. When she reached it and heard the sound of voices from within, she had the tiniest moment's hesitation.

Doubt swam through her, briefly, but insistently.

Lex was hurting and feeling unworthy. But would he really do something as destructive as trying to compound the hurt, for both of them, by picking up another woman?

"No way," she whispered, sure down to her bones that he wouldn't.

She lifted her hand and knocked. The voices immediately lowered in volume. *The television.*

Glad her confidence had been justified, she stared at the peephole, her expression challenging, silently demanding he let her in.

The door swung open. "Hello, Amelia," he said, sounding weary, resigned, but also, she thought, happy to see her, if even against his better judgment.

"Let me in," she ordered, not waiting for him to agree. She simply pushed past him and strode into his room, then spun around to look at him. "You've got a lot of nerve."

He shut the door and crossed the room to lean against the desk, crossing his arms over his chest, waiting for her to continue.

"How dare you decide who I can and cannot love."

"Amelia..."

"I'm not finished," she snapped, the nice girl gone, the fire-breathing one who was ready to fight for what she wanted fully in charge. "How dare you assume that you're not worth loving, not worth staying with?"

"I didn't say..."

"You didn't have to. Do you think I don't know you, Lex? The *real* you?"

He huffed out a breath. "You don't."

She literally growled. "I most certainly do. You're a playboy, and you've been a womanizer."

He straightened, his spine straightening. "So you do know the real me."

"I'm not finished," she snapped, indignation warring with frustration. Both were surpassed by a helpless longing to wrap her arms around him and hug the abandoned boy he'd been, to convince him he was worth loving.

She found strength and went on. "You let women into your life whom you could never love, fully expecting things to go wrong. It seemed easier that way, easier to protect yourself from any hurt you might feel the next time someone walked out the door."

He clenched his jaw. A direct hit, as she'd known it would be.

"But those things don't define you, Lex. Because you're also funny, tender, thoughtful, smart. All the hours we've talked, the time we've spent together, do you really think I never saw the man underneath?"

He looked away, not giving an inch. But she wasn't about to give up.

"Do you imagine I'm so blind, so gullible, that I couldn't distinguish you from the character you played for your own protection? If you believe that, am I supposed to believe that you never saw the real woman hiding behind the mask of nice craft-store owner?"

His mouth opened and closed as he tried to come up with a reply. But he had nothing, obviously thinking about her words, letting himself start to believe them. He relaxed his posture slightly and loosened his stiff jaw—he was finally starting to listen. And to *hear*.

Not wanting to throw her words at him, to attack him with what she knew and what she felt, she crossed to him. She lifted her hands to cup his cheeks, rubbing her fingertips across the faint stubble. Her voice low, tender, she said, "I know you, and I have fallen in love with the man I know."

He covered one of her hands with his own, staring down at her, his handsome face racked with indecision. "You don't understand. Some of the things I've done…"

"Of course I understand," she insisted, aware of what was weighing on his mind. Swallowing, not wanting to embarrass him, but certain she had to put it all on the table, she went on. "Your father understands, too. Brittani told him how she'd met you."

He closed his eyes and jerked back, so obviously ashamed, her heart broke for him. "God almighty, what a mess."

"Yes, a mess, but one from your past. Everybody has a past. Everybody makes mistakes."

"My father…"

"Has given up," she said sadly, accepting in her heart

it was true. "He doesn't even want to try to be optimistic anymore, doesn't want to ever expect anything good to happen. But that doesn't mean you can't."

"I started to think it was possible," he admitted, hoarseness in his tone revealing his churning emotions. "You made me believe it."

"I'm glad." She twined her arms around his neck and leaned close to him. "You deserve happiness, Lex. You deserve love." With a slightly cocky smile, she added, "You even deserve *me*."

He brushed his fingers through her hair, sliding his other hand to her waist and holding her hip. "I doubt I'll ever really deserve you," he said. "But the truth is, I'm selfish enough to want you anyway."

Her heart started fluttering again, her entire spirit buoyant, lifted by the certainty that she hadn't been wrong.

He did love her.

She didn't need to hear the words he hadn't yet voiced. She knew it was true, knew he wanted to make this work, as she did.

With a happy sigh, she rose on tiptoe and pressed her mouth to his, kissing him with all the love she felt for him. He gave up all resistance, wrapping his arms around her, hauling her tightly against his body.

They kissed deeply and said so much in that kiss. He silently vowed to trust her, she promised to stay, they swore to give their relationship the best they both had to give. They made plans and considered the future, all in one long sweet embrace that they'd been moving toward since the moment he'd bumped into her on that dance floor.

When they finally drew apart, Lex stayed close, his

cheek touching hers. Still holding her, he whispered, "I love you, Amelia."

She almost purred with happiness. "I love you, too." Then, licking her lips and eyeing him with mischief, she said, "But do you think sometimes you might call me Lia?"

He threw his head back and laughed, squeezing her even more tightly. "Honey, I'll call you whatever you what. Just please, don't ever ask me to give up loving you. Because I suspect that's one resolution I would never be able to keep."

* * * * *

Dear Reader,

I originally had the idea for this romantic comedy years ago, when I was pregnant with my first child. In fact, an early draft of chapter one was given the Maggie Award of Excellence the week before my son was born. (My daughter came a year later, and it's safe to say a lot of my ideas were lost to lack of sleep during that time.) But this story idea would periodically, stubbornly, resurface and I am thrilled to finally share it with readers, especially in a collection with two other authors whose books I admire.

My heroine Erin Cross is about to make a New Year's resolution that leads to mistaken identity, chaos, danger and, ultimately, love. Whatever your resolutions are this year, I wish you luck in achieving them! With determination and effort, I believe anything is possible. (Even outsmarting the bad guys and winning the heart of an emotionally guarded but undeniably sexy federal agent.)

If you enjoy my novella, I hope you'll let me know on Facebook or Twitter and that you'll check out my Harlequin Blaze debut title, *Good with His Hands*, available in April 2015.

Happy reading!

Tanya Michaels

JUST A FLING

Tanya Michaels

For Pam Hopkins.
Thank you for a decade of great advice
and unfailing support.

CHAPTER ONE

BRUSHING AWAY THE snowflakes dotting her face, Erin Cross waited for her best friend to answer the door. She was surprised not to hear any of the usual rowdy laughter from inside and equally surprised that hers was the only car in the driveway.

When Bethany opened the door, her cute pixie features, which made her look a decade younger than mid-thirties, wrinkled in confusion. "What are you doing here?"

Erin held up the bottle of champagne she carried. "Um…happy New Year's Eve?"

"You're supposed to be on a date." As she spoke, Bethany moved aside so Erin could come in from the cold. The flurries that had been dusting North Carolina all day were beginning to stick.

Handing over the champagne so that she had both hands free to unbutton her coat, Erin sighed. "I know I said I'd go to that party with the man from my building." She hadn't meant to say yes, but he'd caught her off guard. "He's…nice, but the idea of kissing him at midnight was painfully awkward. Literally painful. It made my stomach hurt. So I told him I wasn't feeling well and decided to join you for girls' night."

Since Bethany's husband, Jason, an ER doctor, had to work tonight, Bethany had invited her three closest friends over, teasing that they had to make themselves scarce by 2:00 a.m. because that's when Jason would be home. They had their own private celebration planned.

"Ironic," Bethany said, "that the one person who RSVP'd no for girls' night is the only one who shows. Gemma called this afternoon to say the adorable nephews she played with at Christmas gave her a not-so-adorable flu. And Dee ran into Chad while she was getting coffee this morning. He talked her into going to his company party tonight."

They exchanged glances of sympathy and exasperation. Dee and Chad, who'd been stuck in the same on-again, off-again loop for three years, were crazy about each other. But, ultimately, they wanted different things out of life.

Bethany shook her head, her long blond hair swinging in a pendulum of disapproval. "To break free of each other, one of them is going to have to move to a different time zone."

Erin had already hung up her coat, but now she hesitated in the foyer. "If girls' night is a bust, do you want me to go?"

"Are you kidding? I have three bottles of champagne chilled, not including this one. Get your shapely butt in here."

"You know you don't have to pepper *every* conversation with ego-boosting compliments, right? I'm not as fragile as when we first met." The two of them belonged to the same gym. After Erin's divorce, she'd gone to burn off calories and hostility. Her self-confidence had been damaged not only by her husband's affair but the cruel things he'd said to her. Bethany had started as a casual workout partner but eventually became the big sister Erin never had.

At the kitchen island, Bethany filled a champagne flute for each of them. Erin sipped her drink, keenly aware of her friend's scrutiny. There was obviously something Bethany wanted to say, and she wasn't the type to censor herself. Trying to hold in an opinion might cause her brain to explode.

"Whatever it is," Erin prompted, "spit it out."

"You and Dee are exactly the same! Except for being total opposites."

Well, that made a ton of sense. "How much bubbly have you already had?" Erin teased.

"Dee knows what her long-term goals are but keeps sabotaging herself by falling into bed with Chad. You, on the other hand, say you're ready to date, that you've wasted enough time on the faithless ex, but you also keep sabotaging yourself. By *not* falling into bed. You haven't had sex in how long?"

That was too depressing to answer. "I want to have sex. In the abstract."

"Honey, that's not how it works. Sex is supposed to be tangible."

"I just meant I haven't met the right guy. I've gone on a couple dozen dates this year, but the chemistry… it's never felt natural or like the right time."

"But the faithless ex was the only guy you ever slept with," Bethany countered.

Erin, who'd skipped a grade early in her school career, had always been younger and shyer than her classmates. She'd just turned seventeen when she went to college and met her future husband.

"So being with someone else, *anyone* else," Bethany

said, "is bound to be a little awkward the first time. The longer you wait, the more pressure you put on yourself. Plus, even though you're a lot more outgoing and feisty since the divorce was finalized, I know that stuff he said hurt you."

"If we're going to rehash that, I might need something stronger than champagne," Erin grumbled. Learning of Steve's affair with his French receptionist—which confirmed the "paranoid" suspicions Erin had fought for months—had merely been the first blow. Equally painful had been the criticism he'd used in a petty attempt to justify his cheating. He'd called Erin dull and predictable, practically lifeless in bed.

"Maybe *he* was a terrible lover," Bethany said, "and you just didn't have enough experience to know better. What you need is a basis for comparison."

A startled laugh caused Erin to choke on her champagne. "So what are you suggesting, some kind of comparison study where I seduce guys in my building as research? That could make the tenant meetings a little awkward."

"So look beyond your building. There's got to be someone who revs your motor."

A number of television actors came to mind, but a full DVR was no substitute for a love life. Technically, there was *one* real-life possibility, but... Erin's cheeks heated.

"Yes!" Bethany pumped a fist in triumph.

"Don't get too excited. He works in the West Coast office." She was a service manager for a tech company, and Mike was one of their programmers in Seattle. "We've never actually met, but we've had to phone each other about various projects. Our conversations have been getting flirtatious."

"You do realize this proves my point? You feel safe responding to him because he's so far away, because there's no chance of anything physical happening. You have to get back in the saddle, so to speak." She frowned. "Although, Seattle's a little far for a fling. Especially since you don't fly."

Erin had only been on a plane once, as a little girl. Engine trouble had forced a harrowing emergency landing that had been just a few degrees shy of a crash. Following that traumatic ordeal, her parents had rented a car to complete the rest of the journey. She still had nightmares about flying. Or, rather, plummeting.

"I don't suppose this guy will be visiting North Carolina anytime soon?" Bethany asked hopefully.

"Um…no."

"Then why are you blushing like you're guilty of something? Man. Your parents must have busted your every lie when you were a kid."

"What lies? I wasn't exactly a reckless, sneaking-out-to-parties kid."

"It's time to make up for that by having a little reckless adult fun! Now, what aren't you telling me?"

"Mike will be in Cancun in a few weeks," Erin said. "The company's bringing together representatives from all our offices for a strategic convention. My boss asked if I wanted to go."

"To Cancun? During the bitter cold of winter? Of *course* you do! I'm dying of jealousy. Who's lucky enough to have a convention in Cancun?"

"Must happen more than you think, or they wouldn't have built the convention and exhibition space." Looking out the kitchen window at the fat snowflakes blanketing the yard, Erin imagined a warm beach. "I *want* to attend, especially if it means meeting Mike face-to-face, but—"

"Hold it right there. I am not letting you self-sabotage this time."

"I'd have to fly."

"You can do it! Mind over body, just like at the gym. I've seen you push through grueling workouts. We just need to psyche you up, bolster your resolve." Bethany grabbed the pad of paper that sat next to her kitchen phone and scrawled something across the top sheet. "Tape this to your bathroom mirror. Make it your mantra."

Erin read the sheet of paper.

NEW YEAR'S RESOLUTIONS:
1. Get on plane.
2. Get some action.

In black-and-white, it seemed so simple. "Okay," she heard herself say. Opportunities for adventure in her life were few and far between.

I deserve some excitement. And she planned to find it in Cancun.

CHAPTER TWO

RISK AND REWARD. Erin had overcome her first hurdle—
white-knuckling her way through a seemingly endless
flight—and now she was on a beautiful, sunny beach.
Get on plane. Get some action. She was halfway there.
So far, she had no regrets.

Who knew late January could feel like this? She
doubted she'd actually get in the water, but more intrepid tourists had. She fit right in among them in an
electric-blue bikini, beaded flip-flops and a skirt that
tied at the waist. She'd almost pulled on a shirt over the
bathing suit, but Bethany's drill-sergeant condition-
ing echoed in her head. It was time to be the *new* Erin.

Bethany had helped her shop for the trip, vetoing Erin's more conservative choices, arguing that her friend
was in the best shape of her life. "You won't be twenty-
six forever. You really want to look back later and regret that you wasted prime bikini years?"

Frankly, Erin doubted her deep future regrets would
involve swimwear, but she'd be covering up plenty once
the business meetings started tomorrow afternoon.
Today was for her. In anticipation of meeting Mike,
she'd splurged on a mani-pedi and a sassy new hair-
cut, the shortest she'd ever worn it. Would he like what
he saw?

They'd agreed to have their first meeting at the open-air bar behind the hotel, rather than in the lobby where they would be in view of any colleagues checking in. Too anxious to sit with nothing to do, Erin had already ordered the house specialty—a frothy, rum-based drink sporting a paper umbrella. Reminding herself to sip it, rather than gulp it down in an attempt to fortify her nerves, she scanned the beach from behind white-framed sunglasses. She wished Mike had sent a picture that allowed her to get a better look at his face.

He'd emailed a photo with the teasing subject line that even programming geeks had their athletic moments— it was a slightly blurry group shot of a sweaty company softball team hoisting a trophy. Clearly taller than most of his coworkers, he'd been placed in the back row. He was dark-haired and seemed attractive under the smudges of dirt on his face, but it was hard to make out much detail. She'd almost asked him to send a differ-ent photo, but she hadn't wanted to seem hung up on physical appearances.

Hopefully, there'd be chemistry between them, but if not…well, New Year's resolutions weren't blood oaths. No matter what Bethany said about the wisdom of a tropical fling, Erin wasn't obligated to invite him back to her hotel room. She was only obligated to keep an open mind and see what developed.

It was a gorgeous day, and she was about to meet a guy who never failed to make her smile when they talked on the phone. What was the worst that could happen?

FINALLY. AFTER AN hour of pretending to read a book while surreptitiously studying the beach, FBI Agent Campbell Foster had a solid prospect. The fidgety woman in the bright blue bikini top radiated tension, clearly waiting for someone. He couldn't see her expression behind the huge sunglasses, but whenever she set down her glass, liquid sloshed as if her hands were shaking. The sun glinted off the coppery red highlights threaded through her auburn hair. Her height and build were right.

Ellen Hodge, I presume.

Unlike so many in the current "selfie" culture, Ellen was camera-shy. Not because the journalist was modest, if the rumors about her flirting to get close to sources were true, but because it was more difficult to snoop when people recognized you. The official ID shot Foster had been given of the disgraced reporter was a couple of years old. In it, her hair had been a more brilliant red, curling past her shoulders. Now that she was on Lance Balducci's bad side, she'd been wise to change her appearance.

Wiser still would have been to dress differently. While a bikini wasn't out of place in their surroundings, the bright top hugging her perfectly curved chest was like a beacon to any red-blooded male. Even from here, Foster could appreciate—

He abruptly switched gears, determined to view her with professional detachment. *Focus on the job.* He only had a few weeks left, and he was going to leave the Bureau on a victory—not that arresting Balducci would erase past mistakes, but maybe Foster would start sleeping better at night. All he needed was to escort the reluctant witness safely back to Atlanta. By this time next month, he'd be standing at the front of a college classroom. No more crime bosses and serial killers.

No more worrying that an error on his part could get someone killed.

Leisurely, as if there were nothing more important beckoning him than a frosty beer, he tossed the paperback novel into his beach bag and rose from his chair. He kept his pace relaxed as he approached her, but she lacked his training in discretion. She jolted in her chair when she saw him, and swallowed hard. Balducci was a formidable man. Would she try to run again, rather than return with Foster and testify?

He stopped by her chair, keeping his voice low and soothing. "You must be—"

"Erin," she squeaked, quickly cutting him off. So that he wouldn't have the chance to call her Ellen? It made sense she'd be traveling under an alias, although she should have picked something further from her real name. "I've been expecting you." She pressed her palm to her forehead. "That sounded like a line from a bad movie. Sorry. I'm a little nervous."

A little? She looked as if she was on the verge of cardiac arrest.

"Completely understandable." He slid into the chair next to her, taking the opportunity to check the perimeter. "I wasn't sure it was you at first—you've changed your hair."

As she babbled an answer about not being used to the new hairstyle herself, his attention snagged on two large men on the other side of the bar. Both wore flower-print shirts and held full glasses. Which neither of them drank from.

They kept eyeing "Erin." Guys admiring a woman who looked like her wasn't out of the norm, but when the breeze ruffled one man's hideously bright shirt, it revealed a suspicious bulge strapped to his side. A bulge that looked a lot like the one strapped to Foster's side beneath his rayon button-down.

The worst thing he could do would be to panic Erin or suddenly drag her from the beach. They needed a casual cover that would help them blend with the other tourists. It would be best if they appeared to be vacationing lovers, rather than reluctant witness and federal agent. And if he kissed her, it would prevent the goons from getting a good look at her.

He leaned toward her. In a voice so low it was nearly inaudible, he whispered, "Trust me." Then he cupped his fingers in her short, silky hair and slanted his mouth across hers, stealing her opportunity to protest or ask questions. In her own way, she'd been "undercover" before; she should have the sense to play along.

He meant to keep his concentration on the men across the bar, but, damn, she was distracting. She tasted like rum and sunshine and woman. When her lips parted beneath his, he reflexively deepened the kiss. But her sudden shoving him with both hands helped kill the moment. The woman who'd kissed him back so sweetly had murder in her eyes.

So much for playing along. "I can explain—"

She shot to her feet. "No need. I know *exactly* what you were thinking! And, okay, maybe I've thought about it, maybe I even… But a few phone flirtations aren't carte blanche to pounce on me like I'm some desperate, sure thing!"

"Ellen—"

"It's Erin! At least get my name right, you pig."

Whirling around, his best shot at putting away Lance Balducci did exactly what she'd done two weeks ago. She ran.

As SOON AS THE elevator doors opened, Erin hurried onto the third floor, frantic to get to her room and regain her composure. She wished her cellular plan included long-distance calls. She'd never needed Bethany's advice more.

Did I overreact? Bolting because of a single kiss wasn't the most sophisticated thing she'd ever done, but, between hormones and rum, she hadn't been able to think clearly.

On the one hand, ohmigod, was Mike gorgeous. Tall and broad shouldered with black hair and penetrating blue eyes. But on the other hand, given that he'd kissed her less than sixty seconds after meeting her, he obviously had other penetration in mind. *Slimeball.* She was not some skank who jumped into bed after barely exchanging hellos.

Another few minutes of that kiss, and I might have been. What had panicked her more, his presumption or her own unexpected reaction? At the touch of his lips to hers, unfamiliar heat had surged through her.

Her hand trembled as she pulled the key card out of her skirt pocket. Behind her, the elevator doors chimed.

"Ellen! Wait, we have to talk."

Now a different kind of fear snaked through her. That was the second time he'd called her by the wrong name. Something felt off here, and she was no longer safely in public with the guy.

"Go away," she ordered. Relief swelled within her as she stumbled through the doorway of her room, but he was right on her heels. He blocked the door with his arm and invaded her room, closing the door behind them with an ominous click.

Oh, God. Her New Year's resolution had gone terribly wrong. *Get on plane. Get murdered in hotel room.*

"You're safe with me." He spoke in a calm, comforting tone.

Funny how she didn't feel calm *or* comforted.

"I'm not one of Balducci's men," he said. "I know you have good reason to be afraid, but I'll take care of you. The plane tickets are right here in my bag."

The phrase "plane tickets" jumped out at her. He wasn't just trying to seduce her, he was trying to abduct her! She grabbed the closest thing she could use as a weapon—a small umbrella—and brandished it at him. "I'm not going anywhere with you! I told all the girls in my department I was meeting you today," she lied. "If I don't show up for the team-building session tomorrow—"

Moving so quickly her eyes could barely follow him, he seized the umbrella and disarmed her. "I'm Agent Campbell Foster, with the FBI. You weren't waiting for me?"

She shook her head wildly. "I was waiting for a computer geek from Seattle!"

"Seriously? You aren't lying because you're afraid for your life?"

"Why would I be afraid for my life? Except, of course, that I'm trapped with a maniac."

"I'm not a maniac, I'm a federal agent. And we need to get out of here." He grabbed her arm, tugging her toward the balcony. "Two men with guns are on our trail. I'm only one man with a gun. And a hysterical woman."

"You have a gun?" Hearing her own shrill words, she realized he might be right about the hysteria.

On the other side of her door, there was metallic rattling. As if someone were messing with the lock. A fresh spike of adrenaline shot through her.

Okay, *now* she was afraid for her life.

CHAPTER THREE

FOSTER'S MIND RACED. Later, he'd sort out how a screwup of this magnitude was even possible—and what in the hell had happened to the real Ellen Hodge?—but for now, he had a civilian to save. One who was currently ranting about the consequences of hooking up with a stranger and swearing that no sex was worth this amount of trouble.

Her balcony was semiprivate, with a solid ledge in front and boxed plants on either side. Over the inset hedges, he could glimpse the adjacent balconies. "We're going next door. It's only about a five-foot wall." The five feet up was nothing compared to the fifty feet down. He gave her a boost, then hoisted himself over. An elderly woman in an orange caftan dropped the book she was reading and gaped at them.

"American federal agent, ma'am." Keeping his voice low, Foster fished out his badge. "No time to explain, but we have to borrow your room for a minute. You could really help us if you keep reading and act normal."

At her stunned nod, he jerked open the door to the room and shoved Erin inside.

"Is it safe to leave her out there?" she whispered.

"Should be. No one's after her." With any luck, the bad guys would assume they went to the right, away from observers. But Foster had his fingers curled around his gun, prepared for any eventuality.

"Why the hell would anyone be after me?"

"I was supposed to meet a witness here and give her protective escort back to Atlanta, Georgia. You fit her description. The people she's running from thought so, too. Simple case of mistaken identity."

"A *simple*—"

Foster silenced her with a hand pressed to her mouth. "Lady," he whispered, "there's no point in hiding from the bad guys if you plan to make enough noise for them to find you."

She pulled away from him and plopped down on the bed with an angry thud, but when she spoke again, it was a murmur. "Do these bad guys think I'm her because they saw me with you?"

"I don't know." Everything about this was wrong. They shouldn't have known who he was or that he was supposed to meet Ellen here. Balducci had deep pockets—enough to buy an informant in the Bureau?

"You probably endangered my life just by talking to me!"

His jaw clenched. "Or I saved your life. They might have come after you anyway, and you wouldn't have had my protection."

"What now?"

"We wait. If they see the little old lady out there and she remains calm, they'll assume we went the other way, which buys us some time."

"And if she gives us away?"

He glanced pointedly at the gun.

A door creaked open behind them, causing Erin to

jump, but she didn't let out a sound. Foster pivoted, his finger on the safety.

An elderly man wearing a robe with the hotel emblem emerged from the bathroom and jerked his hands into the air. "Our money's in the room safe! What have you done with Gloria?"

Foster lowered his gun. "Take it easy, sir. Gloria's out on the balcony, and we're not here to rob you." Dammit, he was supposed to be undercover. Announcing his presence to every guest in the hotel hadn't been in the plans. He was reaching for his badge to reassure the man when Gloria came inside, looking smug.

She winked at Foster, then rushed to the old man's side. "Oh, Arthur, this is the best anniversary ever! You didn't tell me you got us one of those Murder Mystery Vacations!" She planted a loud kiss on his cheek, and Arthur reddened.

"Yes, well…only the best for you, dear. I, uh, know how much you love that Agatha Christie collection of yours."

Gloria turned back to Erin and Foster. "Two guys popped up over the plants, but I was cool as a cucumber. They said they were hotel security, but I didn't like the looks of 'em. They're playing the bad guys, aren't they?"

"Yes, ma'am." That's how this was beginning to feel—like a surreal play in which Foster didn't know his lines. But he gave Gloria an encouraging nod.

"They asked if I'd seen anyone, and I told them Arthur and I saw flamenco dancers last night and that I'd highly recommend the show. Of course, it wasn't nearly as exciting as *this*. What else can I do to help?"

"YOU READY?"

Erin felt as if she were lip-reading rather than actually hearing Agent Foster's words. He was probably whispering because of how sound reverberated in the stairwell. Then again, even if he'd spoken in a normal tone of voice, the sound would have been muffled by her pounding heart.

She didn't bother answering his question. How could she possibly be "ready" to leave the comparative safety of her hotel with a man she didn't know and cross the lobby while armed men lurked somewhere nearby, wishing her harm? Her life would be a hell of a lot simpler if the bad guys and good guys bothered with minor details like positive identification.

Trying to distract herself from impending doom, she adjusted the fuchsia-and-lime-print fabric weighing her down. "What's that sweet old lady going to do when she doesn't get her clothes back?"

"Judging from her closet, she had muʻumuus to spare." Agent Foster had asked if they could borrow one of Gloria's caftans, which Erin had thrown on over her bathing suit. He'd refused to let her go back to her own room for a change of clothes or anything else, warning that at least one of the men was probably waiting in there.

Her sole possessions were the few things she'd had in her pocket earlier, a blue bikini, a pair of flip-flops, a mile-long beach dress and another woman's floppy straw hat. "I feel like an idiot." She envied his simpler disguise, a ball cap and pair of shades he'd pulled from his duffel bag.

"Better a live idiot than a dead babe in a bikini."

It was almost startling to hear someone besides Bethany compliment her. "You think I'm a babe?"

He snorted. "Women. Men are trying to kill you, and you're worried about what you look like. No wonder I never got married."

She resented the implication that she was shallow. "Or maybe you never got married because no woman would put up with you."

"A strong possibility," he admitted. "Now, when I open this door, your instinct will be to haul ass outside and throw yourself into a cab. But walking quickly or acting furtive will draw notice. It's imperative you be nonchalant, just another tourist headed out for the evening. Eyes forward. Casual and relaxed."

He'd just reminded her men wanted to kill her, now he wanted her to relax. "Tell you what," she snapped, "I'll shoot at you and *you* be nonchalant." Hearing the unfamiliar bite of sarcasm in her voice, she sighed. "I normally have a very sunny disposition."

"I know you're scared, but I won't let anything happen to you. Until this is over, sunshine, I am your personal bodyguard." Then he reached for the door handle, and it was go time.

Mind over body. She took a step forward. *Deep breaths. Try not to think about the thugs who want to permanently end your breathing.*

When she'd checked into the hotel, she'd been charmed by the airy, flower-bedecked lobby with its festive atmosphere and bright colors. Now the expansive room seemed like a death trap. She battled the urge to flinch at her own staccato footsteps on the marble tile.

Covering the distance to the revolving glass door was the hardest thing she'd ever done. On top of everything else, she couldn't fathom that she was leaving her belongings behind. Her passport, an heirloom pearl necklace. *What am I doing?*

She turned to tell Agent Foster she'd changed her mind, that she wasn't comfortable leaving with him, but when she looked back, she saw a man sprinting toward them, shoving a luggage cart out of his way as he gained speed. His vacation clothes were bright and festive, but his expression was steely.

"Go!" Agent Foster gave her a little push, propelling her outside, and the next thing she knew, they were in a cab.

ERIN SPENT THE entire cab ride braced for danger, half expecting the sound of squealing tires and bullets behind them. But it appeared they'd made a clean getaway. Agent Foster had the driver take them to a hotel several miles inland. But once they'd been dropped off, instead of going inside, the agent knelt on the sidewalk as if he were tying his sneaker.

After the taxi was out of view, he stood. "C'mon." He led her across the street with one arm around her shoulders. To anyone watching, it would be a casual, affectionate gesture but she recognized it as protective. After so many months of physical intimacy limited to occasional hugs from Bethany, his closeness was overwhelming. It was impossible not to think about their kiss on the beach. And, although it was a ridiculous detail to notice under the circumstances, she liked the way he smelled, a combination of deodorant and his own earthier male scent.

They walked about a block, until they reached a shabby motel. The sign out front proclaiming Rooms

Available didn't surprise her. Why would anyone stay here voluntarily?

The inside was as dismal as the exterior. The lobby floor was cracked, with some tiles missing completely, and the registration desk was flanked by two faded pots sporting a pair of ferns in varying stages of death. Not the kind of establishment that offered room service.

Maybe not even the kind of establishment that offered indoor plumbing.

Her self-proclaimed bodyguard approached the clerk who was thumbing through a magazine. "Need a room."

The man's eyes flicked to the two of them and their luggage, consisting of one duffel bag. "You paying by the night or by the hour?"

"My wife and I would like to stay the night."

There was a brief exchange of cash and room key. She'd never stayed anywhere before where a photo ID and credit card number weren't required. Then again, today had been full of unprecedented circumstances.

When they entered the shoe-box-size room, she flicked the light switch. Only one of the bulbs in the overhead fixture illuminated. Erin removed her sunglasses to better see in the dim lighting, then wished she hadn't. Furnishings were comprised of a lone bed that barely qualified as a double and a bulky television set on a folding card table. There was no nightstand or chair or even a phone, which she supposed cut down the number of complaint calls to the front desk. The ugly shag carpet was an indeterminate brown, and there appeared to be a cigarette burn in the plaid comforter across the sagging mattress.

"Oh, shoot," Erin said mildly. "We forgot to ask the manager if they have free Wi-Fi."

Agent Foster's lips twitched in a half smile. "Pretty sure continental breakfast is out of the question, too."

She shuddered. "I don't think I'd eat anything they serve in this place."

"Well, I've got dinner in here, but it'll have to tide us over for tonight." He pulled two protein bars and small bottles of water out of the duffel bag.

She accepted them almost numbly. "Got anything stronger than water in there?" To think, a couple of hours ago, she'd been happily sipping a frothy drink with a high rum content and waiting to meet her potential fling. *Bethany would be so proud—here I am, right on schedule, shacked up in a hotel room with a hot guy.* A high-pitched laugh bubbled up, at first just a stray giggle, but once she started, she couldn't stop.

Clapping a hand over her mouth, she tried to stifle her inappropriate amusement. "I'm sorry…" She gulped for air, trying to calm herself. "N-none of this is funny. I… You must think I'm unhinged," she said when she was finally able to regain some control.

"On the contrary, I think you've held up pretty well, all things considered." His indigo eyes were full of understanding. "You haven't cried. You apparently haven't lost your sense of humor. Pretty impressive, sunshine."

"Thank you." If the situation had gone according to plan, and she'd had her rendezvous with Mike, would *he* have been impressed with her? Would he have found her as appealing in person as he seemed to over the phone, or would he have shared her ex-husband's disappointment? Ludicrous thoughts, given her predicament, but it felt safer to dwell on Mike's reaction than her sudden life-or-death need to flee the country. She still wasn't sure how she was going to manage that without a passport.

Her earlier hysterical laughter had faded, replaced with wry disbelief. "To think, when I got up this morning, my biggest concern was whether my blind date would be happy with what he saw." Crap. That probably sounded frivolous and vain.

Agent Foster's dark brows shot up. "You worried about whether he'd be happy with you? In that blue bikini top?" His gaze scorched a trail from the top of her head to the pedicured tips of her toes. He made her feel like the sexiest woman alive—which was quite a feat given her floppy hat and glaring muumuu.

"Th-thank you, Agent Foster."

"Just call me Foster. Everyone does. And it seems silly to stand on formality if we're going to be sharing a bed tonight."

CHAPTER FOUR

GET A GRIP, MAN. Seated on the creaky bed, Foster curled his hands into fists atop his thighs. What was wrong with him? Granted, the woman whose kiss had short-circuited his brain earlier today was currently naked on the other side of the paper-thin wall. He could hear the groan of pipes as water rained down on her in the shower. He could easily imagine—

No! No imagining. Had he learned *nothing* at Quantico? It didn't matter how appealing Erin was, he was on a mission: get enough evidence on Lance Balducci to put the crooked businessman behind bars. Lusting after an innocent bystander was not part of Foster's job description. Neither her delectable curves nor her meadow-green eyes factored into the equation. He was a trained professional, and he knew better than to buy into the sense of false intimacy just because they were trapped in a shared hotel room for the night.

Tearing himself away from thoughts that could only lead to trouble, Foster pulled an untraceable burner phone from his duffel bag. He dialed a number from memory. The original plan had been to fly home with Ellen tonight but, not knowing if there was someone on the inside feeding Balducci information, he was having to go off script.

His supervisor, special agent in charge Morgan Brenner, answered immediately. "Brenner here."

Foster took a deep breath. Despite the possibility of a leak in his department, every cell in his being told him he could trust Brenner. Which meant his boss would likely go ballistic when he heard about the change in plans. "I don't have Ellen Hodge," he said without preamble.

"No kidding," Morgan answered. "She's here in Atlanta, and she's in critical condition. We've got a problem."

"*A* problem?" Foster pinched the bridge of his nose, thinking over the best way to tell Morgan about Erin and the possible informant who'd led Balducci's men to Cancun so quickly. "We should be so lucky."

TO ERIN'S SURPRISE, the hotel actually had running water. It just couldn't be described as warm.

She'd hoped for a hot shower to ease some of the tension from her rigid muscles, but the sputtering stream coming through the nozzle could most generously be labeled tepid. *Does it really matter?* If she were honest with herself, standing under the shower spray was only her way of stalling. And even if she stood here until kingdom come, it wouldn't erase the memory of the way Campbell Foster had looked at her. Chemistry had sizzled between them, unexpected and unwanted.

Sure, he was a completely sexy man. And, sure, he was a hell of a kisser. But...

Erin blinked, wiping water out of her eyes. Where had she been going with this train of thought? Nowhere, she told herself sternly.

To Agent Foster, she was a...mission. Nothing else.

He probably rescued damsels in distress all the time. She was attaching more importance to him than was warranted simply because he'd saved her life. Understandable, really. But she wasn't going to confuse gratitude with anything more meaningful.

Resolute, she reached for the knob and shut off the water. Unfortunately, there were no thick, downy soft towels awaiting her, as there had been in her previous hotel room. Instead, she grabbed a ragged cloth the color of yellowing ivory. Her clothing options were severely limited. She didn't even have proper underwear! She would have to wear her bikini bottoms underneath the cotton T-shirt Foster had produced from his bag. She knew it was meant to be his change of clothes, but he'd given it to her.

The soft, faded cotton slid over her skin, falling past her thighs and practically to her knees. There was something ridiculously personal about wearing a man's clothes. The shirt was blue. She found herself wishing she could see him in it, betting the color brought out his eyes. The fabric smelled faintly of the same soap she'd breathed in when he kissed her on the beach.

Erin glared at her reflection. "No more thinking about that!" Yeah, she'd just wipe one of the hottest kisses she'd ever experienced from her mind. Easy peasy.

Feeling oddly exposed even though all the pertinent bits were covered, she exited the cubbyhole of a bathroom. Foster was sitting on the edge of the bed, his head in his hands.

She drew up at the sight of him. His position made him seem almost...vulnerable. He sighed. "You are definitely not Ellen Hodge."

If not for the note of defeat in his voice, she might have made a joke about that. Had there really been any lingering question about her identity?

He met her gaze. "Not that I thought you were, intellectually. But hearing my screwup confirmed… The real Ellen isn't even in Mexico. She was rushed to an Atlanta hospital midmorning after a car accident. Well, 'accident' isn't entirely accurate. There were bullet holes in the vehicle."

Cold fear skewered her. There'd been talk of men with guns all evening, but now it was real, not just abstract conversation. "Is she…?" She couldn't bring herself to say it, not even about a faceless woman she'd never met.

"She's alive," Foster said. "But unconscious."

"I don't understand." She paced the shag carpet. "If this man—what did you say his name was?"

"Lance Balducci."

"If Balducci got to her today, then he obviously knows she isn't here. He had time to call off his men before you and I met this afternoon. Why would anyone be after *me*?"

"To be honest, I don't know yet how this went wrong. Ellen Hodge was a reporter, briefly, but she was known to put ambition before integrity. She's not thirty yet, and she's worked at three different papers. She was fired from at least one. We know she was following a senator's aide, hoping he would lead her to a sex scandal, but instead she saw him assassinated by Balducci. She contacted the Bureau days later, saying she'd skipped the country but would be willing to come back and testify if we gave her protective escort. Only, if she was driving around Atlanta today, it looks as if she never intended to make our meeting."

Before she could respond, he let loose an explosive oath that made her jump. "I can't believe this is happening. I thought I'd botched up before, but this..."

She sat next to him, oddly compelled to comfort him. "It's not your fault. You stuck to the plan."

"It was supposed to be simple. Bring her in to testify, then I was getting out. Retiring. Leading a nice, dull life."

"I've had nice and dull. You aren't missing much." Her gaze locked with his. "I know it's none of my business, but aren't you way too young for retirement?"

Something haunted and bleak flashed in the depths of his eyes. "You're right. It's none of your business." He stood abruptly, saying nothing else. The decisive click of the bathroom door closing spoke for him.

FOSTER WAS LEANING into the water, lathering shampoo into his hair, when he heard the scream. *Erin!* Without pausing to question how they'd been found or what danger might await him, he lurched out of the shower and grabbed his gun off the counter. Suds dripped into his face and stung his eyes. He grabbed one of the ridiculously small towels and swiped it across his face. He had no time for anything else. Every second counted, and he'd sworn to protect her.

Throwing open the bathroom door, he cocked his gun. Dimly, he made out the image of Erin standing on the bed, but saw no one else in the room. She spun toward him and screamed again.

"Ohmigod! You're *naked*!"

He lowered the gun and scrambled for the discarded

towel, holding it in front of him as he demanded, "What are you screaming about?"

She waved a hand at something on the other side of the bed. "That!" The single word was infused with terror.

He stalked over to the side of the bed, where a spider nearly the size of his palm scuttled across the floor. "But it's just a—"

"A spider!" She sounded far more upset about the arachnid than about Foster not being dressed.

He was aiming his gun when common sense caught up with him. Shooting the bug was definite overkill. He grabbed one of his shoes.

Erin was still talking, her voice quivering. "It was coming right at me! And it's huge! It's probably some poisonous, tropical variety! It's—"

Thud. "A stain on the wall," he finished for her. "You okay?"

He held the towel strategically in front of him and waited for confirmation that she was all right. Now that the crisis had passed, he felt ridiculous, standing there dripping wet and naked. The towel didn't cover much, he knew, but it at least allowed him the illusion of dignity.

Erin finally took a deep breath. "I—I'm fine now, Agent Foster."

"Foster," he reminded her. "No need to stand on ceremony now that you've seen…" Well, everything there was to see.

"Thank you. Foster."

He was stunned by the breathy gratitude in her voice. By his count, he'd saved her life three times today, but she'd yet to look at him with that particular glint of hero worship in her eyes. Apparently, smashing eight-legged bugs was the way to this woman's heart. But if he stood here any longer, the appreciative expression in her eyes was going to cause a reaction the threadbare terry cloth couldn't mask. Throwing a strangled "you're welcome" over his shoulder, Foster beat a hasty retreat back to the bathroom.

She's an assignment, just part of the job. You cannot be attracted to her. Definitely not. Despite the judgment errors he'd made in the past, not even he was that stupid.

ERIN PULLED THE sheets down and inspected the bed thoroughly.

From behind her, an amused masculine voice asked, "What are you doing?"

She stiffened. She hadn't realized Foster was finished in the bathroom. *Please, God, when I turn around, let him be wearing clothes.* She glanced over her shoulder and wasn't disappointed. Or...maybe she was. His shirt, the same one he'd worn earlier, hung unbuttoned over his bare chest, and he'd put on a pair of gym shorts.

While the clothing was far better for Erin's peace of mind than his nudity, she knew from her earlier glimpses that Campbell Foster had the type of body it was almost a crime to conceal.

She squeezed her eyes shut, hoping it would blot out the mental image of his naked body. Instead, her imagination summoned new images, this time of both of them naked and...

Her eyes flew open, and she prayed she wasn't blushing. Finally, she remembered his original question. "I'm getting ready for bed." How in the hell were they going to share the small mattress? Her entire body buzzed with the memory of the way he'd kissed her, to say nothing of how he'd looked when he'd raced to her rescue, every muscle primed for attack, water coursing down his torso.

With an unexpectedly affectionate grin, he waved her aside. "Better let me do that. You're obviously looking for more eight-legged visitors," he deduced. "What are you gonna do if you actually find one?"

She stepped away from the bed so quickly she almost lost her footing.

He rifled through the covers and assured her the mattress was uninhabited. Then he just stood there, between her and the bed, regarding her with a bemused expression. "You're an interesting woman."

The corners of her mouth lifted in a wan smile. "I don't know, some men find me distinctly dull."

"Some?" He peered at her. "Or one in particular?"

"My ex-husband, not that his opinion counts. It's funny, I barely even miss him—except when it comes to killing certain bugs—so why would anything he said have the power to hurt me?"

"Maybe because he was the person who was supposed to know you better than anyone else, so deep down you wonder if his words have any merit," Foster speculated. "But you are not dull. Eccentric, maybe, but—"

"Me?" There was a word that had never been used to describe her.

He nodded. "You barely blinked at executing a daring balcony escape, yet a mere spider—"

"It was the size of a cat!"

Foster chuckled, and she realized it was a laugh she could grow to like. She thought of the kiss they'd shared and the way he'd rushed to her defense in the middle of his shower. There was a lot about him she could like. Suddenly, the already miniscule room shrank even smaller. Desire tingled through her, making her shiver. It was a tiny movement, but Foster caught it.

"Are you okay?" He came to her side, studying her with concern.

"I…" After everything that had happened today, there was no way she could convincingly say she was all right. But she couldn't tell him what she'd really been thinking, either. "Guess I'm just tired. It's been a draining day."

"And we'll be flying out early. Let's get you into bed."

Hearing him mention her and bed in the same sentence made her knees go liquid. She'd been celibate since her divorce, and largely celibate during the last few months of her marriage. Now she was spending the night with one of the most intriguing men she'd ever met. The thought of making up for lost time in Foster's arms, imagining everything he could do to her right here on this mattress, made her tremble.

"You're in shock," he pronounced.

"No, I'm really not."

"You keep shivering, and it can't possibly be because you're cold. It's a sauna in here. The air-conditioning unit must be older than both of us put together."

She swallowed. "True. It's very hot."

"I know you're probably keyed up after all the adrenaline today, but you should try to get some rest."

When she lay down, it emphasized how small the bed was. Bigger than a single, but not by much. It would be difficult to keep space between them. Foster must have been thinking along the same lines.

"Would you sleep better if I crashed on the floor?" he offered. "It wouldn't be the worst place I've ever bunked."

She glanced at the hideous carpet. "I have trouble believing that. You saved my life today, the least I can do is give you half the bed."

"Okay." He drew the sheet over her, then surprised her by smoothing the hair away from her face.

He went to the light switch and a moment later, the room was pitch-black. She followed the sound of his footsteps as he returned, and the mattress groaned as he stretched out on top of the sheet. Earlier, when they'd been walking to the hotel, she'd noticed he smelled good. Fresh from the shower, he smelled even better. Resisting the urge to inhale deeply, she rolled on her side, facing away from the agent with the incredible blue eyes. Not that she could see them in the dark, but when she closed her own eyes, his face was vivid in her imagination. The tiny crinkles at the corners of his eyes when he smiled at her, his strong jaw. His lips.

Of all the things she could regret about today, the one that stood out in her mind was how quickly she'd shoved him away when he kissed her at the bar. If she had to do it all over again, she'd let herself savor the experience.

Next to her, Foster yawned. "Sweet dreams, sunshine."

With the immediate danger past and her adrenaline subsiding, fatigue came in their place. Lassitude seeped through her. With the heat of Foster's body against her back and the memory of his mouth on hers, she fell into very sweet dreams, indeed.

CHAPTER FIVE

EITHER ERIN WAS overcoming her fear of flying—especially impressive on this small plane, which jostled with every air pocket—or she was so humiliated by the way her day started that plummeting out of the sky didn't seem much worse than facing Foster.

She'd awakened more or less wrapped around him. The sheet had been displaced during the night. They lay in the middle of the bed, limbs entwined. Half-asleep and confused by her surroundings, she'd clumsily tried to extricate herself from his embrace. When her thigh came into contact with something hard, she'd unthinkingly blurted, "You sleep with your gun?"

"My gun," he'd answered in a strained voice, "is up by my pillow."

Hours later, the memory still suffused her face with heat. Too bad she hadn't stayed in the tropics long enough to pick up a tan; a little bit of color might help hide her blush.

When the pilot began their descent, she found herself clutching the armrest between her and Foster. Okay, maybe she wasn't completely over her flying phobia. But she'd made real progress. She'd been in the air twice in as many days, definitely fulfilling the "get on plane" part of her resolution. She tried valiantly not to think about the unfulfilled other half.

They landed at a small airport north of Atlanta amid drizzle and predictions for heavier rain later. The January sky was dark with bloated clouds, and wisps of fog surrounded them. She hoped the bleak weather wasn't an omen.

"The fog is creepy." She shivered, wishing she weren't wearing short sleeves. "A person expects to run into Jack the Ripper with ambience like this." But she didn't need to worry about a long-dead London killer. She had corrupt businessman Lance Balducci after her. According to what Foster had told her, the rich and powerful Balducci was based in Atlanta but had offices in multiple cities and spent a few weeks out of the year in DC.

As she and Foster crossed the parking lot, he placed his arm around her in that same protective, shielding gesture as when they'd walked to their hotel yesterday. It had stirred her senses then, but the effect was even more potent now, after seeing him naked and waking in his arms. Trying to regain her composure, she reflexively shied away from him.

"Sorry." She met his reproving gaze. "I didn't mean that to be rude."

"You didn't hurt my delicate feelings, sunshine. But until I'm confident that you're out of danger, your instinct should be to move closer to me, not farther away."

"I understand. It was involuntary. Since my divorce, I'm just not used to people being in my space." Well. That probably told him more about her embarrassing lack of a sex life than he needed to know.

What about *his* love life? she wondered suddenly. Despite his occasionally gruff manner, he had some very attractive qualities. "You don't have a girlfriend, right? I know that when you kissed me yesterday, it wasn't real, and maybe the girlfriend of an FBI agent has to accept some undercover moments most lovers wouldn't, but I would *hate* to be—"

"Calm down, there's no girlfriend." He steered them toward a car with tinted windows, unlocking the doors with a key remote when they were a few steps away. "But I'm guessing by your near-stroke on the subject of fidelity that your ex-husband cheated?"

With the exception of some cathartic venting to Bethany, Erin hated discussing the affair. It should be a source of shame for Steve—*he* was the one who broke his vows—but the fact that she hadn't been able to hold her husband's attention sometimes felt like failure on her part. "Yes. He did."

"Ass," Foster said succinctly.

A grin tugged at her lips. "Yes. He is."

Minutes later, they were on the road. The first order of business was finding the nearest restaurant drive-through.

"I don't know about you," Foster said as he rolled down the window, "but I plan on getting one of everything on the menu." He'd managed to keep them from starving, but neither of them had eaten a bona fide meal since they'd met on the beach yesterday afternoon.

Their next stop was one of those twenty-acre "super" stores that sold everything, including big-screen TVs, smoked gouda and blue jeans. The bright beach clothes that had worked as adequate camouflage in Cancun made her stick out like a sore thumb in Metro Atlanta in January. Plus, she was freezing.

"I realize the options aren't exactly high fashion," he said as he swung a left into the parking lot, "but we need to get you some essentials, then meet with Morgan. Aside from me, he's the only person I'm comfortable with you talking to until we know more."

It was insane how radically her universe had narrowed. Last week, she had a group of regular girlfriends and enough clothes that she'd been able to cover her bed with options when deciding what to pack. Now she owned one outfit and her personal interaction stopped and started with Campbell Foster.

"I don't suppose there's any way I can call my best friend and let her know I'm—"

"No. She'll be full of questions you can't answer. And you don't want to put anyone you care about in the position of trying to lie for you if someone comes looking."

"In North Carolina?" Was that really a possibility? Her heart thudded frantically against her ribs.

"Once they knew your hotel room in Mexico, figuring out who you are wouldn't have been hard. A bribe to an unprincipled desk clerk could get them your address in under ten minutes."

Oh, God. She'd been clinging to the half-formed notion that she was reaching the end of her surreal adventure. With Foster back among his fellow agents, they'd figure out how to take down Balducci, and she'd be on her merry way. That hope had helped her endure the past twelve hours. But she'd known deep down, like a kid who's outgrown Santa Claus but isn't ready to admit it, that her overly simplistic scenario wasn't going to happen.

As if realizing that his bald assessment of the situation had upset her, he injected a deliberate note of cheer into his voice. "At least you have shopping to look forward to," he said as he parked the car. "Or are you not one of those women who subscribes to retail therapy?"

"Actually, I prefer a good workout to clear my head."

He nodded. "Works wonders, doesn't it? After my last ca— Sorry. We're supposed to be focusing on getting you what you need, not discussing my favorite pieces of gym equipment."

Although she didn't pry, curiosity gnawed at her. What had he been on the verge of saying about his last case? He'd hinted before that it hadn't gone well. She fervently hoped it hadn't included someone under Foster's protection getting hurt. *Or worse.*

Inside the store, she went for some basics—a package of socks, jeans, a pair of inexpensive black miniboots that would work with a range of pants and skirts. When she strode into the lingerie section, Foster faltered.

"I can't just keep wearing this bikini under my clothes," she pointed out.

"Right. I hadn't thought much about what was under your clothes." He shot her a disarming grin. "But I am now."

When he closed the gap between them, her concentration scattered. The sensible thing to do was grab a couple of basic bras and move on, but her imagination was getting the best of her. Would Foster prefer a woman in underthings that were frilly and dainty, or bold—like the bright red satin on the Valentine's endcap display? Did he care whether it had a traditional back closure or a front clasp? Great. Now she was preoccupied with the idea of him removing a bra...

"Need some help?" he offered after she'd been standing there a full minute. "Just let me know your size, and I'll throw a couple into the cart."

Oh, hell no. "Like this situation isn't already making me self-conscious enough?"

He cocked his head. "Why would a number and letter make you feel self-conscious? Perfection is perfection. What's printed on the tag is irrelevant."

Heat flared through her, but she couldn't tell if it was from embarrassment or wayward lust. Possibly both.

"I think I'm just going to duck into the dressing room." And hide until her pulse returned to normal. "And, uh, try a few things on."

He gave her a smile of patently false choirboy innocence. "If you change your mind about needing help, you know where to find me."

ONCE ERIN DISAPPEARED into the changing room, Foster began to feel conspicuous standing alone in the middle of the lingerie section. He moved a few feet away and texted Morgan, letting him know to expect them soon. He also asked Morgan to follow up with the local police department near where Erin lived. Would Balducci have any further interest in her with Ellen Hodge in the hospital?

After he finished his texts, he waited, trying his damnedest not to look back at the rows of lacy, silken underthings. Trying not to imagine Erin in them…or out of them.

He had no trouble justifying his audacious teasing. She'd been through a major ordeal, and it wasn't over yet. While he wanted her alert, he didn't want her panicked. Fear caused people to do dumb things. So, yeah, he flirted with her some, distracted her. Coaxed smiles and those charming blushes that singed her fair skin. But he couldn't rationalize standing here fantasizing about her when he should be keeping an eye on their environment, aware of anyone who looked like they didn't belong.

Thankfully, Erin appeared a few minutes later, confirming that all but one article of clothing had worked. At checkout, Foster told a sympathetic cashier that their luggage had been stolen the last day of vacation and asked if Erin could change in the store's restroom and wear some of her new purchases. It wasn't until Erin emerged in normal, flattering clothes that he realized how truly hideous the caftan had been. He'd reached a point where he hadn't even registered her outfit, he'd only been seeing *her*. Now she wore a pair of hip-hugging jeans and a dark green, scoop-neck sweater that accentuated her eyes and her cleavage.

He bit back an admiring comment. Harmless flirting was one thing, but maybe he needed a reminder of the boundaries.

For her part, Erin was mostly quiet on the ride downtown. She only grew talkative again as they entered the FBI offices.

"Not what I pictured," she muttered.

"How so?" He looked around at the fairly conventional setting, trying to see what was amiss.

Her tone was sheepish. "You're the FBI! I guess on some level, I envisioned a labyrinth of unmarked doors or taking a mysterious elevator to a floor that doesn't officially exist. At the very least, looking into a laser that confirms your identity with a retinal scan."

"Maybe you should lay off movies of the week," he teased.

If she was vaguely disappointed with the office, perhaps special agent in charge Morgan Brenner lived up to her expectations. He was an imposing figure. The black man was nearly six-foot-four with a deep, resonating voice.

"You must be Ms. Cross." After shutting the door to the conference room, Morgan shook her hand. "While it is the official position of the FBI that you are not in this unfortunate situation due to any actions of this office, let me extend my personal apologies that you've become entangled in this mess. We will do everything possible to see you safely home as quickly as is feasible."

Foster barely refrained from rolling his eyes at his friend's polished speech. "You practice that in front of a mirror?"

Morgan arched an eyebrow. "I will be so glad when you retire."

Once they'd all taken seats, Morgan's expression turned grim. "I'm afraid I have some bad news. Ms. Cross, it seems your house was vandalized last night."

Erin straightened with a gasp.

"It's not uncommon for break-ins to occur while home owners are on vacation," Morgan continued. "It is uncommon, however, for nothing to be stolen in a burglary. The police say all the obvious valuables are in place, but someone highly motivated to find something went through your belongings. Thoroughly."

"Someone was in my house?" Though she was trying to stay calm, her voice had taken on a shrill edge. And she was blinking rapidly, clearly trying not to cry.

Foster squeezed her hand in wordless encouragement. He didn't even realize he'd done it until Morgan's gaze dropped to their laced fingers in surprise. As discreetly as possible, Foster pulled away.

"I don't understand," Erin said. "Foster said they

went after Ellen Hodge. Who do they think *I* am? And what do they think I have?"

"That is the million-dollar question," Morgan said. "I should tell you, Ms. Cross, while I don't think it would be a good idea for you to go home, if you'd rather be in North Carolina than Atlanta, we do have a field office in Charlotte. I could coordinate—"

"She's staying with me." Foster spoke softly but with resolve. Technically, she didn't fall under their jurisdiction—she wasn't actually involved in any way with the case or with Lance Balducci. They could try to talk her into a safe house, but if there was a leak in the department, would any place really be safer than with him? He'd promised to protect her.

"Unorthodox," Morgan commented.

True, but everything about this situation was. And Foster only had a few weeks left on the job. It wasn't as if getting fired was a daunting consequence.

"Would that arrangement be all right with you?" Morgan asked Erin.

She chewed at her bottom lip. "How long are we talking?"

"I'm not 100 percent sure, but I did hear from the hospital that Ellen Hodge's condition is improving. She sustained some serious head injuries in her car accident, but hopefully I'll be able to speak to her soon. That should clear up some of the confusion. And if she's willing to testify against Balducci…"

"See?" Foster said, trying to project confidence. "Things are looking up."

DURING THE DRIVE to his place, Foster explained the setup of his apartment building. Every tenant had his or her own floor. The parking lot had a security gate, and the lobby had both security officers and cameras. When the elevator stopped on a specific floor, a person had to have a key to get off on that floor or have the tenant buzz them in. And then of course, there were locks on the entrance door to each individual apartment.

"You sure went to a lot of trouble to find a secure place," Erin remarked, relief evident in her voice.

He decided not to tell her that time with the Bureau had taught him no place was ever totally secure. Sometimes it all came down to luck.

Unlocking his front door, he announced, "Well, this is it. Home sweet home." He flipped on the light switch.

Dropping one of the shopping bags she carried, Erin let out a muffled shriek. "Dear Lord, Foster! They got to your place, too."

"Um, no. This is pretty much how it looked when I left." He hadn't entertained a lot of guests since his last case went south. Suddenly, he saw his apartment through someone else's eyes.

"I don't suppose you're lying to me to make me feel safer?"

"It's not like I left for Mexico knowing that I'd be gaining a roommate," he added defensively. "I would've cleaned up." Probably.

"Sorry. Didn't mean to sound ungrateful. I know this must be an imposition on you."

It *should* feel like one. She'd commented earlier that she wasn't used to people being in her space. Truthfully, Foster had been adept at keeping his distance from people since the death of his sister. Aside from a college roommate and the occasional long weekend with a lover, he'd never lived with anyone. Why didn't the idea of having her here bother him more?

Because you're a sensible person and you know this is temporary. He may have invited her to stay with him, but he hadn't asked her to help pick out curtains.

As she explored the living room, he followed at a guilty distance, assessing the clutter. The cream-colored carpet went well with the green-striped ivory sofa, but the light floor had lost a few fights with red wine and pasta sauce stains. Textbooks and articles covered most surfaces; ever since he'd agreed to fill in for a criminology professor going on maternity leave, he'd been prepping for the class.

Back issues of *Sports Illustrated* competed for space on the coffee table with his collection of unopened, cellophane-wrapped fortune cookies that routinely came with his Chinese takeout even though he told the restaurant not to send them. He'd accumulated enough cookies to supply his own Chinese restaurant if he ever opened one. Since he never used the brick fireplace at the far end of the room, the hearth had become a resting place for laundry. He glanced to make sure there was nothing too personal atop the pile, like the jockstrap he used for playing racquetball.

"Um, let me show you to the room you'll be staying in." The guest room would be dusty but otherwise clean because it hadn't been used since he moved in.

Foster's long-standing philosophy was that as long as he didn't leave food out, didn't attract bugs and nothing smelled, then his apartment was reasonably clean. The look on Erin's face forced him to reconsider his position.

But her expression melted into a smile when she studied the guest room. "This is nice!" She couldn't quite mask the note of amazement. The furniture was decent. There were a few cherrywood pieces his parents had given him when they'd downsized and moved into a condo, pieces that would have gone to Lia.

"Foster?"

He shook off thoughts of the sister he hadn't been able to save. For years, he'd dealt with her loss by pushing the pain as far away as possible. In the past few months, that technique had become less effective, but he was stubborn enough to keep trying.

"I'm a little fried," he said. "Would you mind if I catch a quick nap? There are DVDs and books in the living room if you get bored."

She gave a bark of startled laughter. "I've experienced about a thousand emotions over the past day but, trust me, boredom wasn't one of them."

CHAPTER SIX

EVEN THOUGH FOSTER had graciously offered her access to his movie library or a novel, assuming she could find one amongst the debris, Erin was too keyed up for something as passive as sitting in front of the television or thumbing through a book. As she'd told him earlier, she was at her calmest when she had some kind of physical activity to occupy her. And it didn't take her long to settle on a course of action.

She lost track of time but estimated that little more than an hour had passed when he appeared in the doorway between the living room and his bedroom. He glanced around, his expression groggy as he asked, "What the hell did you do to my apartment?"

"You like it?" she asked hopefully. Considering everything he'd done for her, helping him tidy up seemed like the least she could do in return.

"I don't... What happened to my fortune cookies?"

"I threw them out." He couldn't possibly be upset that she'd gotten rid of a bunch of stale cookies he hadn't wanted in the first place. So why was he scowling? "Look, Foster, I didn't repaint the place. I just straightened up a little, mopped the kitchen floor—"

Scratching his head, he interrupted, "I own a mop?"

"I was shocked, too. Now that you're awake, I can vacuum." At his mutinous expression, she added, "Please?"

Ever since she'd first learned she was in danger, she'd thought longingly of the time when she could return safely home. But now the thought of being there made her skin crawl. The idea of someone rifling through her cabinets, upending drawers, digging through her closets…she felt violated.

"I need a physical outlet," she admitted. "And I guess I needed to feel like I had some control again. Sitting around and hoping Ellen Hodge is lucid enough to talk soon doesn't feel like much of a plan."

Foster gave her a sympathetic smile. "Actually, waiting can be a major part of law enforcement. But I get your point. And I may have an idea that will help."

WITH MOST OF the building's residents at work in the middle of a weekday, Foster and Erin had the private gym to themselves. She was glad she considered workout clothes essential enough to have thrown a pair of cotton shorts and a sports bra into their shopping cart.

Foster led her past weight machines, ellipticals and stationary bikes to the mats used for stretching and free-weights. "So you've never had any kind of self-defense?" he clarified. "No classes at the rec center or even a big brother teaching you how to throw a punch?"

"It was just me and my parents," she said. "And they would have been horrified at the idea of my needing self-defense. They would have encouraged me to run rather than fight."

"They would have had a point—running is a completely legitimate option. Fighting back is a last resort. Preventing an attack in the first place is always preferable. Even when you do fight back, you want to keep as much distance as possible."

Fight back from a safe distance? "Sounds counter-intuitive."

"It'll make sense later when I show you what I mean. Let's start with something simple, breaking a wrist hold. An assailant could grab your wrist like this to pull you where he wants to take you." Foster clasped his hand above her wrist.

She knew she needed to concentrate—she was genuinely invested in learning what he was trying to teach her—but it was difficult with him touching her. His fingers were the slightest bit rough, nothing smooth or delicate about them. The hint of friction against her skin sang along her nerve endings. Her pulse sped up, and she wondered if he could tell.

"Okay, some creep grabs you like this, and the weakest part of his grip is going to be between his thumb and fingers. So you…" Foster looked up at her, and when their eyes met, she felt the moment of connection as if it were physical.

She had no doubt the reaction she'd been having to him was reflected in her gaze. He was trained to observe people, to discern the truth even if someone were trying to hide it. And, frankly, she hadn't been trying that hard.

"Damn," he swore. "Lost my train of thought. Maybe this wasn't such a good idea," he added guiltily, releasing her arm.

"Don't give up on me yet!" She'd been going crazy cooped in his apartment. The opportunity to learn useful skills—especially if it meant his hands on her body—was a hell of a lot more enticing than looking for something else to clean in his apartment. "Please."

"Okay." He ran a hand through his hair. "Let's try this again."

This time, she braced for his touch, trying to think past the attraction simmering between them. He showed her how to pivot her arm and break the hold, praising her when she quickly developed a feel for it. After they'd practiced a few times, he launched into the description of different strikes she could use against an opponent. He pointed out that while the eyes and nose were widely recognized as vulnerable, they were also small targets. It was often easier to strike out at someone's neck or knee.

"You can gouge with your fingers if you have to," he said, "but that requires close contact. Better to kick or swing your purse at an attacker's head. The closer you are, the more vulnerable you are."

He demonstrated his point by trapping her against him. Even though she'd expected it, had tried to prepare herself mentally, being pressed against him left her adrift in sensation. Close enough to feel the muscular planes of his chest beneath his T-shirt, she was transported back to waking with her body wrapped around his, his erection hot and hard against her thigh.

"Erin? You aren't trying to get away." His breathing had grown labored, as if he'd just finished a grueling hour on a stair-climbing machine, rather than a fifteen-minute lecture on personal safety.

Get away from him? It was all she could do not to lean into him, reveling in the surge of desire. "I'm trying to remember why I'd want to," she said candidly.

He stared, his gaze dropping to her mouth. "You make it very difficult not to kiss you."

Anticipation shimmered through her. Her body swayed closer to him. Her lips were sensitive, as if she could already feel his kiss.

"The Bureau frowns on agents making out with wit-nesses," he said, his voice low.

"Technically, I didn't witness anything," she re-minded him. "And aren't you leaving the Bureau?"

"Erin." He groaned in defeat.

He meshed his fingers in her hair, cradling her head as his mouth locked on hers in an intense, sear-ing kiss. His tongue met hers boldly. She hadn't been this turned on in years, and it felt *glorious*. She nipped at his lower lip, running her fingers up and down his tightly muscled arms. His hand slid to her butt, pressing her even closer to him. The desire was so overwhelm-ing she could barely process it. Her skin was feverish. Her breasts felt full and deliciously heavy, her nipples taut and aching.

"A-hem." A voice thick with disapproval asked, "Am I interrupting?"

Yes, go away. Erin would have been content to keep kissing Foster for another hour. Maybe another week. But he'd already bolted into action, springing between her and the interloper, a thin man with a goatee and a sneering expression.

"I realize sex burns calories," the man said, "but maybe you could conduct your 'workout' in a more ap-propriate place?"

Sounds good to me. She reached for Foster's hand. "Let's go."

He evaded her reach—and her gaze. "Good idea. I think we were about done here."

FURY PULSED THROUGH FOSTER. He didn't think he'd ever been more disgusted with himself, not even after he'd failed to pull his older sister from the wreckage of their boat crash. After all, he'd only been thirteen then, disoriented and spluttering water. He was a grown man, now, and a trained FBI agent. Yet he'd gotten so caught up in kissing Erin that he'd missed a potential threat entering range!

What if the snippy resident with the goatee had been one of Balducci's thugs? It didn't matter that such a scenario was improbable, requiring bad guys to not only bypass a number of security measures but have some way of knowing he and Erin were in the top-floor gym. The principle of the thing was galling. He'd promised to protect her. Considering the way he'd felt in there, barely stopping himself from tossing her down on the training mat, maybe what she really needed was someone to protect her from him.

She spoke first, slicing through the tense silence in the elevator. "Tell me you aren't beating yourself up over kissing me."

"What happened back there was a mistake." He'd known that even before he reached for her. Foster knew he had flaws, but being weak-willed had never been one of them.

"The only mistake was our location," she objected. "That guy was right. Instead of making out in the gym, we should have stayed in your apartment."

His apartment. Where they would both be sleeping tonight with one wall separating them. The idea of being trapped in such close quarters with her was as torturous as it was tantalizing. If they picked up where they left off…

Absolutely not. Ignoring the protests of his body and the arousal pounding through him, he told himself that a good agent—one who cared more about Erin's safety than about getting laid—would reclaim some professional distance.

"Going forward, we keep our hands to ourselves." Grating out the words took every last ounce of willpower he had, which made him sound harsher than he'd intended. "I was an idiot to let you distract me. It won't happen again."

She drew back, hurt in her eyes. But anger quickly replaced it. "Got it," she said tightly. "I shouldn't touch you and I shouldn't touch your stuff, because heaven forbid anyone disturb your collection of antique fortune cookies. I should just sit quietly in your guest room and passively wait for someone to neutralize Balducci."

Actually, that would make his life a lot easier. But since she was eyeing him as if she were on the verge of trying out that knife strike punch to the throat he'd taught her, he refrained from saying so.

EVEN THOUGH FOSTER knew her parting words before disappearing into her room had been sarcasm, so far, Erin had made good on her offer. She'd been in there for over an hour. The total silence from the other side of the door was deafening. He supposed she could be reading, but from the look she'd shot him when they entered the apartment, it was equally possible she was in there plotting his death.

When Morgan showed up with a large pizza, a bag of groceries and an update, Foster couldn't remember the last time he'd been so happy to see someone. His boss could help defuse the palpable tension in the apartment; not to mention, his presence would be a tacit reminder that Foster needed to conduct himself as a professional.

Setting the pizza on the table, Morgan looked around

in frank surprise. "Damn. Place looks good, man. You cleaned up this well for her?"

"She cleaned up. Nervous energy. We have to get enough on Balducci to make an arrest soon, or she and I will end up—" in bed together "—stir-crazy. Were you able to see Ellen Hodge today?"

"Yes."

"And?" Erin asked from the entrance to the kitchen. She looked so excited by the possibility of good news that she was practically bouncing on the balls of her feet. With both men's attention focused on her, she added, "Sorry to interrupt. The smell of pizza lured me into the kitchen. Nice to see you again, Agent Brenner. Now, what were you saying about Ellen?"

As Foster tossed a salad to go with the pizza, Morgan filled them in on his visit to the hospital. "There have been periodic allegations against Ms. Hodge that she glosses over fact-checking and is willing to embellish her stories for a price. She's lost the respect of many of her peers. Hoping for a big enough story to change that, she was following a senator's aide. She snapped some pictures of him meeting with Balducci. Unfortunately, when she saw the man get shot, she panicked, drawing attention to herself as she was running away and failing to capture actual evidence on camera."

"But she did see the crime?" Erin pressed hopefully. "Surely she'll testify now that she knows she's in danger already? She'd be safer with him off the street."

Morgan sighed. "All true. But we don't have the weapon or any concrete evidence putting Balducci at the scene. It's the word of a woman with a reputation for dishonesty against a well-connected pillar of the community. And I'm sure Balducci will have his own

'eyewitnesses' that place him at a business meeting or
charitable event.'"

Accepting a cold bottle of beer from Foster, Morgan added, "But we do know where *you* come in to
all of this now, Ms. Cross. Ellen Hodge never went to
Mexico—she arranged that meeting with Foster as part
of a wild-goose chase. Instead, she decided it would
be more lucrative to blackmail Balducci than to testify against him. You can see why she's not the most
credible witness in the world," he grumbled. "She told
him that for a quarter of a million dollars, she would
disappear. When he hinted that she could be made to
disappear for a lot less than that, she bluffed an insur-
ance policy, figuring she could keep both the feds and
Balducci's goons safely away from her. She told him
she'd given pictures of the aide's murder to a friend who
would turn them over to an agent in Cancun if anything
should happen to Ellen."

"And they thought I was that friend?" Sitting back
in her chair, Erin scowled darkly. "I think I hate this
woman."

"To be fair," Morgan said, "I doubt she expected
Foster to find anyone close to her description waiting
to meet someone."

Foster wished he had it to do over again. He wished
he'd realized sooner that Erin wasn't a match. He wished
he'd tripped on his way down to the beach and broken
his leg. Anything to have kept her safely out of this.

Of course, that meant he never would have met her.
The thought gave him a weird pang in his chest that
felt a lot like heartburn. He pushed away his half-eaten
slice of pizza.

"So...Balducci thinks I have these incriminating pictures," Erin said thoughtfully. "That's why he sent guys to ransack my house? If he still believes the photos are in my possession, is there any way to use that to our advantage? To force his hand?"

Morgan looked intrigued. "What did you have in mind?"

"Well, I could always take a page out of Ellen's book. What if *I* tried to blackmail him? I could meet with him—"

"Like hell," Foster thundered, sitting bolt upright. "The last woman who tried to blackmail him is still hooked up to IVs and lucky it wasn't worse!"

"She took him on alone. Dumbass move," Erin scoffed. "I would have the FBI to back me up. He's a businessman, right? If I made a legitimate appointment through his receptionist to see him during regular work hours, it's not like he could blow me away in his office. Maybe you could do that thing like on TV where you monitor me from a surveillance van? I wear a wire and if I get in trouble, I use a code word and you swarm."

Foster smacked a palm to his forehead. "No more TV for you. If getting him to admit wrongdoing were easy, don't you think we would have accomplished it before now? And he had his office constructed with special materials. The walls interfere with audio. Morgan, tell her she's insane and that there's no way—"

"It might be worth trying," Morgan said. "He knows who you are, so he'll definitely take the meeting."

"But…" Even knowing he was outnumbered, Foster couldn't help pointing out the obvious. "It's too damn risky."

"I've been at risk since you first walked up to me," Erin said softly. "Please, let me do this. I can't just sit around your apartment and wait to be rescued from this."

She was paraphrasing her earlier statement, what she'd said when she'd been hurt by his rejection. *This is my fault*. He'd made their situation too uncomfortable, and she was eager to escape. His gut clenched. This was worse than his last botched assignment.

Then, he'd been too blinded by a personal connection to see clues sooner. People had been hurt because of him indirectly. Now he was an active catalyst. Driving someone to confront a dangerous murderer was a new low.

CHAPTER SEVEN

As the door closed behind Agent Brenner, Erin could feel the electric crackle of Foster's unspoken words gathering like a distant storm front. The air in the living room grew charged as he stalked toward the couch where she sat.

"You'll just be wasting your breath," she warned him. "My mind's made up." That had been one of the liberating side effects of her divorce—rediscovering her stubbornness. She'd always applied steadfast determination in academics or career advancement, but in her marriage, she'd often comprised. She'd wanted to be a good wife.

But there was certainly nothing between her and Foster that required her to placate him. She put her hands on her hips, almost eager for a fight. He'd controlled their every move so far—and she appreciated his keeping her safe—but dammit, this was her life. She intended to reclaim it.

He stopped a couple of feet from the couch, eyeing her warily. "Whatever I say, I'll likely make a mess of it. I'm used to working alone. I don't have a partner, I don't have a roommate and the last time I dated someone for more than a few weeks, there was a different president in office. What I'm trying to say is, my people skills may be even rustier than my housekeeping skills. There was probably a better way to handle our conversation after I kissed you."

"Probably half a dozen better ways," she said, "but that's not why I'm doing this. It's not some petty revenge for you not wanting me."

"I *never* said I didn't want you. I just don't want to lose focus, be the reason someone gets hurt."

Hurt *again*, she deduced. "Foster, what happened on your last case?"

He flinched. "I don't normally talk about that."

She stared him down, clinging to her newfound tenacity. "Has anything been normal since we met? You might be surprised—talking can be extremely effective therapy." She scooted over to make room for him, holding her breath as she waited for him to make a decision. Asking him to reveal his past felt even more intimate than the physical contact they'd shared.

When he sat next to her, warmth blossomed inside her—in its own way, as powerful as the intense heat that consumed her when they touched.

He took a shuddery breath. "Wanting to join the FBI was…an inherited dream. It wasn't originally my goal. I had an older sister, Lia. She was spunky and intelligent and fearless. You would have liked her." His mouth twisted in a bittersweet smile. "I idolized her. She was fascinated by true crime and unsolved cases, talked about becoming an FBI agent someday. So I decided at a young age, that's what I was going to do, too. The summer before Lia started college, she and her boyfriend were killed in a boating accident."

Sympathy squeezed Erin's heart, but she was hesitant to say anything. Now that the pent-up words were spilling free, she was afraid that if she interrupted Foster, he wouldn't resume his story. And she sensed that he truly needed to, whether he knew it or not.

"I was in that boat crash, too, but escaped relatively unscathed. Since I survived and she didn't, I resolved to realize our shared dream. I was going to become one hell of an FBI agent. In some ways, it was the perfect job for me. It reinforces compartmentalizing emotions."

Compartmentalizing, or repressing?

"My last case was undercover at a company where someone was selling technology secrets to bad people. Because of the type of access necessary, we suspected the culprit was someone high-ranking, but I should have kept an open mind. There was a young woman there, bright and ambitious—barely past entry level but with obvious potential. She reminded me so much of what Lia would have been like if she'd lived to see her twenties. My irrational fondness for her not only kept me from recognizing the truth but lulled me into letting down my guard. She realized my identity and panicked, taking hostages. Another agent got shot in the cross fire. A pregnant agent."

Erin sucked in a breath. "Was she—"

"She's fine now, due to give birth to her daughter around Easter. But for a moment, seeing her hit the floor, I imagined having to tell her husband that he'd lost his entire family because I hadn't been observant enough, *objective* enough."

"You're assuming too much guilt for someone else's actions." She hated to compare it to her failed marriage, because Steve's infidelity seemed downright trivial compared to a woman who'd almost been killed in the line of duty. But the blame Foster was assigning himself seemed vaguely familiar. People screwed up—that was indisputable fact—but no one should waste his life kicking himself for someone else's bad choices.

Now, she just hoped Foster wasn't making bad choices of his own. Would he regret leaving a position he'd worked so hard to attain? "Are you sure you want to quit the Bureau because of one case gone wrong? Maybe this woman did get under your skin, but she made you aware of a vulnerability. I doubt anyone would be able to exploit that in the future, no matter how much they looked like your sister."

"No, I don't think I'd make the same mistake twice. But that hasn't stopped me from making new mistakes." His gaze dropped to her lips. "Or from making myself vulnerable to different problems."

Their eyes locked, and Erin struggled to find a response. If he considered her a vulnerability, then he must care about her. That gave her a rush of joy like nothing she'd felt in months. On the other hand, it wasn't very flattering to be considered a mistake or liability.

He straightened, raking a hand through his hair. "As long as I manage not to fall for one of my students—or give someone an undeserved A because she reminds me of Lia—I think teaching will be a good fit for me. I'm putting my knowledge of criminology and abnormal psych to worthy use without shackling myself to someone else's dream."

"Well, good luck, Professor. But I'm damn glad you haven't left the Bureau yet, that you're the agent who found me." She couldn't imagine sharing the experiences of the past couple days with anyone other than Campbell Foster.

He might have only been in her life a brief time, but he'd made an impression that would last forever.

ERIN HOPED SHE didn't look as nervous as she felt. She had the urge to wipe her palms, which were damp with perspiration, on her skirt. But the outfit she had purchased specifically for this occasion was expensive silk. She conjured a smile and tried not to feel alone.

Even though Foster had mocked her interpretation of what an FBI operation was, there really were two surveillance vehicles outside Balducci's building. She was not wired, but there was a tiny recorder in her purse cleverly disguised as a feminine hygiene product. Although probably a long shot, Morgan hoped Lance would admit to some of his illegal activities on tape.

"Doesn't necessarily have to be the murder of the senator's aide," Morgan had said. "After all, they got Capone on tax evasion."

Foster had been almost manic that morning, trying to cram in a bunch of last-minute self-defense advice. "If it comes to actual violence, remember to hold back a little bit."

"You mean only *sort of* kick his ass?" she'd joked weakly.

"A lot of victims, in their panic, wear themselves out too quickly. You want to conserve enough energy that, when you have the chance to run away, you can run far and run fast."

So her plan, loosely, was to ask Balducci about his tax returns and approach hand-to-hand combat in a mellow, leisurely manner? Yeah, 007, she was not.

"Ms. Cross?" The secretary cut through her musings about life as a superspy. "He's ready to see you now."

Erin was shown into a plush office with a desk the size of her queen bed at home. Behind the polished desk sat a broad-shouldered man with a square chin, dark hair and dark eyes.

He's handsome! After all the repugnant things she'd learned about him, she supposed she'd expected someone oily and cruel looking. Or perhaps someone who looked more like Brando in *The Godfather*.

He flashed a smile. "I'm Lance Balducci. Please, have a seat. Can I have Diana bring us any coffee or sparkling water?"

Right, like I'm gonna willingly eat or drink anything in this joint. "No, thanks. I think it would be best if we just conducted our business, don't you?"

After waving his secretary from the room, he raised his eyebrows in challenge. "I wasn't aware we had any business dealings together, Ms….Cross, was it?"

"Well, we may not have any business together yet, but we have a mutual friend. Ellen Hodge."

"I'm afraid you're mistaken. I don't know Ms. Hodge. But I believe I saw in the news that she's in the hospital? Car accident." He shook his head in faux sympathy. "I certainly hope she drives more carefully in the future. What about you, Ms. Cross? Are you a careful driver?"

Gulp. "I'm a big fan of public transportation."

When he chuckled at that, she continued. "Ellen and I actually have a lot of differences of opinion. We aren't as close as we used to be, but she did give me…a present. It might be of interest to you."

"I think *you* are of interest to me." His gaze dropped over her, lingering at the collar of her blouse and the hem of her skirt with obvious appreciation.

Okay, this she hadn't counted on. None of the women in her circle of friends would believe the week she was having! In the space of a few days, formerly abstinent and shy Erin Cross had made out with a hot FBI agent and been hit on by a crime lord. "I'm—" *repulsed* "—flattered."

"You should be. I'm rich, powerful and good-looking. Have dinner with me. And maybe breakfast."

She couldn't help wondering what Foster's reaction to that would have been if she *were* wearing a wire. For a second, she allowed herself to indulge in the pleasant fantasy of Foster bursting through the door and decking Balducci. Then again, as long as she was fantasizing, why not picture herself kicking his ass? After all, Foster had said she had a natural athleticism and aptitude for the self-defense moves he'd been showing her.

Taking a deep breath, she forced herself back to the present and the cocky SOB waiting for a response. "Mr. Balducci, I think we've gone off topic. Let me be blunt. I came here today because, through no fault of my own, I happen to have information that would be to your benefit to purchase."

He gave her a coy smile. "Information? I should warn you that insider trading is illegal."

"And you, of course, are a law-abiding citizen."

"Of course."

"That's disappointing." She lowered her voice to a confidential murmur. "I've always thought the law is for people who lack…imagination. I figured an enterprising man such as yourself must be full of ideas." *Come on, admit you've done something wrong. Anything! Admit you ran a stoplight in 2010!*

He was silent for a moment. "I like to think I'm a very creative man, within legal limits. Just for curiosity's sake, what is this information you have?"

She'd hoped he would be the first one to acknowledge the photos, but obviously that wasn't going to happen. "Pictures," she said boldly, "that were accidentally taken of a certain business transaction. I believe the deal took place not far from here, in an industrial park warehouse." She held his gaze, determined not to show fear.

"Industrial warehouse?" He wrinkled his nose. "Call me a snob, but I prefer doing my business in office suites. Or over expensive dinners. Join me tonight?"

Hell, that hadn't been part of the plan. Was he trying to draw her out as a target? And, if he made any attempts against her, would Foster and Brenner finally have unshakable grounds for an arrest?

"Dinner tonight?" Not wanting to lose this opportunity, she made a snap decision. "Absolutely. But, fair warning, I may bring up the subject of our doing business again. I'm persistent."

He spread his hands in an accommodating gesture. "I like a woman who knows what she wants. When should I pick you up?"

"I'll take a cab and meet you there. Depending on how the evening goes," she drawled, "maybe you can take me home."

"IT WAS BAD enough that we let her meet with the bastard, but now we're allowing her to date him?"

There were times Erin found Foster high-handed and infuriating, but right now, his opinionated shouting didn't bother her. Not when she clearly heard the concern beneath his irritation. Leaning across the kitchen table, she squeezed his arm. "I'm going to be all right." He'd made her believe that the day they met. *I won't let anything happen to you, sunshine.*

Weirdly, she was less afraid of dinner with Lance

Balducci than she was of spending more nights in such close proximity to Foster. He'd said she should keep her hands to herself, but now that he'd opened up to her, he was more appealing than ever. Too much prolonged exposure in his company, she might decide to hell with her pride and make another move on him.

Bethany would be so proud.

Morgan sat between them at the table, occasionally glaring when Foster's bluster got out of hand. "You heard the tape. We can't make a case on anything he's said to her so far. She'll be in a controlled environment. It's a public restaurant."

"It's lunacy."

"I don't want a loose cannon on my team. If you're not okay with this," Morgan said calmly, "you can always stay here tonight. We've got it covered without you."

"Like hell!"

"Can you believe this is the same man who used to value his ability to be stone-cold and emotionless?" Morgan grinned in Erin's direction. "He's gotten louder since he's met you."

She couldn't help returning the man's smile. "I must be a good influence."

"If the two of you don't stop talking about me like I'm not here, I'm reaching for my gun."

Ignoring the idle threat, Morgan summarized the highlights of tonight's setup. The Bureau had flown in an agent from their Dallas field office to act as Erin and Lance's waiter. The man had been hand-selected by Morgan and his being from out of state minimized the odds that Balducci had any association with him or might recognize him. The taxi driver would also be an undercover agent. She couldn't be seen with the special agent in charge dropping her off at the front door.

"Now remember," Morgan said, "you can leave with him if you have to. We'll have you discreetly tailed, and there's a tracking device in the heel of your shoe. It won't provide us any sound, but we'll be able to tell where you are. Just don't take your shoes off."

"Don't take *anything* off," Foster growled.

Was it wrong that Erin liked his possessive tone?

"You have your recorder back in your purse," Morgan continued. "All of us hope you get the SOB to talk, but the most important thing is your safety. If you get out of visual range, I'm not comfortable with the two of you being alone any longer than five minutes."

She exhaled slowly, trying not to think about all the things that could happen to a person in five minutes.

"Last thing. Balducci knows you've had contact with the FBI. His guys saw Foster hustle you out of the hotel. Don't try to deny contact with us, just play it off. We pushed, but you refused to cooperate. He'll be predisposed to believe you since, if you had given us the alleged pictures, he'd already be in prison. Any questions?"

"No. But if I'm going to get appropriately dolled up I should start getting ready." She shook her head ruefully. "Figures that my fanciest postdivorce date is with a murderous crime lord." Guess that's what happened when you used FBI cases to arrange a night on the town instead of going through Match.com.

Morgan had sent a female assistant out with sizes earlier in the day, then brought a selection of three dresses to Foster's. They hung in a clear garment bag from the door of Foster's laundry room. As Morgan left the apartment, she stood regarding her choices. Classic little black dress, a slinky blue number or a red sweater dress. "What do *you* think I should wear?" she asked Foster.

"Body armor."

She gnawed at her lower lip. "Is there something specific that you're worried will go wrong tonight?" The way Morgan outlined the plan, it sounded relatively safe. Obviously there were no guarantees, but that was true of life in general.

"Yeah." He stepped closer, cupping her cheek. His hands were big, powerful. She almost shivered with the desire to feel them across her body. "*Specifically*, I'm worried you'll get hurt. This isn't worth it."

"Not even to take down Balducci?" She wanted Foster to be able to leave the Bureau at peace, with this success blotting out his previous case. "I know how important this assignment is to you."

"Not as important as you are." The unexpected depth of emotion in his voice cut her to the quick. She wanted to tell him she'd changed her mind, that she'd stay here with him all night if he'd keep looking at her like that.

"Careful," she said breathlessly. "You talk like that, a girl might think you care."

"God knows I tried not to." Pulling her against him, he captured her mouth in a hard, deep kiss that left her dizzy. When he let her go, his breathing was ragged. "I need you safe, Erin. Get your butt back here in one piece tonight."

If another kiss like that was her incentive, she'd have Balducci's confession by the time appetizers were served.

CHAPTER EIGHT

ERIN STEPPED INTO the restaurant, recalling the undercover cabbie's final snippet of advice. "You'll want to reassure yourself by spotting our guys. Don't. Balducci notices, and the whole operation is a bust. Just know we're there for you."

Supposedly, the small, handpicked team was comprised of men and women both inside the restaurant and out. But her mind was centered on one man. Somewhere out there, Foster had her in his sights. Knowing he was there both steadied *and* unnerved her. She'd learned to trust him in a very short time and knew he'd do everything in his power to keep her safe. But he also created a chaotic swirl of emotions and desires inside her. She never knew entirely what to expect from him, never knew what to expect from *herself* when she was under his influence.

Considering the distance he'd been careful to put between them after their session in the gym, she wouldn't have predicted that kiss he gave her tonight. Arousal still buzzed through her system like a drug. But she needed to collect her thoughts and play a part convincingly if she was going to fool a seasoned criminal. Lord knew Lance Balducci had more experience with lies than an introverted service manager whose steady Friday night date was Netflix.

He was standing at the bar, and she forced herself to sashay up to him even though her instinct was to run the other way. "Lance," she purred. "I hope I'm not late."

For a second, she was terrified, wondering if her disdain for him showed through in any way. How in the hell had her husband cheated without giving himself a stroke, constantly worried about getting caught? When she'd flirted with Lance in his office, she'd been afraid he'd see right through her. Luckily, the man had a healthy ego. He was inclined to believe women wanted him.

"You're right on time." He gave her a predatory smile. "But, looking like that? You would have been worth a wait."

"Very smooth. Bet you're quite popular with the ladies."

"Tonight, I'm only interested in one."

It was all she could do not to shudder when he brushed a knuckle over her cheek. She tried to make herself look regretful as she pulled away. "Unfortunately, I'm interested in money. It's hard to concentrate on pleasure when we still have unresolved business."

For a moment he looked angry, but then he smiled. "You are forthright."

"I believe in being up-front."

"Then why don't you tell me about your recent vacation and your abrupt departure from Cancun?"

Boy, he didn't waste any time making his suspicions known. Thank goodness Morgan had prepared her for this. "I was…intercepted on vacation by a pushy travel companion. He seems to think I know something about your business dealings." She batted her eyelashes at him. "But I keep telling him he's wrong."

"You haven't shared your pictures with him?"

"What good would that do me?" She placed a hand on his sleeve. "I'd much rather do business with you." In the abstract, her lie was believable. Too many people would let themselves be lured by a payoff or intimidated out of their civic duty to testify. "Now, about that business…"

"First, let's eat." He signaled the hostess to show them to a table. "Then afterward?" His gaze seemed to slither over the neckline of her black dress. "I guess we'll just see."

FROM A SHADOWED booth across the restaurant, Foster watched as special agent Murdoch Robelot took dinner orders from Erin and Balducci. Foster's jaw was clenched so tightly his head began to hurt. Or maybe the way Balducci was practically drooling over her had caused the headache. Every time Erin was forced to smile at the man, Foster thought he could feel a blood vessel pop somewhere inside him.

"Is everything okay, sir?" A waitress drifted into his line of sight, frowning.

Her apprehensive expression made him realize he'd been savagely ripping a dinner roll into tiny, doughy pieces. "Just fine." When she continued to stand there uncertainly, he added, "Maybe some more iced tea?"

She hurried off to fulfill his request, leaving him free to once again glower across the restaurant. The nice part was he didn't have to worry about being subtle. Erin was going to "out" him as a way to build trust between her and Balducci. Morgan had thought being in the same room as them would make Foster more comfortable. Not so much. He hated that she was at the same table as that monster.

He didn't even like the idea of them in the same zip code.

He grabbed the second roll out of the bread basket and began systematically shredding it. The repetitive motion helped keep him in his chair. Every cell in his body wanted to drag her out of there, wanted to get her to safety. Then, he wanted to apologize for getting her involved in this mess. And after that, he wanted—

Hell, he wanted her. Period.

He'd felt protective about witnesses and victims before, but never this invested, as if he'd given up part of himself to her and wouldn't be the same without her. The thought was terrifying. Even for a man whose job regularly put him in life-or-death situations.

Erin waited until the moment the waiter set down their plates to put the next piece of Morgan's advice to use, disassociating herself from agents in case Balducci identified any of them.

She lowered her voice to a frantic whisper. "Lance, don't be obvious, but you see that guy? That's the agent I had to put up with in Cancun! I've already told them I can't help, but he's dogged. What if he tries to follow us when we leave?"

Balducci seemed pleased that she planned to leave with him. "Do you think he's here with other agents?"

Taking her time, she pretended to think this over. "Probably not. His boss more or less told him to stop harassing me. If I describe his car for you, can you pull something out of the engine or deflate his tires or something?"

He chuckled. "Well, I'm not going to go out in the parking lot and play mechanic, but I believe I can have it taken care of."

She described the car Morgan had requisitioned expressly for this purpose, and Balducci excused himself to speak to his driver. Balducci had seemed flattered when she'd deferred to his taste and let him order for both of them. Now she seized the opportunity to switch their identical plates. As eager as he seemed to get her into bed, it was probably wildly paranoid to think he'd have her poisoned. But after he'd had Ellen Hodge shot at and hospitalized, why take chances?

When he came back to the table looking smug, Erin wondered if he knew how much less attractive it made him.

"All taken care of," he assured her.

They began eating, but the company had more or less ruined her appetite. After a few bites, she gave up trying. "So, Lance," she drawled, "why don't you tell me about your business?"

He eyed her suspiciously. "I don't like talking shop on dates."

"Oh." She thought fast. "That's too bad. Because there's no aphrodisiac like money and power."

"In that case, let's save the shoptalk for dessert. Somewhere private."

Dammit. She'd wanted so badly for him to say *something* Foster and his colleagues could use while she was safely surrounded by so many witnesses. Then she would have been free to fake a headache or excuse herself to the ladies' room and never return.

"If we go back to my office," Balducci suggested, "we can get that money you want from my safe." He let his dark eyes trail down from her mouth to her neck to where the neckline of her dress curved up over the swell of her breasts.

She felt like slugs were crawling on her skin.

"Then," he continued softly, "perhaps I can get what *I* want."

Smile, Erin! Try to look like a woman overcome with lust, not *a woman who wants to stab him with her dinner fork.* "Ready whenever you are."

God help her. Even with the tracker in her shoe, she really didn't want to go anywhere with this man. But, to accomplish what she'd come here to do, it was beginning to look as though she didn't have a choice.

As SHE CLIMBED into the limousine, Erin's heart beat like a crazed metronome, getting faster and faster. Her mind was full of Mafia movies. She expected Lance to turn to her at any second and announce, "We're gonna go for a little ride, Joey." Not that there were a lot of dense forests in downtown Atlanta in which to bury her, but she was sure he could come up with somewhere to hide a body.

But his thoughts seemed to be on a different path than hers. He poured them both champagne from the limo's minibar, then began telling her about his college years, when he decided he was going to become an Important Person. His hand dropped to her thigh, and she cringed inwardly. During gym workouts, Bethany had commented more than once on Erin's self-discipline. But no grueling exercise in existence took more willpower than not squirming away from Balducci's touch.

As they neared his office, she felt sorry for the feds who would have to sort through the audio recordings.

This much self-aggrandizing, egocentric prattle was a crime in itself. Maybe Brenner could add that to the other charges.

I can't believe this bozo thinks he's charming.

Then again, listening to him drone on about himself was better than, say, kissing him, so she'd tried to look as though she were hanging on his every word.

At night, the office building looked far more ominous than it had during the day. The chauffeur opened the door for them, and Balducci instructed the man to stay with the car.

"I'm not sure yet how long we'll be," Lance added, a smirk in his voice. Surprisingly, it was almost a relief when he took her hand. Without him leading her toward the entrance, Erin wasn't sure she would have been able to make herself go inside.

Don't panic. You know Foster would never let you be alone with this man for long. The agents would be here soon. Besides, even if Balducci did still want to kill her, he definitely wanted to sleep with her first.

Funny how that thought wasn't actually comforting.

While Balducci unlocked the door to his personal office, Erin tried to stall him from getting cash from his safe and moving to the next step—seducing her. "Instead of a lump sum of cash," she said, "what if we discussed a more long-term business arrangement? I'd love to work for a man like you. I realize you already have an army of employees, but I'm not without…talents."

With his hand on the small of her back, he gave her a light push. "Long-term, huh? And here I thought you were just out to blackmail me."

She wrinkled her nose. "Blackmail is so low class."

"How true. I said something very similar to Ellen. Right before I ordered her killed."

Little dots appeared in front of her eyes as her blood pressure rocketed. Was his admission because he had decided to trust her—or because he'd decided to kill Erin and knew she wouldn't be able to spill his secrets?

His voice hardened. "It's nice to know you aren't going to repeat your friend's mistakes, but tell me the truth. This sudden interest in working with me? Is that your ploy to get me talking about what I do for a living? How do I know you aren't working with the cops, that you aren't wired?"

Breathe, breathe, breathe. She pouted. "The cops can't help an ambitious girl like me get where she wants to go, and I'm hurt that you would think otherwise. But if it puts your mind at ease, how about we have a couple of drinks and then I can remove this dress? You can check for wires yourself." *Foster, if you don't hurry up, I will shoot you with your own gun.*

"A perfect plan." Instead of moving toward the liquor bottles displayed on the other side of the executive suite, as she'd hoped, he took a step toward her. "Except I'm not thirsty. Let's skip the drinks." His expression was commanding. Now that he'd abandoned his self-centered attempt at charm, she suddenly missed it. "Come here, Erin."

She was paralyzed, as if her mind was racing with so much energy that none was left to power her body. When she didn't comply, Balducci impatiently grabbed her arm. Instinct kicked in. Without thinking through the consequences, she rotated her arm the way Foster had shown her during their self-defense sessions and yanked free. She was already raising her arm for the follow-up knife strike punch when she realized she'd blown her cover irreparably.

Balducci sprang back, snarling, "You bitch. I—"

Whatever vows of vengeance and murder he was about to make were interrupted by the door being knocked open. Morgan Brenner announced, "FBI!" and ordered Lance Balducci to freeze. The man had other ideas, however, and lunged for Erin. Suddenly, Foster was there between them. With a roar, he swung at the other man, knocking him to the ground with a single punch. Relief flooded Erin, so sharp it almost bowled her over.

"He ordered the assassination attempt on Ellen," she blurted. "He admitted as much."

"What about you?" Foster asked, scanning her with worried eyes. "Did he hurt you? Are you—"

"Fine." She exhaled a breath. If she wasn't entirely fine, she was getting closer to that state. "At least, I am now that you're here."

Later, as a handcuffed Balducci was being led away by agents, Erin could no longer resist the impulse to hurtle into Foster's arms. She wasn't sure how long she'd been shaking, but she couldn't stop. Having his arms around her felt like her only chance of holding herself together.

"I don't know how anyone does this job," she mumbled into the front of his shirt. "I would make a terrible agent."

"Oh, I don't know." He rubbed his hand up and down her back, clearly trying to be soothing, but she heard the emotion in his voice. The mix of concern and pride and relief that it was done. "After all, you got a taped confession on your first night out. Nice job."

"And I remembered what you taught me about breaking a wrist hold," she added. "You're a good teacher."

"See? If we'd been ten minutes later, you probably would have subdued him all by yourself." He was joking, trying to lighten her mood, but the idea of how ten more minutes would have played out made her stomach clench in pure dread.

"I need to get out of here." She was sure there was some kind of FBI debriefing thingy and paperwork that had to be filed. Tomorrow, she'd be happy to answer any further questions Morgan and his team had. But for tonight… "Take me home?"

Foster's arms tightened around her. "You got it, sunshine."

CHAPTER NINE

As FOSTER ESCORTED Erin into the apartment, he fretted over how quiet she was being. Partly because he worried she was still shell-shocked, partly because in the silence, he found it impossible to think of anything except the ice-cold fear that had flowed through his veins tonight. Extracting Erin from the building had required stealth, first taking care of the chauffeur, then double-checking building security. If Balducci had been alerted, he could have taken Erin as a hostage. But stealth required time and patience. Every agonizing second that had passed had been hell for Foster. He'd been in a frenzy to reach her. If he hadn't thought it would put her in jeopardy, he would have said screw stealth and driven a truck through the front doors of the place.

Now that it was over, he should feel calmer. He shouldn't feel eaten alive by this need to hold her tightly and never let her go. He wanted to explore every creamy millimeter of her skin to assure himself there were no bruises. He wanted to kiss away the memory of every minute she'd had to spend undercover.

Insensitive ass. Tonight had probably scared a year off her life. She needed a hot shower or a cup of tea, not another guy pawing at her.

She sat on the sofa, looking dazed.

"Are you *sure* you're okay?" Foster asked.

"He may have permanently put me off dating, but otherwise I'm fine."

Dating. It felt like a lifetime ago that he'd found her waiting for her date in Cancun. Had it really only been a matter of days? Would she contact the man she was supposed to have met once she'd returned to her real life? Foster's hands squeezed into fists even as he acknowledged that he had no right to be jealous.

"I...was scared," she admitted suddenly, a slight crack in her voice. "I shouldn't have been, I *knew* you were coming for me, but—"

"Hey, don't beat yourself up." He sat next to her, putting an arm around her shoulders. "You were brave and wonderful. But you don't have to be scared now. It's over."

Morgan was jubilant. Earlier today, Ellen had looked through photos and identified the two men she'd seen with Balducci in the warehouse the night the aide was killed. One had already been brought in, and Morgan was hoping to convince him to cut a deal in exchange for information on Balducci. Between Ellen's eyewitness testimony and Erin's tape, they finally had the slippery bastard.

Erin sniffed. "You're right. It is all over. I guess I'll be leaving soon."

"Yep." For her sake, he tried to sound cheerful. "Headed back home. But before you do, you should steal time for something fun—maybe the aquarium or a Hawks game, if you like basketball. Your trip so far has been very 'I went to the ATL and all I got was this lousy T-shirt and dinner with a murderer.' You need something good to remember."

Her gaze collided with his, full of emotion. A sec-

ond passed, stretched into another, and the air around
them was so charged he could almost see sparks. "I have
something good to remember, Campbell."

"That's the first time you've used my first name,"
he said gruffly. "No one ever does." Then again, Erin
wasn't like anyone else.

She moistened her lips, looked away nervously. But
then she lifted her chin and resolutely returned his gaze.
"There is one more memory I'd like to make."

He froze, torn between the urge to be noble and the
urge to bury himself inside her. After her harrowing
evening, she was emotionally vulnerable. If he acted
on the desire he'd felt since the moment he'd met her on
the beach, would he be taking advantage of her? Would
she regret a one-night stand with him in the morning?

An inarticulate noise of exasperation rose in her
throat, and she shot to her feet. "When will I learn? I
must be a sucker for rejection. This is the second time
I've thrown myself at you, and—"

"My silence wasn't a rejection." He stood. "I just
want you so badly I couldn't think straight enough to
speak."

Fierce joy lit her expression, making her green eyes
sparkle. "So we won't talk, then."

He scooped her into his arms and carried her toward
his bedroom. It was the only room she hadn't entered
during her stay here, as if they'd both recognized the
invisible boundary and known what would happen if
she crossed it.

In his room, he set her down next to the bed so that
his hands were free to turn on the lamp on his nightstand. He wanted to see her, had dreamed of seeing her.

"Kiss me?" she whispered. There was a tremor of

nervousness in her voice. Because it had been so long since she was intimate with someone, or because she was afraid Foster would push her away again? As if he could. No power on Earth could convince him to let her go tonight. He kissed her like a man possessed, and she answered his fervor with her own. She sucked at his tongue, drawing him deeper and setting his body on fire.

When his hand moved to the zipper on her dress, she lowered her head, kissing his throat, lightly raking her teeth over his skin. Beneath the dress, she wore a matching set of violet lingerie—a bra and pair of panties that they'd purchased on their shopping expedition.

He palmed her breast through the satiny material. "I've imagined you in these," he admitted hoarsely, "but it was nothing compared to the reality. You're beautiful."

Her smile was pure sunshine, but her voice was scolding. "And you're overdressed."

Barely taking the time to undo the top button, Foster yanked off his shirt. Erin helped him with the pants. When her hand slid over his erection as she tugged down the zipper, he thrust his hips, seeking her touch. His blood was pounding so hard he could hardly see clearly. Which was a damn shame, because he planned to memorize every inch of this woman's body before the night was over.

He reached for the hook on her bra. The scrap of violet fell to the floor, and her breasts were bared to him. Full and tempting, her coppery nipples hardened into tight peaks begging for his touch.

He swallowed. "Did I already mention you were

beautiful?" He pulled her onto the bed with him, rolling so that he was above her.

Erin couldn't believe she was here with him, finally in his bed. The avid way he looked at her seemed too good to be true. And his touch...

He used the side of his hand to trace a wide, slow circle around the outside of her breast, tantalizing her. The circles got smaller and smaller until his finger brushed over her sensitized nipple. She whimpered. How was it possible for something to feel that amazing yet equally inadequate? She needed *more*. She arched her back, her hips writhing beneath his. Foster lowered his head to her breast. His tongue stroked over her, and she thought she would spontaneously combust.

But she needed to know that he was caught up in the same hailstorm of desire that she was. She wanted to give back the incredible sensations he made her feel. Rolling on her side so that he could keep kissing her but she had more freedom of movement, she trailed her hand over the ridged muscles of his abdomen and inside the waistband of his boxer briefs.

When her fingers brushed across him, he groaned and went completely still. Then he recovered, shoving down the boxers to give her more access. She wrapped her fingers around him, tentatively at first, then harder as he continued suckling her breasts. By the time he pulled a condom from the nightstand, she'd already been at the brink of orgasm twice.

She was restless and aching with need as he rose over her. Holding her breath, she met his gaze, knowing this single sliver of time would be imprinted on her forever. With one swift motion, he thrust his hips forward and filled her. She gasped at the invasion. There was no pain, but the tightness reminded her of how long she'd waited for this.

"You feel…" His voice was strangled as he withdrew, pulling back with exquisite slowness before rocking forward again. "So. Good."

Each stroke was measured and patient, amplifying the sensations that thrummed through her body, making her nearly delirious with pleasure. Then he cupped her butt with his hands and raised her so that he could surge even deeper. Biting back a cry, she raced to meet his thrusts, each movement sending her closer to the precipice of a Technicolor abyss. Then her body buckled, her muscles clenched and she splintered into a thousand pieces in his arms.

Campbell gave a hoarse shout and collapsed against her. She ran her hands over his sweat-slicked skin and embraced him tightly.

"I'm so glad it was you," she murmured, thanking her lucky stars that while she'd waited for one man in Mexico, fate had steered her onto a different path. "I got on that plane to Cancun expecting just a fling, but now I know I want so much more than that."

She felt his muscles stiffen beneath her hands. He was practically rigid in silent protest of her words.

Disappointment crashed through her. She'd realized tonight that she had fallen for him. Was she alone in that epiphany? She recalled the way he'd crushed her to him before she'd left the apartment, admitting that he cared even though he'd struggled against it. After Balducci's arrest, she'd seen the naked fear in Foster's eyes as he'd sought to make sure she was unharmed. His concern for her had seemed personal, not part of the job.

And the way he'd propelled her to breathless orgasm? That was pretty freaking personal.

But apparently it wasn't enough. He was obviously okay with the idea of her walking out of his life, might even be counting on it. She shoved at his shoulders, needing to get out of the bed, needing to be alone before the familiar sting of rejection drove her to tears.

"Erin." There was sympathy in his voice, and she hated him for it.

"Don't!" She scrambled to the edge of the mattress.

"You know I care about you. At least, I hope you do. But it's not uncommon for people in dangerous situations to develop infatuations with those protecting them. It's something agents are taught about when they join the Bureau. Whatever you think you're feeling for me now, you might—"

"I said, *don't*." She got to her feet, fuming. Her hands were shaking so much that she didn't think she could manage her bra or the zipper on her dress. Well, to hell with it. She'd worked hard in the gym, and she wasn't ashamed of her body. She was comfortable with who she was and what she felt—which was more than she could say about her lover. He'd finally let her into his bed, but then panicked at the prospect of letting her into his life.

Had he always been wired to push people away, or was it a reaction to losing the sibling he'd been so close to? Or maybe a reaction to all the cases when he'd had to deny his own emotional responses?

"You're a coward," she accused. "In our self-defense lessons, you said that getting too close makes you vulnerable. And you're right. But life isn't hand-to-hand combat, Agent Foster. If you can't let yourself be vulnerable, you're not really living. You think I'm not afraid to get involved again after my divorce? Because I am. I have emotional baggage. Everyone over the age of three has baggage! But I don't plan to let mine stop me from being happy."

He sat up, looking angry. "It's not that simple."

"It could be," she argued. "But not if you aren't brave enough to take chances."

Mustering as much dignity as a naked woman on the verge of tears possibly could, she strode from his room. By the time she reached her own room, her cheeks were wet and her eyes burned. Ironic—she'd spent the first half of the night alarmed that something could happen to her, but, in the end, it wasn't the callous criminal who'd hurt her.

FOSTER SUPPOSED THAT a lot of mornings-after were awkward, but this one was particularly bad. Over coffee, he'd tried to apologize for making a mess of things last night, saying that he'd wanted to exercise caution since she was emotional. That had only ticked her off further.

"At least I *have* emotions!"

The drive to the FBI office had been conducted in frigid silence, and there was no question that Morgan and other agents had noticed the newfound hostility between him and Erin. Maybe once they were finished here, Foster could buy her lunch, try again to repair the damage. He could make his peace with her leaving, but he didn't want their goodbye to be like this. He wanted her to remember him as—

On second thought, after everything she'd been through, it would probably be better if she put this entire experience behind her. But, in the privacy of his own thoughts, he could admit he was too selfish to want that.

Morgan sat back in his desk chair, smiling at Erin. "It was a genuine pleasure meeting you, Ms. Cross. If you ever change your mind and decide to go into this line of work, you give me a call."

Her laugh was brittle. "Fat chance."

"In all seriousness, you have my number. Don't be afraid to use it if you have questions or you get a case of the heebie-jeebies. Now that we're punching holes in Balducci's empire and his own people are rolling on him, you should be safe. But if someone seems suspicious to you or you think anyone is following you, don't dismiss your instincts. And don't forget we have a field office in Charlotte. I can ask some people there to look in on you if you have concerns."

"Thank you."

Morgan nodded. "Next order of business is booking you a flight home. Agent Foster thought you might like to wait a day or two so that you can see something in the city besides this office and his place. If—"

"Today," she insisted, the vehement word like a gunshot.

Foster straightened in his chair. "You want to go today?"

She sent him a look full of the same pain and accusation he'd glimpsed last night. "I don't have a good reason to stay, no offense to the fair city of Atlanta. I want to go home. I want to sleep in my own bed. And I want to forget that any of this ever happened."

It was dark outside when Erin's flight touched down at Raleigh-Durham International. The descent, which had startled her as her plane landed in Cancun and again when she arrived in Atlanta, barely registered now. She could tell Bethany with pride that she'd fully conquered the first resolution on her New Year's list. Technically, she'd even managed to fulfill the second resolution, but the one-night stand she'd shared with Foster didn't feel like a victory.

Get on a plane.

Get your heart broken.

Earlier today, after Morgan had insisted on driving her to Hartsfield airport rather than let her take a cab, she'd called Bethany from the gate. The story was too convoluted to spill in such a short time, but she'd promised her friend she was alive and well, giving her a bare-bones version of being confused for a fugitive witness and staying under the FBI's protection while it was all sorted out. She glossed over mention of Foster, but when her friend had asked about the FBI agent, Erin's voice broke.

Her friend knew her far too well not to notice. She hadn't pressed for details over the phone, but Erin knew Bethany would have a mile-long list of questions when she picked up Erin in a few minutes. They were meeting at baggage claim—not that Erin actually had any luggage checked, but it was as convenient a place to find each other as any.

In some ways Erin looked forward to spilling the whole sordid story. A verbal purge might do her some good. It was like she'd told Foster when she'd coaxed him to open up about his last case...

Dammit! She couldn't go sixty seconds without thinking about the man in some way. Why torture herself? Her husband hadn't wanted her, and she got over that. She wasn't going to pine over yet another man who didn't care enough about her.

His feelings were perplexing. She knew how rarely he spoke about his sister or the case that had compelled him to quit the Bureau. Yet he'd confided in Erin. The deep emotion reverberating in his voice when he'd said she was more important than the case, more important than bringing down Balducci? Didn't that *mean* something?

One of the two people in this scenario is an idiot. It was either her, for believing they shared something truly special, or him, for not being able to admit it.

Confused and exhausted and heartsick, she made her way to the baggage area of the airport.

"Erin!" Bethany's cry of greeting rang out, her sisterly expression full of welcome and curiosity and worry.

The two women met in a hug, and Erin's throat burned with emotion. This would be the second time her friend had nursed her through a broken heart. Why did this feel so much worse than when her marriage had ended?

Maybe because then, she'd had such a long time to realize that their relationship was ending. With Foster, she'd barely had time to process anything. It had been rapid and intense and the most unforgettable experience of her life.

Hot tears spilled down her cheeks, and she tasted salt.

"Oh, honey." Bethany squeezed her shoulder. "I'll drive. You tell me all about it."

EVEN THOUGH HIS office hours were posted so that students could find him, Foster was surprised by the knock at his office door. He'd only been in the job a week. If anyone had a question this soon, he wasn't sure he'd have an answer.

But it wasn't a criminal justice major who stood on the other side of the door. Morgan the traitor smiled at him. Rationally, Foster knew he couldn't have kept Erin in town against her will, but it rankled that his turncoat friend had actually taken her to the airport.

"Don't look so happy to see me," Morgan complained. "Can I come in?"

"If you want to." Foster turned away, sinking like a stone onto the small leather couch next to an overcrowded bookcase.

"I came to give you good news. You look like you could use some." Morgan raised an eyebrow. "You also look like you could use a shave, man."

Foster glared. "I hope you weren't planning to stay long."

"All right, I'll cut to the chase. Balducci's lawyers are desperate to make a deal. They're volunteering information in an attempt to make their client look cooperative. Of course, we told them there won't be a deal, but they have no ethical problems giving us a few names in the hopes we get hungry for more and change our minds. We've already picked up the two clowns that were tracking you and Erin in Cancun."

Hearing her name aloud made Foster's heart lurch. He tried, with dogged determination, to put her out of his head every single day. And each morning when he woke up, there she was again.

"Foster, you even listening to me?"

"Yeah, sure. You were talking about Erin," Foster muttered.

Morgan shook his head, radiating unwelcome pity. "No. Actually, I was talking about Agent Cole Markus."

"What about him?"

"You know how we've questioned before whether Balducci's pockets are deep enough to buy an agent? Well, they were deep enough to buy Markus. The man has helped Balducci elude us on multiple occasions, and Balducci's lawyers gave him up. And I'll tell you something else that should make you feel better. Markus is the reason your last undercover assignment fell apart. You didn't give yourself away because you got careless or too emotionally invested in a suspect. Markus identified you for a price."

Foster waited for the relief to come, but, oddly, he was too swamped by other emotions to really care. He tried to conjure a ghost of a smile in response to Morgan's news, but he failed.

The other man sighed. "If you're this miserable, why did you let her go?"

"Says the man who escorted her out of my life."

"From the chilly atmosphere between the two of you that last morning, it looked as if you'd already done a thorough job of exiling her. The plane ride was just a formality."

"Morgan, we had a doomed affair with no real future. I'm sure by now she realizes that her so-called feelings for me were only generated—"

"Spare me. The real issue is that you screwed up, and you're using this bogus theory as an excuse for not sucking up your pride and going after her."

"You don't know what the hell you're talking about. I'm already over her."

CHAPTER TEN

"PLEASE," FOSTER PLEADED.

"Are you out of your damn mind?" Morgan leaned against the corner of his desk, looking caught between laughter and exasperation.

"Fine." Foster paced anxiously. "How about you just tap her phone so I can find out if she's dating anyone yet?" Thoughts of her with the unknown Mike plagued him. His only consolation was that Mike lived in Seattle. Then again, maybe *Mike* had been smart enough to realize that Erin was worth the difficulty of a long-distance relationship.

"I can't believe you're wasting my time like this. What are you even doing in my office? Aren't you supposed to be teaching a class or something?"

"Independent study day." The dean had suggested Foster leave because he looked unwell. That was a tactful way of putting it. Foster had felt wildly unhinged for the past few days. He doubted they would be offering him a permanent position on campus. "Come on, Morgan, you're supposed to be my friend!"

"And *as* your friend, I'm not going to let you break federal laws. Weren't you the same guy who said you were over her?"

"I lied! I can't stop thinking about her," Foster admitted. "I've even been keeping my apartment clean in her honor. I may actually be losing my mind wondering whether she's with someone or whether we could have made it work. You were right, okay? I'm crazy about her."

"Very good—" Morgan applauded "—but don't tell me. Tell Erin."

ERIN KNEW EVEN before she glanced at her cell phone that the caller would be Bethany. "This is the fourth time you've called today," she told her friend. It might be exasperating if it weren't evidence of how much Bethany cared.

"Are you still at the office? I know you're at the office."

"I am, but I was finishing up," Erin promised, watching her computer screen as it went through the stages of shutting down. She envied it. She wished she could log out of her emotions—and her date with Bethany. Her friend had refused to let Erin be alone on Valentine's Day. And since Bethany's husband had pulled a shift at the hospital, Bethany had suggested a decadent night out.

Normally, Erin could muster enthusiasm for an evening that started with cheese fondue appetizers and ended with chocolate fondue dessert, but the last thing she wanted was to be out on the town, surrounded by happy couples.

"I'm on my way to the restaurant," Bethany said. "If neither of us is there on time, they might give our reservation away. You'd better be there soon! Or I will track you down."

"Understood. But if, at any point during the meal,

you pull out a figurative or literal list of eligible men, I am out of there."

"Understood," Bethany echoed. "Drive safe."

Erin shrugged into her jacket and gathered her stuff. On the drive to the restaurant, she debated telling Bethany about the phone conversation she'd had today. It was the first time she and Mike had spoken since before the convention. Frankly, when she'd returned to North Carolina, she'd been afraid she wouldn't have a job anymore. But Morgan had promised to take care of that, and he'd kept his word. She'd sent Mike a very short email apologizing for standing him up in Mexico and glossing over "an emergency situation." Three words that did absolutely nothing to cover the unexpected events that had unfolded or the emotional turmoil she'd been through. Mike had not replied.

But when they'd talked today, he'd said that even though they still hadn't met in person, she'd influenced his life. He'd admitted that he was shy, better with computers than people, and that it had been easier to flirt with her than the neighbor he had a crush on. When he'd returned from Mexico after Erin's no-show, he'd realized that if he was willing to fly to a different time zone for personal interaction with a woman, he ought to be willing to brave a cup of coffee with one.

Tonight, he was cooking a Valentine's dinner for his neighbor, nervous about their first real date but sounding optimistic. Erin had said she was happy for him and tried to mean it. She only wished she could rebound so quickly.

At the fondue restaurant, the valet opened her car door and she handed him her keys. But she hadn't gone three steps when someone grabbed her wrist. She turned, automatically pivoting her arm to pull away when she heard her name.

"Erin."

Her heart stopped. Foster looked devastatingly handsome in a black suit, no tie, his blue eyes bright with emotion. He'd lost a little weight in the days since she'd seen him last. And he was holding a bouquet of roses.

"Wh-what are you doing here?" The flowers suggested this was not official FBI business.

"Praying, mostly. Praying that I'm not too late, that I still have a shot with you. That you can loan me some of your bravery." His smile, laced with vulnerability, rocked her to the core. "Because I am scared out of my mind here."

Foster was saying he wanted to be with her? Her mind reeled. There was so much to say, so many feelings to sort through that she didn't know where to begin. "How did you know I was here?"

"The woman who lives across the street from you marched up to me on the sidewalk with a German shepherd and a cell phone poised to dial 9-1-1. She said it looked like I was casing your place and that, as a diligent member of the neighborhood watch, she was calling the police if I didn't have a damn good reason to be there."

Erin laughed out loud. Starting a neighborhood watch had occurred to her after the break-in at her house. Millie Abrams, who'd been bored since retiring from teaching last May, had taken to it as if she'd been assigned security detail to the president.

"I told her I did have a good reason—falling in love. And needing to grovel for your forgiveness. That and the flowers convinced her to tell me where you were planning to be tonight."

Erin smacked her forehead. "I don't think providing information about a person's whereabouts is very— Wait. You said love!" It took her brain a moment to catch up with what she'd heard. "You love me?"

"Crazy isn't it? But you made more of an impact on me in a matter of days than some people have in years. You made me reexamine the way I live my life and relate to others. And if you don't say something soon…" Uncertainty wavered in his voice, evidence that he was overcoming a great deal of doubt in order to reach out to her.

"Oh, Foster." Her chest tightened, her heart pounding with love for this man. "I don't know what to say."

Tossing the flowers onto the valet stand, he pulled her into his arms, his lips quirked in a wicked half smile as he lowered his head. "So we won't talk, then."

Foster's kisses had always been sensual and consuming. But now she realized he'd been holding himself back before, unwilling to fully connect. Unwilling to make himself vulnerable. Now he kissed her as if his life depended on it, with a passion that made her insides quake and her toes curl.

As he slowly pulled away, he whispered, "Happy Valentine's Day."

Yes, but Valentine's was only one day. She needed more than that. As ecstatic as she was that he'd come to see her, she needed to make sure he wouldn't retreat again. "So what's the plan exactly? We see each other on weekends and talk in between—or we have an incredible night of make-up sex, then you push me away in the morning?"

"I couldn't push you away. I'm too miserable without you. As for just seeing each other on the weekends, would you be open to more than that? I'm…kind of between jobs. The college replaced me with an adjunct who doesn't scare the students with his foul mood. And Morgan reminded me there may be a happy medium between fieldwork and leaving the Bureau entirely. There are plenty of desk jobs, and I thought I'd talk to some people in the Charlotte office."

Joy bloomed inside her. "You'd consider staying in North Carolina?"

He pressed a kiss to her forehead. "I'm afraid you may be stuck with me, sunshine."

She was suddenly eager to get him inside the restaurant, to introduce him to Bethany and share her happiness. "You have to meet my best friend. I warn you, though, her interrogation techniques are tougher than anything the Bureau employs."

He chuckled. "Let her do her worst, I'm not worried. After all, I have you to protect me."

* * * * *

REQUEST YOUR FREE BOOKS!

2 FREE NOVELS
FROM THE ROMANCE COLLECTION
PLUS 2 FREE GIFTS!

YES! Please send me 2 FREE novels from the Romance Collection and my 2 FREE gifts (gifts are worth about $10). After receiving them, if I don't wish to receive any more books, I can return the shipping statement marked "cancel." If I don't cancel, I will receive 4 brand-new novels every month and be billed just $6.24 per book in the U.S. or $6.74 per book in Canada. That's a savings of at least 22% off the cover price. It's quite a bargain! Shipping and handling is just 50¢ per book in the U.S. and 75¢ per book in Canada.* I understand that accepting the 2 free books and gifts places me under no obligation to buy anything. I can always return a shipment and cancel at any time. Even if I never buy another book, the two free books and gifts are mine to keep forever.

194/394 MDN F4XY

Name	(PLEASE PRINT)	
Address		Apt. #
City	State/Prov.	Zip/Postal Code

Signature (if under 18, a parent or guardian must sign)

Mail to the Harlequin® Reader Service:
IN U.S.A.: P.O. Box 1867, Buffalo, NY 14240-1867
IN CANADA: P.O. Box 609, Fort Erie, Ontario L2A 5X3

Want to try two free books from another line?
Call 1-800-873-8635 or visit www.ReaderService.com.

* Terms and prices subject to change without notice. Prices do not include applicable taxes. Sales tax applicable in N.Y. Canadian residents will be charged applicable taxes. Offer not valid in Quebec. This offer is limited to one order per household. Not valid for current subscribers to the Romance Collection or the Romance/Suspense Collection. All orders subject to credit approval. Credit or debit balances in a customer's account(s) may be offset by any other outstanding balance owed by or to the customer. Please allow 4 to 6 weeks for delivery. Offer available while quantities last.

Your Privacy—The Harlequin® Reader Service is committed to protecting your privacy. Our Privacy Policy is available online at www.ReaderService.com or upon request from the Harlequin Reader Service.

We make a portion of our mailing list available to reputable third parties that offer products we believe may interest you. If you prefer that we not exchange your name with third parties, or if you wish to clarify or modify your communication preferences, please visit us at www.ReaderService.com/consumerschoice or write to us at Harlequin Reader Service Preference Service, P.O. Box 9062, Buffalo, NY 14269. Include your complete name and address.

ROM13R

Newly promoted Nathan Garrett is eager to prove he's no longer the company playboy. His assistant, single mom Allison Caldwell, has no interest in helping him with that goal, despite the fiery attraction between them. But as Nate grows closer to Alli's little boy, she wonders whether he might be a family man after all…

Read on for a sneak preview of THE DADDY WISH, by award-winning author Brenda Harlen, the next book in the miniseries THOSE ENGAGING GARRETTS!

***

Allison sipped her wine. Dammit—her pulse was racing and her knees were weak, and there was no way she could sit here beside Nate Garrett, sharing a drink and conversation, and not think about the fact that her tongue had tangled with his.

"I think I'm going to call it a night."

"You haven't finished your wine," he pointed out.

"I'm not much of a drinker."

"Stay," he said.

She lifted her brows. "I don't take orders from you outside the office, Mr. Garrett."

"Sorry—your insistence on calling me 'Mr. Garrett' made me forget that we weren't at the office," he told her. "Please, will you keep me company for a little while?"

"I'm sure there are any number of other women here who will happily keep you company when I'm gone."

"I don't want anyone else's company," he told her.

"Mr. Garrett—"

"Nate."

She sighed. "Why?"

"Because it's my name."

"I meant, why do you want my company?"

"Because I like you," he said simply.

"You don't even know me."

His gaze skimmed down to her mouth, lingered, and she knew he was thinking about the kiss they'd shared. The kiss she hadn't been able to stop thinking about.

"So give me a chance to get to know you," he suggested.

"You'll have that chance when you're in the VP of Finance's office."

She frowned as the bartender, her friend Chelsea, slid a plate of pita bread and spinach dip onto the bar in front of her. "I didn't order this."

"But you want it," Chelsea said, and the wink that followed suggested she was referring to more than the appetizer.

"Actually, I want my bill. It's getting late and…" But her friend had already turned away.

Allison was tempted to walk out and leave Chelsea to pick up the tab, but the small salad she'd made for her own dinner was a distant memory, and she had no willpower when it came to three-cheese spinach dip.

She blew out a breath and picked up a grilled pita triangle. "The service here sucks."

"I've always found that the company of a beautiful woman makes up for many deficiencies."

***

Don't miss THE DADDY WISH by award-winning author Brenda Harlen, the next book in her new miniseries, **THOSE ENGAGING GARRETTS!** *Available February 2015, wherever Harlequin® Special Edition books and ebooks are sold.* www.Harlequin.com

HSEEXPO115R

Read on for a sneak peek at
THE TWINS' RODEO RIDER
by USA TODAY *bestselling author Tina Leonard,*
part of the **BRIDESMAIDS CREEK** *miniseries.*

"Kiss me." He leaned close to the window to give her prime access.

"Why would I want to do that?" Suz's blue eyes widened.

"Because I have nice lips. Or so I've been told. Pucker up, dollface."

"I don't pucker for anyone who calls me 'dollface,' unless you want me to look like I bit into a grapefruit. Now *that* kind of pucker may be available to you."

He laughed. "So much sass, so little honesty."

She sniffed. "I'm trying to *save* you, cowboy, not romance you. Don't confuse this."

He sighed. "No kiss? I really feel like I need to know if you're the woman of my dreams, if you're determined to win me. And a kiss tells all."

"Oh, wow." Suz looked incredulous. "You really let that line out of your mouth?"

"Slid out easily. Come on, cupcake." He closed some distance between her face and his in case she changed her mind. *Strike while the branding iron was hot* was a very worthwhile strategy. It was in fact his favorite strategy.

"If I kiss you, I probably won't like it. And then what motivation do I have to win the race? I'd just toss you back into the pond for Daisy."

He drew back, startled. "That wouldn't be good."

Suz nodded. "It could be horrible. You could be a wet kisser. Eww."

"I really don't think I am." His ego took a small dent.

"You could be a licky-kisser."

"Pretty sure I'm just right, like Goldilock's bed," he said, his ego somewhere down around his boots and flailing like a leaf on the ground in the breeze.

"I don't know," Suz said thoughtfully. "Friends don't let friends kiss friends."

"I'm not that good of a friend."

"You really want a kiss, don't you?"

He perked up at these heartening words that seemed to portend a softening in her stance. "I sure do."

"Hope you get someone to kiss you one day, then. See you around, Cisco. And don't forget, one week until the swim!"